The Time
of My
Life

BOOKS BY TILLY TENNANT

The Summer of Secrets

The Summer Getaway

The Christmas Wish

The Mill on Magnolia Lane

Hattie's Home for Broken Hearts

The Garden on Sparrow Street

The Break Up

The Waffle House on the Pier

Worth Waiting For

Cathy's Christmas Kitchen

Once Upon a Winter

The Spring of Second Chances

An Unforgettable Christmas series

A Very Vintage Christmas

A Cosy Candlelit Christmas

From Italy with Love series

Rome Is Where the Heart Is

A Wedding in Italy

Honeybourne series

The Little Village Bakery

Christmas at the Little Village Bakery

TILLY TENNANT

The Time of My Life

bookouture

Published by Bookouture in 2021

An imprint of Storyfire Ltd.
Carmelite House
50 Victoria Embankment
London EC4Y 0DZ

www.bookouture.com

ISBN: 978-1-80019-245-4
eBook ISBN: 978-1-80019-244-7

For my family. Please forgive all the burnt dinners and Sunday afternoons spent locked away from you. I hope you approve of the result.

Chapter One

'A letter's more personal, right?' Bonnie stood in front of the mirror and scraped her hair back into a ponytail. 'If I take the time to write an actual letter, he'll see just what a nice person I am. Maybe he'll decide to get his bodyguards or whatever to bring him round to say hello?'

Bonnie's reflection offered no reply. She was right, though, because it was a stupid idea and even her reflection knew it. Holden Finn was no more going to visit her home than Bonnie was going to get a job with the FBI. She sighed and fastened her tabard, grimacing as a new grey in her fringe caught the light. At thirty-five she was already battling the silvers in her ash blonde hair; her mum hadn't had to colour until she was well into her fifties. Bonnie winced as she tugged the offending hair out.

Her mind returned to her mission. So, a letter was not going to get Holden to notice her, but working quietly and anonymously in a greengrocer's shop wasn't going to either. She had already tried emailing his management company *and* the record company to no avail, had tracked his mum down on Facebook and sent her what she thought was a polite and perfectly reasonable request (which had got her blocked the next day) and had tweeted him, which got lots of questionable replies from his other followers but none from him. Perhaps that alone ought to tell her something.

Devoid of a better solution, Bonnie went to the drawer in the kitchen table to fetch the matching floral paper and envelopes she had bought the previous day.

Passing Paige's open bedroom door, she noticed that her daughter had managed to turn the alarm off and go back to sleep. Paige hated going to her grandmother's house for the day and had clearly ignored the alarm in a cunning attempt to make Bonnie so late that she would have to leave her at home. There was no way that was going to happen. Paige might have been fifteen but Bonnie still wasn't comfortable with leaving her alone in the flat all day; she had, after all, been fifteen once too. And keeping this tiny flat and their meagre income meant Bonnie keeping her job at Applejack's, and that was not going to happen if she couldn't even turn in on time. Whether she liked it or not, Paige was going to have to get up.

Bonnie's gaze travelled around the rest of the room with a deep sigh. The floor was littered with clothes – many of them obviously dirty – a plate full of toast crumbs peeped out from beneath the bed, a mug that Bonnie didn't even dare look inside sat on the bedside table. It was just another teenage bedroom – Bonnie recalled her own being more or less the same, the décor and the styles of clothing the only clue that they were generations apart.

Just as she was about to shake Paige again, her gaze was drawn to the poster above her daughter's bed, the young, impossibly attractive man posing on it smiling down at her with a cheeky yet seductive look in his eye. What did it matter if Holden Finn was almost young enough to be her son? There was nothing wrong in wanting to meet him, to say hello and tell him how much she admired his music... was there? It had nothing to do with the hair that begged to have her hands run through it... and the eyes that twinkled with barely-disguised sexual dynamism, perfectly controlled so that his teenage fans couldn't yet identify what it was that stirred them to a frenzy at the mere mention of his name. Suddenly noticing that her mouth was hanging open, Bonnie shook herself. She had definitely been on her own too long, and if her brain was functioning as it should, she'd be able to do something about this ridiculous and not entirely appropriate obsession.

'Paige, get up.'

Paige rolled over. 'I am up,' she replied groggily.

'Looks like it. You know we have to leave for your gran's house in half an hour and you haven't even showered yet.'

'I can shower there. There's nothing else to do.'

'She said last week that she was going to get some DVDs for you.'

'That pile of crap she picks up from the market stall? Most of those films were made before I was born.'

'Maybe they were, but they would be things you wanted to see if you'd give her some sort of clue what you're into.'

'Ugh.' Paige pushed herself to sit. 'It's not my fault her voice turns into a boring noise after two seconds of speech.'

'That's my mother you're talking about.'

'Yeah, that's where you get your boring voice from then.'

Bonnie's eyebrows knitted together. The urge to smack her daughter's legs still rose from time to time, despite the fact that Paige was far too old. But then she took a deep breath and gathered all her dignity. 'Well… it almost certainly means you'll have a boring voice too!' She turned to leave, giving the frozen poster-Holden one last longing glance. 'If you're not at the table in ten minutes you're going without breakfast.'

'Whooo big deal…' Paige's voice faded as Bonnie trudged through to the kitchen.

*

'So, what time are you going to rescue me from Jeanie's?' Paige mumbled through a mouthful of cornflakes.

'Don't call her Jeanie. It's grandma or gran, or nan or something similar to you.'

'She likes Jeanie; she says gran makes her feel like an old lady.'

'No she doesn't, you decided that.'

Paige looked up and flashed a lopsided grin. Dark brown eyes, olive skin, thick black hair, cheeks just a little too plump for the thinness of her face but somehow it worked. It was at times like this when Bonnie realised just how much Paige looked like her dad and not really like Bonnie at all. Maybe she had Cartwright in the build – curvy but just on the right side of slim – but everything else was Henri's. She pushed the thought to the back of her mind. Paige's dad had left them and gone back to France and he was never coming back.

'Nanas are supposed to be all sensible, anyway, like bake you cakes and stuff,' Paige continued. 'Jeanie doesn't do any of that, so why would I call her nana?'

'There is no rule that says nanas have to do anything. They're still people with their own likes and interests.'

'Well,' Paige continued stubbornly, 'I don't know anyone else at school whose nan moshes to Motorhead, or pulls out Ouija boards to contact dead rock stars.'

'I bet all their grandparents have some unusual hobby or habit if you ask them. People aren't always what they seem on the surface. Now eat your breakfast. I'm late enough as it is.'

*

The autumn winds swirled leaves up the drive and around Bonnie's feet as she hurried to Jeanie's front door, dragging a reluctant Paige behind her. She rapped on the door with an impatient fist, stamping and huffing as she waited.

Bonnie had always loved this house, and despite her annoyance at running late this morning, she couldn't help a sweeping glance at the garden, noticing with affection the gnarled, stunted old pear tree that she used to play under with her dad, and that, much to her dad's annoyance, never seemed to bear more than the stingiest handful of pears. And there were the same old rose bushes where she had collected the delicate pink petals to make perfume for her mum. It never smelt like any perfume that Bonnie had ever sniffed while out shopping with her parents, but her mum had always taken the reused shampoo bottle full of water and mushed up petals (not to mention the odd unfortunate squashed bug) with a fond smile.

Life had seemed so simple back then (apart from some of her mum's odder hobbies) though Bonnie suspected, looking back, it was only her youth that had made it seem so. Then Henri had walked into her life one day – or rather, she had wandered into his while on a holiday to the Vendée as he backpacked across France – and it seemed that things had been complicated, in one way or another, ever since.

'Hey, Paige! How's my favourite granddaughter?' Jeanie opened the door with a broad smile, pushing a blonde dreadlock from her forehead.

'I'm your only granddaughter,' Paige said, pushing past her into the hallway before disappearing into the house.

Bonnie shrugged. 'She's a bit tired this morning.'

'That's because you let her stay up till all hours on chat rooms.'

'Have you ever tried stopping Paige from doing something she wants to?' Bonnie frowned.

'You don't show her enough authority; head in the clouds yourself all the time.'

'What, like you did with me?' Bonnie retorted, hands on her hips. 'If authority means her hanging around at rock festivals while her mother flirts with band members then no, I don't.' She sighed. 'I don't have time for this, Mum, I'll be late for work.'

'What time will you be back?' Jeanie called down the driveway after her.

'The usual.'

*

Fred Black glanced up at the clock as Bonnie hurried through the doorway of Applejack's, shrugging her coat off. 'Just about, lass,' he warned in a gruff voice. 'One more minute and you'd have had a late mark.'

'Sorry Fred. I'll be with you in two ticks, just hanging up my bag,' Bonnie said, ignoring the impulse to say something much more insulting to her vertically-challenged, overweight boss.

'Fridges need emptying before we open, you know, I've been waiting for you to get the cold stock out,' Fred continued.

'Couldn't Linda have done it?' Bonnie called from the cramped staff room at the back of the tiny shop.

Applejack's was one of those little backstreet places that every town has; it seemed to have completely missed the arrival of the twenty-first century. They still closed at lunchtimes and had the same sun-bleached advertising posters hanging in the windows as they'd had when they first opened. Faux dark wood panelling lined the walls and the floor was tiled in scuffed and chipped terracotta. Somehow, though, the people of the small town of Millrise loved it and the shop still managed to thrive in the face of the out-of-town supermarkets that squeezed the town centre a little more every year. Nobody could quite say why the people of Millrise viewed Applejack's with such affection; it was a dump in anyone's honest opinion.

'She's out back fighting with some cockroaches that arrived with a box of bananas this morning. Opened the blasted thing and there they were – scuttling like mad all over the place. The size of my fist, some of them,' Fred huffed as he came through to the back room and stood in the doorway.

Bonnie glanced at him. It was on the tip of her tongue to ask why he couldn't get the fridge stock out while he was waiting for her to arrive, but she thought better of it. 'Okay,' she said. 'I'll do that first, then I'll go and see if Linda needs a helping machete to take out those cockroaches.'

*

As she lugged out trays of peaches and crates of grapes, Bonnie's mind wandered to the letter she was going to write as soon as she had five spare minutes at break time.

Dear Holden,

You don't know me, of course, but I just wanted to let you know what a huge fan of yours I am. It would make me so happy to meet you…

No, too formal and not eye catching enough.

Dear Holden,

Do you believe in fate? I do, and I believe that although we have not met yet, and you don't even know who I am, we are destined to meet…

No, too melodramatic and made her sound slightly unhinged. The only thing that letter would persuade Holden to do was double his security arrangements.

Dear Holden,

I know you don't know me, but do you fancy a drink sometime? I wouldn't tell a soul about it, obviously…

Too… well, just ridiculous. As if he was going to say yes no matter how much she promised not to tell.

Dear Holden,

My daughter is a huge fan. She's had a really tough time lately, what with her dad abandoning us and everything, but meeting you would make her so happy…

It looked better, the favour being for Paige, and Paige would love it, but, in reality, what would he care about just another fatherless fifteen-year-old? The world was full of them. And it wasn't really for Paige, was it? If anyone knew how ridiculous and juvenile her own obsession was, it was Bonnie. Even Paige, as much of a fan as she was, didn't pine after meeting Holden Finn in the way that Bonnie did. But there was a part of her that couldn't let it go. Perhaps, she and Jeanie, who had spent many of her prime years chasing after rockstars, weren't that different after all. If nothing else, at least that thought gave Bonnie someone to blame. But she knew that her mum wouldn't have developed an obsession this unhealthy, and even when she did get near to the object of her affections, she always went home to Bonnie's dad satisfied with an autograph and a peck on the cheek. Bonnie pretended to herself that this was all she wanted, but deep down, she knew it wasn't true.

Okay, so the letter was stupid, and being in love with a boy barely old enough to wipe his own nose was stupid, and writing actual letters to *anyone* these days was stupid. Bonnie knew all this. But who could tell where it might lead? If she could get him to notice she existed it would be enough. Since Henri had left her she'd felt invisible. It was all she wanted: just for someone to notice, just to feel young and sexy again.

As she pulled out a tray of plums, Fred popped his head around the doorway of the vast, walk-in fridge.

'Are you nearly done in here, lass?'

'Yep, almost, Fred.'

'So I can open the doors?'

'You could have opened the doors anyway. I can't imagine we'd have a huge queue outside waiting for greengages and even if we did, I'm sure they'd wait for a moment or two without rioting.'

Fred grunted a reply, but as he lumbered away rattling the shop keys Bonnie failed to catch what it was.

Linda came through from the outside yard wiping sweat from her round and very red face. 'My God! You should see the size of those buggers! You know what they say about cockroaches being the only creatures to survive a nuclear attack? Well, I think those ones outside already did!'

Bonnie laughed. 'Alright, Linda?'

'I will be as soon as I sweep up all those bug bits and get a cup of tea.'

'I'm not sure Fred will let you do that, he's afraid that we're going to be overrun by a horde of rampaging shoppers desperate for leeks as soon as we open.'

'Not let me have a cup of tea? After the act of genocide I've just committed for him out back? I've seen enough tropical banana box stowaways to last me a lifetime. Let him try and stop me!' Linda disappeared into the staff room, scraping her shoe clear of insect legs as she went.

*

Break time came and Bonnie sat on her own in the dark and dank staff room with a cup of tea and a blank flowery page in front of her. She'd been staring at it for ten minutes, and her break was only fifteen; she'd have to think of something to put in this damn letter. Lunch was always taken up with Linda, so there wouldn't be time to do it then without attracting unwanted curiosity. She began to write…

Dear Holden,

This is going to sound like a ridiculous request, and I'm sure you get a thousand like it every day, but I'd love to meet you.

There, I've said it and that's it. I have no special reasons, no terminal illness, I'm no pillar of the community or doer of great deeds or talented or famous or rich. I have nothing to offer you but my affection and a wish to tell you face to face how I feel about you and how much just seeing a photo of you lightens my otherwise gloomy life.

I know that I will never get a reply to this letter, and you'll never even get to read it, but I've written it anyway.

Love, Bonnie Cartwright.

Bonnie read the letter through again and sighed deeply before screwing it up and putting it in the bin.

Just then, Linda came in wiping her hands down her tabard. 'Ugh, just put my fingers straight through a rotten satsuma.'

Bonnie wrinkled her nose. 'God, you can tell by the stink!'

Linda went to the tiny sink and washed her hands. 'I know, they're the foulest smelling things known to man. Prisoner of war – rotten orange under his nose and he'd tell you anything.'

Bonnie drank the last of her tea.

'And Fred says you're due back out, by the way,' Linda added.

'I'll bet he does,' Bonnie mumbled. 'He must have a stopwatch surgically implanted in his brain, and if he doesn't, I bet he's after a Harley Street specialist to do it.'

Linda wiped her hands on a tatty towel. 'Fred would never pay Harley Street prices. I'm sure he'd know some Del Boy down the pub who could smash a watch into his brain on the cheap.'

Laughing loudly, Bonnie pushed herself up from the chair and took her cup to the sink. 'I'll rinse this at lunch,' she said, putting it down. 'Right now I'd better get back out before he blows a gasket.'

'I'll do it for you,' Linda said, flicking the kettle on.

'Thanks, Linda; I don't know what I'd do without you.'

'You'd still be chasing cockroaches around the back yard for a start.'

Bonnie, still looking back and laughing, almost bumped into someone as she made her way out from the tiny kitchen into the warehouse, beyond which lay the main shop.

'Oh God, Max, I didn't see you there!'

'I'm pretty hard to miss.' Max grinned down at her. 'All six-foot-two of me.'

'That's true.' Bonnie smiled. 'Please don't tell me you've got more stock to bring in, I've lugged enough Spanish strawberries to last me a lifetime today. And I'm pretty sure we're going to have to reduce the buggers by the end of today, which always makes His Royal Fredness in there as grumpy as hell.'

Max pushed a hand through his wind-tousled locks. His cheeks were a little ruddy from the autumn chill. Along with his golden hair, naughty smile, and lean height, his current flush made him look like an over-grown and mischievous schoolboy. 'I'd hate to be the cause of that. You've no need to worry, though; I've just come to drop off an invoice.' He leaned closer and dropped his voice. 'Unless, of course, you've changed your mind about that drink?'

Bonnie laughed. 'No I haven't. I'm sure I couldn't keep up with you.'

'Probably not,' he said, grinning and straightening up. 'You are, like, a hundred years old.'

Bonnie slapped his arm. 'That's no way to persuade me either.'

Every week Max asked her and every week she gave the same reply. They always laughed it off. But today, Bonnie thought she caught something else in his expression, something sad. She shook the thought away. This was Max, the wise-cracking, whistling delivery driver. She didn't think he would know sad if it slapped him in the face. Not like Bonnie, of course, she and sadness were best friends these days.

'Linda's on the hunt for a man,' Bonnie said. 'Her John is driving her mental and she's looking for a younger model.'

Max laughed. 'And I'm on the hunt for a woman. But much as I like Linda, there's only one that I want.'

'I bet you say that to all the girls.'

'I do. Just ask in Cherry Ripe across town, they've all been subjected to the Delaney charm. It takes years of practise to come across this desperate.'

'Max.' She smiled up at him. 'I'm sure there are girls queuing around the block for you.'

'Queuing around the block to get away from me, more like.'

Bonnie's reply was cut short by Fred's sweaty face at the doorway. 'Any chance of a hand out here?'

He disappeared again and Bonnie looked at Max, shrugging apologetically. 'I'd better get back in. Anyone would think it was the first day of the Harrods sale in there. I bet he's got old Mrs Simkin asking for the plums on top of the display that he can't reach. He hates that, makes him feel all emasculated.'

Max chuckled. 'In that case, I'll just leave this on his desk and sneak out. I'm sure an invoice won't improve his mood.'

'Probably for the best,' Bonnie said as she made her way back out to the shop. 'See you later, Max.'

'Yeah,' Max replied as he watched her go. 'See you later.'

*

Linda turned the closed sign on the shop door and locked it as Bonnie waited on the pavement. The day was cold and blustery but the late autumn sun on their backs was warm and comforting.

'So…' Linda asked as she and Bonnie made their way to the delicatessen down the street for lunch. 'Did Max ask you out again?'

'Not really.' She looked across and caught Linda's raised eyebrows. 'Okay, sort of. It was a bit half-hearted though.'

'It's not going to be anything else if you keep saying no.'

'I know; but he's not really my type… and I don't think it's such a good idea anyway, with him being in here every day. What if it didn't work out? I'd still have to see him all the time and that might be very awkward…'

'You know Henri is not coming back, don't you?' Linda asked serenely.

Bonnie looked at her sharply. 'I'm not stupid.'

'I didn't say that. What are you waiting for then?'

'I have to say yes to the first man who asks me?'

'When he's that nice and asks that often, maybe you should at least think about it.'

'He's too young. And there's Paige to consider too.'

'He's about six years younger than you, but I don't see how that's a problem. And Paige is going to hate whoever you bring home, because Paige hates everyone, so that's no reason to stay single. You're making excuses.'

Bonnie shrugged and looked away, unable to hold Linda's questioning gaze.

Linda plunged her hands into her coat pockets and shot a wry glance at her friend. 'Henri has been gone for two years. He wasn't that much of a catch when he was here…' Linda didn't flinch under the sour look that Bonnie gave her. 'I'm just saying…'

'And you think our delivery driver is?'

'He's lovely. And he's not just a delivery driver, is he? He owns the firm.'

'That wasn't what I was getting at. It doesn't bother me how much money he earns.'

'Clearly, as Henri was quite content to laze around and let you bring in all the money and you were happy to let him get away with it.'

'He had... issues. Being French and all, it was hard for him to get a job. You know he didn't get many clients for his language lessons either. And there was his depression too.'

'Made everyone around him depressed, that's for sure.'

'Linda!'

'It's true. Bloody cock.'

They arrived at *The Bountiful Isle* delicatessen and sandwich shop, a place that was referred to locally simply as 'The Bounty'. As they walked through the door they were greeted by a loud voice with a strong Greek accent.

'Ladies! What will it be for the beautiful workers today?'

'Hey, Stav,' Linda said, looking down the board. 'Flattery won't get us spending any more money, you know.'

The deli owner pulled a face of mock affront. 'Perish it! Every word from my mouth is truth.'

'Yeah, right. So what's going on with your nose then, Pinocchio?' Linda replied.

Stavros laughed. 'You are beautiful to me, fair Linda.'

'How's your Mama?' Linda asked, ignoring the backhanded compliment.

Stavros pulled his face. 'Getting uglier by the day.'

'Poor woman,' Bonnie giggled. 'I hope Paige never talks like that about me.'

'Come on,' Linda turned to Bonnie, 'what are we having?'

'I'll just have a cheese sandwich,' Bonnie said, looking into her purse.

'Right,' Linda said to Stavros. 'I'll have a Cajun wrap special and Bonnie will have the same.'

'But –'

'It's on me.'

'Linda!'

'Shut up and put your purse away. John got his annual bonus this week, so I'm flush. You're the only thing that makes working in that bloody shop bearable so if I can't treat you once in a while, it's time to pack in.'

Bonnie was about to argue, then her face relaxed into a smile. 'Thanks Linda. I don't know what I'd do without you.'

'Yeah,' Linda said, giving her a wry sideways glance. 'You keep saying that. Let's hope you don't have to find out.' She looked up at Stavros, who was watching them with a grin on his face. 'What are you standing around for, we only have half an hour, you know!'

Stavros erupted into a hearty laugh. 'Oh, just like Mama! Marry me, Linda!'

*

Bonnie trudged up the path of her mother's house. Her hand reached for the bell and stopped, mid-air, as a pounding bass erupted from within and the first strains of *Another One Bites the Dust* by Queen travelled out to her. Bonnie smiled to herself, imagining Paige's face as Jeanie gyrated around the living room doing her best Freddie Mercury impression. Realising that the bell was as likely to be heard as a hamster with laryngitis, Bonnie hammered at the front door instead.

Moments later it was opened by a red-faced Paige.

'Mum!'

Bonnie raised her eyebrows. Paige was sweating, her ponytail was coming loose, with half her hair hanging out at one side, and she was clearly out of breath.

'If I didn't know better, I'd think you'd been moshing with your nana.'

'Yeah, but she wanted to…' Paige moved aside without another word and let her mum through into the hallway.

Jeanie appeared at the living room door. Freddie was still singing his heart out on the sound system in the living room and the light fitting in the hallway was vibrating with the volume, dust dancing from the tops of the family portraits that lined the walls.

'Alright?' Jeanie shouted over the din, her face split into a huge grin. 'We've had such a laugh today.'

'Have you?' Bonnie looked slyly at Paige, whose gaze dropped to her feet as she wrestled her hair back into a ponytail.

Jeanie disappeared into the living room and Bonnie followed. She watched as her mum went to the CD player and turned down the volume.

'Cup of tea, love?' Jeanie asked Bonnie as she straightened her denim blouse down over skin-tight trousers.

Bonnie's attention was drawn to her mum's bottom half. 'Are those *leather* trousers?' she asked with an incredulous stare.

'Gorgeous, aren't they?' Jeanie said with obvious pride. 'Got them off Ebay.'

Bonnie could think of a lot of words to describe the trousers that her mum had poured over her legs, but gorgeous wasn't one of them. There was no doubt that for someone of her age, Jeanie had a fantastic figure; even so, leather trousers were, in Bonnie's humble opinion, a pretty daring choice – even she, twenty-five years younger, would feel self-conscious in a pair.

'I like them,' Paige said in a stubborn voice from behind Bonnie.

'I'll get you a pair then,' Bonnie replied sweetly.

'Ugh!' Paige turned and swept from the room.

'I'll put the kettle on,' Jeanie said, sharing a wry smile with her daughter.

Bonnie shook her head. 'I probably should get back,' she said. 'Thanks though.'

'What have you got to hurry back for? I was going to tell you about the lovely shopping trip Paige and I had today. I got her some pink hair colour.'

'*What?*'

Jeanie nodded as she squeezed past Bonnie to go to the kitchen.

'She can't use it, school won't let her.' Bonnie followed her mum to the kitchen.

'It'll wash out in no time. It's not permanent.'

'Did she choose it?'

'No, I did. I thought it would look lovely with her skin colouring.'

Paige was already sitting at the kitchen table on her phone by the time Bonnie and Jeanie got in there.

'You know you can't use that hair colour, school won't let you,' Bonnie said to Paige.

'Chill, Mum. I'll just wait until the holidays.'

'You used to dye your hair all the colours of the rainbow,' Jeanie said to Bonnie. 'And permed it too.'

Bonnie sighed and took a seat at the table. 'I suppose it could be worse,' she said to Jeanie, 'you could have tried to get her to have that nose piercing again.' She looked at Paige, whose attention had returned to her phone. 'Who are you messaging?'

There was no reply.

'Paige?'

Nothing.

'Earth to Paige,' Bonnie called.

Paige looked up at her. 'What?'

'Who are you texting?'

'Does it matter?'

'No, but I'm interested.'

'Why?'

'I just am.'

'Well, my text is very uninteresting, so maybe you want to find your entertainment elsewhere.'

Jeanie chuckled from across the room where she was putting mugs out.

'It's not funny, Mum!' Bonnie squeaked.

'You have to admit, if nothing else she's eloquent,' Jeanie replied.

'She's fifteen.'

'Yes, and very like her mum was at the same age.' Jeanie turned and put her hands on her hips as she gazed at her daughter. 'When did you lose that spark, Bonnie?'

Bonnie pushed a hand through her fringe and glanced at Paige, who had returned to her messaging. 'Right about the time that Henri left.'

Jeanie sniffed as she squeezed the teabags in the mugs. 'Him again. I knew he was trouble the minute you brought him home. Your dad said so too.'

'Dad didn't like him because he was French. *Bloody Frog* was the exact term he used.'

'French or not, your dad knew bad news when he saw it; he just wasn't good at expressing his feelings in a PC sort of way.'

'He didn't express anything in a PC way. He thought PC stood for Political Crap.'

'All I'm saying is that you need to move on. Henri's not coming back.'

'I know,' Bonnie said irritably, 'everyone keeps telling me, as if I don't know.'

'Knowing is not the same as accepting, love.' Jeanie crossed the room with two mugs and set one down in front of Bonnie.

'I have accepted it.'

'Then why aren't you dating?'

'Where is the rule that says I have to?'

'There isn't one. But it's normal behaviour.'

'Who says?'

'I do.'

'Ridiculous. Women can manage perfectly well without men these days.'

'Oh, and when did you turn into Annie Lennox, *doing it for yourself*?'

Bonnie couldn't help but grin. 'Be careful, you'll be showing your age: that song is so before my time.'

'*That song* is a classic,' Jeanie retorted, 'old or not you can't argue that. Paige knows it, don't you?'

Paige glanced up, shrugged, and then went back to her phone.

'You must have your eye on someone?' Jeanie insisted, turning back to Bonnie.

Bonnie's thoughts went to the flowery paper in her bag. 'Not really.' She took a sip from her cup. 'Besides, men only let you down. It's just not worth it.'

'Not all of them.'

'*You're* still single.'

Jeanie looked into her cup. 'That's different.'

'How?'

'I'm older for a start. And your dad…'

'Was the love of your life,' Bonnie finished, her tone softening. 'He was, and you were his, but he wouldn't want you to be alone. Even when you went backstage flirting with Whitesnake, he knew you'd always be going home with him. But he also knew how much you liked company, and he'd hate to think of you living on your own like this, year after year.'

'I get plenty of company,' Jeanie said. 'More mates than I can visit.'

'It's not the same, Mum.'

'We're talking about you, not me.'

'Pot… kettle…?'

'Paige!' Jeanie said, turning to her granddaughter in an obvious attempt to change the subject. 'You want a can of coke or anything?'

Paige looked up from her phone. 'Are we staying for a bit?' she asked Bonnie.

'For half an hour, why?'

'I wanted to FaceTime Annabel.'

'And you have to do that right now?'

'Yeah, she's got something important to tell me.'

'Aren't you messaging each other as we speak?'

'Yeah, but…'

Bonnie sighed. 'At least let me finish this drink and gaze upon your beauty for a while, because once we get home, you'll be locked in your bedroom with that iPad and I won't see you for the rest of the night.'

'You were the one saying we couldn't afford it so if you did buy one I couldn't leave it gathering dust under my bed… *like everything else you get a fad for…*' Paige mimicked Bonnie's voice as she finished the sentence.

'Paige, don't be hard on your mum, she's been to work all day to pay for those things that are gathering dust under your bed.'

Paige almost fired back a reply, but then clamped her mouth shut and stared at her phone again.

'Just leave it, Mum,' Bonnie said wearily.

Jeanie shrugged. 'You're not staying for anything to eat, then? I have pork chops that need using up.'

'Do you mind if we don't? I'm really tired and I think Paige has important social networking to do.'

Jeanie frowned. 'If you're sure you won't?'

Bonnie nodded.

'In that case, take the chops with you, even I can't eat as many as I have in and I need to keep my backside tiny if I'm going to fit into these trousers come The Blood Festival next spring.'

'The Blood Festival? Sounds charming. I don't think I want to know.' Bonnie took another sip of her tea and threw a questioning look at her mum over the rim of her mug.

Jeanie laughed. 'It's only a rock festival. I haven't gone all voodoo on you!'

'Glad to hear it,' Bonnie replied. Although, she wondered if a little voodoo in her life wouldn't necessarily be a bad idea. It might fix a few things, and it couldn't make things any worse than she was doing on her own.

*

Bonnie lay in the bath, staring up at the ceiling. It needed painting, she thought vaguely, as she gazed at the bubbled plaster and clouds of mould that had gathered in the corner by the window. The walls weren't much better. If she was completely honest, the whole room needed to be ripped out and started again, but that wasn't going to happen any time soon on her budget. She had dropped massive hints to her mum that she needed a visit from the *DIY SOS* team, but Jeanie had stubbornly refused to notice. Paint was going to have to do, but even that would have to wait. With a school trip to Belgium to pay for and a list of bills that never seemed to be under control, it was just another promise to herself that would not be delivered.

True to her forecast, Paige had taken herself into her bedroom as soon as they walked back into the flat and had been in there for the two hours they had been home. Bonnie could hear the odd stifled giggle, and the low hum of conversation, but what was being discussed she could only guess at and, despite the fact that Paige would probably be unaware of it, eavesdropping didn't seem right. With that in mind, she wasn't rushing to get out of the bath only to sit in front of the TV alone and watch the endless stream of pointless drivel that counted for entertainment. It seemed like a long time since Paige had wanted to sit with her and chat in an evening.

Dear Holden,

Please rescue me.

Love, Bonnie.

Bonnie's thoughts were interrupted by a hammering at the door.

'Mum!'

'What?'

'The internet's gone down again!'

Bonnie frowned. 'What do you want me to do about it? I'm in the bath!'

'I was in the middle of an important conversation with Annabel.'

'And?'

'Well, now I don't know what she wanted to say.'

'Have you turned off the router and started it up again?'

'Yeah, that didn't work.'

'I don't know what it is then. I'll have to phone the cable company or something later.'

'What about Annabel?'

'What about her?'

'I need to speak to her.'

'Phone…'

Bonnie heard a loud, theatrical sigh and then Paige's footsteps as she stomped away.

Wine was in order, lots and lots of wine. Tomorrow was Sunday and there wouldn't be anything better for Bonnie to do than nurse a well-earned hangover.

Reaching for the towel, Bonnie hauled herself out of the bath. She ought to go and look at that router before Paige exploded with rage. Knowing her daughter's volatile temper these days, it wasn't completely unimaginable…

That was when she heard the high-pitched squeal.

Wrapping the towel around her dripping body, Bonnie rushed into Paige's bedroom.

'Mum!' Paige shouted as Bonnie burst in the door. 'What the hell's the matter with you?'

'I could ask you the same thing!' Bonnie thundered as she saw that Paige was lounging on her bed with the phone, just ending a call and clearly not injured or in any sort of peril at all.

'There's nothing wrong with me.'

'I said I would ring the cable company, but you could at least let me get out of the bath.'

'Who cares about the stupid internet? Annabel phoned me when she couldn't get through.'

'What's with the screaming then?'

Paige sat up, her face now glowing and her eyes suddenly alive with excitement.

'Annabel's just told me about an amazing competition.'

'Competition?' Bonnie asked with some exasperation, now aware that she was making quite a wet mess on the carpet.

'Yeah! To meet Holden!'

Bonnie's mouth fell open. Her gaze travelled to the poster above her daughter's bed. She didn't need to ask which Holden. Suddenly, her pulse seemed to run that little bit quicker. 'Holden?' she repeated.

'Yeah, Holden Finn... from *Every Which Way.*'

'I know who you're talking about,' Bonnie said in a dazed voice.

'I'm going to enter; it's dead easy; all you have to do is text his middle name.'

'Gabriel!' Bonnie squeaked. As soon as she had, she felt the colour rush to her cheeks.

'OOOH, get the oldie in the know.'

'I'm not that old,' Bonnie laughed awkwardly, relieved that her moment of embarrassment had gone unnoticed. But inside she was a whirlwind of emotions. She might be as close as a text message away from meeting Holden Finn. But then she saw something of her own excitement reflected in her daughter's face and realisation came crashing in on her. Even in the incredibly unlikely event of her winning if she entered this competition, how could she not give her place to Paige? Paige, who would want her best friend, Annabel, to go with her, not her embarrassing, almost grey-haired mum.

'Anyway, it costs, like, about two quid to text, that's alright though, yeah?' Paige rattled off, already tapping away on her phone without waiting for her mum's reply.

'I suppose,' Bonnie said. 'Maybe I should text too, from my number, double your chances and all that?'

Paige looked up in surprise. 'Would you, Mum? That'd be amazing.'

'Hmmm, *amazing*… I suppose it would be,' Bonnie murmured to herself as she went to get dry.

Chapter Two

Bonnie tossed and turned but sleep wouldn't come. It was ridiculous to get this worked up over a situation that was statistically unlikely to happen. She had sent her competition text, just as she'd promised, and now she almost dreaded a call to say she had won. At least if it didn't come, she wouldn't have to feel guilty about her reluctance to stand by and watch Paige and Annabel take her chance to meet the man of her dreams. Not that she'd register on his radar, even if she did get to go. A thirty-five-year-old mother of one teenage nemesis getting together with one of the country's most sought after young bachelors? It was about as likely as finding a real pea in a Pot Noodle.

If Henri hadn't left her and Paige in the lurch, would Bonnie even be thinking about such a ridiculous scenario? They had been happy; at least, Bonnie had thought they were happy. Henri might not have been the most reliable or caring man in the world, but at least he was there. Until one day he decided he wasn't going to be. Bonnie still had no idea what she'd done wrong; he'd just gone off in that enigmatic Gallic way of his.

She picked up the phone from her bedside table and looked at the display again. Three o'clock. Surely more than ten minutes had passed since she'd last looked at it?

*

'Did you send that text, Mum?' Paige said as she sat down at the kitchen table where Bonnie was already nursing her second cup of coffee of the morning.

'Good morning to you too, Paige.'

'Yeah, I meant that, but did you send it?'

'Yes, I sent it. It'll go in the pot with the million other texts that will never be chosen but I sent it anyway.'

'Last night you said that we had as good a chance as anyone else.'

'Last night I wasn't feeling quite as rough as I do now.'

'Too much booze?'

'Cheek!'

'Just asking.'

'If you must know, I didn't get to sleep till the early hours, which is why I'm up this late but still knackered.'

'Right. But you still had a drink last night, I saw the bottle in the recycling.' Paige reached for some toast from Bonnie's plate.

'Oi, make your own!'

'That's what you're for,' Paige grinned before biting into the stolen slice.

Bonnie sighed. 'Here,' she shoved her plate over, 'I'm not that hungry anyway.'

'That's because you have a hangover.'

'I do not have a hangover. I'm tired, that's all.'

As she munched her toast, Paige's face had that faraway look that used to make Bonnie's heart leap when she saw it on Henri. Seeing it now on her daughter made Bonnie feel very alone.

'What are you thinking about?' she asked.

'Imagine,' Paige said, showing a barely contained excitement that Bonnie knew only too well, 'that we did win that competition and we met the band and Holden actually fancied me!'

'You're a little too young for him, aren't you?'

'He might wait,' Paige replied defensively.

'Okay, he might,' Bonnie soothed.

'You think I'm being stupid.'

'I didn't say that.'

'But you think it.'

'No, but –'

Paige leapt up from the table. 'I've had enough of this.'

She slammed the door as she left the room.

Bonnie sighed. That was another of Henri's traits Paige had inherited, one that she wasn't quite so fond of. She wondered if, just once, she could have a pleasant conversation with her daughter that didn't end up with her flouncing off in a temper. Jeanie would say that it was Paige's age, but Bonnie was pretty sure that wasn't the only reason. She felt that on some level, Paige was still blaming her for Henri's departure. And Bonnie could see why: sometimes, she blamed herself too.

*

Bonnie had just flicked the kettle on when Linda came in shaking rain from her umbrella.

'Cats and dogs out there,' she grumbled. 'Good weekend, Bon?'

'Weekend? You mean that one day I had yesterday cooped up with Paige and her prickly temper?'

Linda raised an eyebrow. 'That good, eh?'

'Yep. Want a brew?' Bonnie asked, fetching another cup from the cupboard without waiting for a reply.

'Does a bear poo in the woods?' Linda hung her coat and nodded her head in the direction of a deathly quiet shop floor. 'Where's Drop Dead Fred this morning?'

Bonnie shrugged. 'Just phoned me early and said he would be late in today so I needed to open up with my keys.'

'Cheeky bugger. I'd have told him where to go. I bet he doesn't pay you any overtime for being in early.'

'Probably not. Which is exactly why he daren't ask you to do it.'

'Too right. I'd squish his little head like those cockroaches he had me chasing around the other day.'

Bonnie laughed and handed Linda a steaming mug. 'That's one match I'd pay to see.'

There was a tap at the back door.

'That'll be Max,' Linda said. 'Want to make yourself scarce so he can't ask you out again?'

'He hasn't asked me out, he just mentioned a friendly drink, that's all.' Bonnie frowned, dragging the bolts back on the door. She opened it and Max grinned on the step. His wet hair had curled at all sorts of odd angles and his cheeks were wind-blushed, so that he looked more like a naughty schoolboy than ever.

'Morning ladies! Who wants to admire my fine plums today?'

Linda sniggered. 'Bonnie doesn't want your plums, that's for sure.'

'Linda!' Bonnie almost choked on her tea.

Linda winked at Bonnie. 'That's what you told me the other day… *if Max offers me his plums once more, I'll stick my foot in them.*'

Max chuckled. 'Now, now. Perhaps I'll just take my plums elsewhere until you're feeling less aggressive.'

'Ignore her,' Bonnie said, frowning at Linda. 'How about a cuppa?'

Max stepped into the tiny kitchen. 'Sounds lovely.' He looked through to the empty shop. 'It's quiet in there this morning. Fred's normally shouting and unfurling the swastika flag around now.'

Bonnie giggled. 'I know, he just phoned me to say he'd be late in today.'

'That's not like him; he usually likes to check everything in.'

'Yes,' Linda agreed, 'it's not like Fred to miss an opportunity to complain he's a potato short in his delivery.'

'I'm glad you said that and not me,' Max laughed, taking a mug from Bonnie with a nod.

'So what did you get up to this weekend, Max?' Linda asked.

'Hmmm, I went skydiving for an hour Saturday morning, that was just after I'd woken at 4.30am and run a two hour marathon, beating the Ethiopian Olympic team. Then I got back home and knocked up a loft conversion just after dinner. Sunday I was out all day hanging around Buckingham Palace gardens while Liz and Phil threw some burgers on the barbie.'

'Pretty quiet then?' Linda grinned.

'Yeah, I actually sat on my arse for most of it.'

'I'd have thought you would have been out with whichever girl had taken your fancy this week.'

'I'm not doing very well with girls who take my fancy. I might have to start settling for the bug-ugly ones soon if I'm gonna make little Maxes.'

'Or Maxines,' Bonnie put in as she rinsed her mug.

'True. Though Maxines are no good for taking to footie matches.'

'Sexist pig!' Linda said.

'That's me. Do you think that's where I'm going wrong? Maybe I'm not being sexist enough. What are the chances of me getting arrested for assault if I go down town on Saturday night and club some woman over the head, caveman style?'

'Club me over the head caveman style and you'd never be able to use your plums again,' Linda remarked as she took her mug over to the sink too.

'So women don't like that sort of thing?' Max said innocently.

Bonnie threw a teacloth at him. 'You're mental, you are.'

'I'm desperate, Bonnie,' he said, pulling the cloth away from his face with a huge grin. 'Come on, take pity on a desperate man and go out for one teensy drink with me. If you don't have a good time, me and my plums will never bother you again.'

'Oh, Max. I'm such a miserable cow these days you'd be begging for mercy within an hour.'

'I'm a good listener,' Max said.

'I'm sure you are. And I'm sure there's a pretty young thing out there who will think all her Christmases have come at once when you ask her out.'

'In that case,' Max said, putting his cup down on the draining board and cracking his knuckles theatrically, 'I'd better get working on these pecs. Where do you want the spuds?'

*

Just as the last sack of potatoes had been hauled in by Max, Fred let himself in at the front of the shop, throwing back the hood of a raincoat that was so old fashioned the only place it was likely to be seen these days was on a fishfinger advert. He gave himself an exaggerated shake, spraying water everywhere. 'Bloody hell, it's like monsoon season.'

'Alright, Fred?' Max asked, wiping his hands on his overalls.

Fred looked up. 'Still here, are you?'

'Nice greeting,' Linda said with obvious sarcasm. 'It's that down-to-earth friendliness that has the customers eating out of his hand.' She grinned at Max as Fred frowned at her.

'I'm just off now,' Max replied, biting back a grin of his own. He handed Bonnie a piece of paper. 'The chitty.' He leaned closer and lowered his voice. 'Though if you look on the bottom of the page, it has my number on it.' He did a telephone mime. 'Call me…'

Bonnie giggled. 'That's your business number; you give it to all your customers.'

'Yeah, but I wouldn't answer to all of them out-of-hours. And when pretty girls ring it flashes like the Bat-phone.'

'Get out you nutter,' Bonnie laughed. 'You'll be late for your harem at Cherry Ripe.'

'I'll come and lock up after you,' Linda said, following him out.

Fred gave Max a short nod goodbye before turning to Bonnie. 'Stock all out, lass, or have you been hobnobbing with himself again?'

'Yes, Fred, the stock is out, as you can see.'

'I'll open up then, no point in the door staying shut if folk can come and part with their money.' Fred shuffled off to the front door.

'You know he's going to stop asking soon?' Linda said to Bonnie in a low voice as she came back in.

'Fred?'

'Max, you silly cow.'

'He's not being serious. It's just Max flirting.'

'He is being serious. And he's lovely. You're mental to keep turning him down.'

Bonnie turned and put her hands on her hips, fixing Linda with a serious expression. 'What if it all turned to crap? How awkward would that be when he calls here every day?'

'It wouldn't turn to crap. Besides, Max is far too nice to get nasty over something like that. I'm sure you could stay friendly.'

'No, Lind. I know what you're trying to do and I appreciate it, but no me and Max, not now, not ever. That's my final word.'

*

Despite her working week being a long and very routine one, it had still flown by and Bonnie found herself with a rare Saturday off. Paige was still in bed after staying up late the previous night, mostly online, Bonnie presumed, although what Paige did behind her closed bedroom door was anyone's guess.

Bonnie sat at the kitchen table, staring into space. She had washed up and cleaned the surfaces, plopped a pile of meat and veg into the slow cooker with a sachet of casserole seasoning for the evening meal, ironed their washing and read every magazine she had from cover to cover and then back again. What did you do on a precious Saturday off when you had no spare money to enjoy it? Linda was working, of course – one of them had to be in the shop helping Fred (who was probably, right now, on his fiftieth grumble of the day, complaining that they were short-staffed and rushed off their feet and he didn't see why the trade unions had ever got involved in the running of businesses, instigating holidays and sick pay and such nonsense) and her mum was on one of her frequent 'cigarette runs' in Spain (whatever that meant; Bonnie had no idea why she would go all that way for cigarettes, but Jeanie just said they were cheaper and left it at that). They seemed to be getting very frequent indeed, Bonnie mused, and although she hadn't really noticed Jeanie's five-a-day smoking habit worsening, she wondered whether she ought to drop some heavy hints about quitting before her mum smoked herself to instant death. All in all, it looked like it was going to be a boring day and Bonnie was beginning to wonder about phoning her boss to see if she could go into work. At least she'd have someone to talk to there.

One more hot drink and she'd go and get sorted, at least pretend she had something worth getting dressed for on a dreary, lonely, boring Saturday morning.

And into this morass of greyness, her phone bleeped. She rarely got texts from anyone, and the few people it was likely to be were all currently busy. Unless Paige wanted a cup of tea and had decided to text from her bedroom. That would be a new low, even for them, but Bonnie wouldn't have put it past her. She reached across the table and picked it up to read the message. For a moment, it didn't register. But then she stared at the screen as she read it again.

Please call us on 07773771771 to hear some exciting news.

It couldn't be...

It had to be a hoax.

Or a sales call, one of those timeshare cons that made you believe something amazing was coming your way when all they wanted was to get you to buy their poxy product?

Or could it be that, for once in her life, Lady Luck had cut Bonnie some slack?

Bonnie placed the phone on the table and pushed herself up to fill the kettle while the information sank in. As she waited for it to boil, her mind wandered to Paige, and how much she would love to win that competition, how much she deserved it for the terrible time she'd had since Henri had left them one grey morning with no explanation and barely a look back. Paige had spent a long time blaming herself for somehow doing something that had upset her dad to the point that he felt he had to desert them. Once she had finished blaming herself, she blamed Bonnie, and then Jeanie, and then finally seemed to accept that Henri himself was the villain of the piece. But it had taken her a long time to get there. All the while, Bonnie had struggled to keep the relationship between herself and her daughter from falling apart too.

Once she had made herself an instant cappuccino, Bonnie sat back at the table, blowing at the froth and staring at her phone again.

Just ring it you silly cow!

'Hello? I'm phoning about a text message I just received.'

She listened as she was fed some spiel, relaxing instantly as she realised that her first hunch had been right. The person on the other end of the line was explaining that she could win a state-of-the-art home cinema system if she turned up at a warehouse in Croydon equipped with a hefty deposit on a holiday home.

'Thanks for that,' Bonnie said, now feeling foolish for the state she had got herself in only minutes before. 'But you're really talking to the wrong woman if you're after spare cash.'

Without waiting for a reply, she ended the call and put the phone back on the table. She was just taking another sip of her cappuccino when she heard a shout from Paige's bedroom.

Within seconds, Paige had raced into the kitchen, bouncing and hyperventilating with manic excitement.

'Annabel just phoned me… We won!'

Chapter Three

'Sooo,' Paige said for what seemed like the hundredth time that morning as she sat at the table with Bonnie and ate her toast, 'I'm defo gonna need a new outfit. Can we go shopping today, seeing as you're off?'

Bonnie frowned as she watched her daughter wolf down some breakfast. In light of the news she had received that morning, Bonnie's stomach was churning so much that the last thing she wanted was breakfast. It was lucky that Paige was so wrapped up in her excitement that she hadn't noticed – Bonnie didn't need awkward questions to push her already delicate emotional state.

'Paige... light of my life, as I said to you fifteen minutes ago when you last mentioned it, I haven't got any spare cash today. Maybe in a couple of weeks, around payday.'

Paige's toast stopped halfway to her mouth. 'But that's ages away. Can't we look today and then buy it when you have the money?'

'What's the point? The thing you choose might be sold out when you go back for it.'

'You always say that.'

'Because it never ceases to be true. Besides, there's a month until you go to the radio station to meet them.'

'I need to get some idea of what I'm going to wear, at least.'

'Get a magazine, it's cheaper.'

'Yeah, but that's a waste in the end. They're, like, five quid and that fiver could be going towards a top.'

'Five quid! What magazines are you buying?'

'Clearly better than that crap you read,' Paige said, angling her head at the pile of crumpled reading material on the table.

'I happen to like these,' Bonnie said, 'they keep me up to date with goings on in the world.'

'What, like Victoria Beckham's new haircut? Hardly breaking news, is it?'

'You read them, I've seen you.'

'Only because there's nothing else in the flat to read.'

'What about that pile of books in your room?'

'If I wanted to read books I'd go into school.'

'The answer is still no, even if you try to talk me round by wrapping me up in an argumentative knot.'

The room went silent for a moment. Bonnie watched Paige carefully. She could almost hear the cogs moving in her daughter's head and waited for her next gem.

'Can I get a Saturday job, then?'

'Why would you do that?'

'To get some money of my own.'

'Have you forgotten the weekend job at the hairdresser's last year?'

'It wasn't my fault,' Paige pouted.

'You practically gave Mrs Squires a cracked skull.'

'She kept telling me to rub harder when I was shampooing her. So I did. How was I to know the silly cow didn't mean *that* hard?'

'You banged her head on the sink!'

'*She* banged her head on the sink because her neck was too feeble to take my rubbing when she'd told me to rub hard!'

Bonnie tried to bite back a smile as she remembered how annoyed Paige had been, coming home early with a blood stained t-shirt, a small amount of cash and a huge amount of wounded pride. After a long lecture from the salon owner, which apparently included some colourful swearwords, Paige had been sent packing. That first foray into employment had been her last so far. Secretly, Bonnie liked it that way. Paige was growing up way too fast and Bonnie wasn't sure she was ready to let go just yet, even though the money would have been handy.

'Paige,' she said affectionately, 'as soon as I have some spare money, we will go out and buy you whatever your heart desires…' she paused with a half-smile, 'as long as it's under twenty quid.'

*

Despite Bonnie's longer than usual break, Monday came round all too quickly.

'Good weekend?' Linda asked as Bonnie flew into work just in time to avoid one of Fred's lectures, the crisp autumn chill still clinging to her like a second coat.

'Weird, actually,' Bonnie replied as she hung her bag on a peg. 'Paige won a competition to meet Every Which Way. Can you believe that?'

'Wow, that's some luck,' Linda acknowledged. She grinned at Bonnie. 'Don't you have a bit of a thing for one of them? Maybe you're about to get that man of your dreams after all.'

'One of them is cute,' Bonnie said, trying to hide the blush that was spreading from her neck. 'But they're all about twelve, aren't they? I'm not even sure it's legal for me to fancy one of them.'

'I highly doubt it,' Linda replied. 'Probably best you don't tell anyone. When is this going to happen?'

'Next month. We rang the radio station and it's all above board as far as I can tell. Paige is taking Annabel.'

'They'll have a whale of a time. Are you chaperoning or Annabel's mum and dad? They'll need someone sensible there to make sure they don't throw themselves at the band and declare their undying love.'

'I don't really know…' It was actually the first time that question had occurred to Bonnie. And if anyone was going to be throwing themselves anywhere declaring undying love, it was more likely to be Bonnie herself than Paige or Annabel. Perhaps, under the circumstances, it was better if Annabel's parents took the girls to the radio station. Much as she had desperately wanted to meet Holden, faced with the sudden reality of it, she wasn't sure that she wanted it at all. She was just someone that he'd laugh about afterwards, some sad, desperate old cow that he'd make fun of as soon as she'd left the building. At least if she was out of the way she could keep herself occupied at home.

There was a roar from the shop.

'BLOODY HELL FIRE!'

Bonnie and Linda looked at each other, half way between shock and laughter.

'THIEVING LITTLE BASTARDS!' Fred shouted. 'BONNIE, GET IN HERE, LASS!'

Bonnie rushed out to the shop floor. 'What's up?'

'What's up?' Fred shouted. 'What's up? I'll tell you what's up! Look down here.'

Bonnie bent to where he was pointing to see a scattering of small black pellets near one of the display cases.

'MOUSE SHIT!' Fred boomed.

'Oh…' Bonnie stood and stared, wondering quite what Fred was asking her to do about it. Apart from dangling a lump of cheese under the unit, clicking her fingers and calling 'here, mousey, mousey' she failed to see what she could do. If they had mice, then it was going to take longer than they had before opening time to sort the problem.

*

Linda started unloading the cold stock, still chuckling to herself as Fred continued to shout in the main shop. As she worked, the familiar morning knock came at the back door. She went to answer it and Max ambled into the tiny stockroom with a huge grin on his face.

'It's a gorgeous morning, Linda!'

Linda threw him a sideways look. 'No it isn't.'

'The crappy weather can't upset me today,' Max replied lightly.

'Oh? Is that why you look like the cat that got the cream and then licked it off his girlfriend's backside?' Linda said nonchalantly, strolling to the kitchenette. She came back to the doorway, shook the kettle at him with a questioning look and he nodded.

'That's because I now have an actual girlfriend with an actual backside to lick it from,' he said, rubbing the chill from his hands.

'You're disgusting,' Linda laughed.

'You brought the whole backside-cream scenario up,' Max retorted.

'That's true. In that case, I'm disgusting.'

Max laughed. An extra loud shout came from the shop floor followed by Bonnie's placating tones.

'What's up with Freddie Flintstone?' Max asked in a low voice.

'He's found mouse droppings,' Linda whispered.

'It's a fruit and veg shop, goes with the territory,' Max replied amiably.

'Yeah,' Linda agreed, 'but, of course, customers don't see it like that and Fred's freaking out trying to find out where they're getting in.'

'Shouldn't he just get the council?'

'Too risky.'

'They'd close you down?'

'No, Fred would have a heart attack when they sent him the bill.' Max chuckled.

'So,' Linda said as she flicked on the kettle, 'getting back to creamy backsides… who is the lucky girl?'

'She's called Sarah. We met on Saturday at a mutual friend's wedding and she gave me her number. Turns out we were at the same college and never even knew.'

'She's not your girlfriend yet then.'

'Oh she is, we went out for a drink yesterday.'

'Bloody hell,' Linda remarked, clearly impressed, 'you're a fast worker.'

'Life's too short to mess around waiting,' Max said in a significant tone. His glance went, momentarily, to the main shop where Fred could still be heard shouting and Bonnie trying to calm him down.

'So, superstud, when are you seeing her again?' Linda asked.

'Hmmmm?'

'I said, when are you seeing this Sarah again?'

'Wednesday.' He paused for a moment. 'You don't think I'm being too keen, do you?' Max asked, suddenly looking concerned.

Linda laughed. 'I think it's men who get spooked by keenness, women generally take it as a flattering thing.'

Max's worried frown relaxed into a grin. 'Probably. I really like her, Linda.'

The kettle clicked off and Linda poured hot water over a teabag before stabbing it with a spoon a few times and lifting it from the mug. 'She must be something pretty special then,' Linda said, raising her eyebrows as she splashed some milk into the mug and handed it to Max.

He paused for a moment, as though reading her mind. 'Bonnie is never going to say yes and there's no point in flogging that poor horse any longer.'

'She doesn't know what's good for her, that's why.'

Max shrugged. 'Maybe. Or maybe she just doesn't like me in that way.'

'I think she does, that's the problem. But she's been hurt, Max, and I think she's afraid to trust anyone again.'

Max's expression became pensive as his gaze travelled to the doorway of the shop where Bonnie flitted in and out of view as she raced around searching under shelving units.

'That might be true. But I can't keep waiting.' He turned to Linda. 'You understand that, don't you, Linda?'

Linda nodded. 'Of course I do. It's a shame, though, because neither of you can see how perfect you'd be together.'

'I could,' Max laughed. 'I'm clearly not Heathcliff enough for her.'

'I'll stick the fan on,' Linda said as she sipped at her tea, 'and you don the frilly shirt and frock coat and run across the windswept shop shouting to Bonnie to let you in.'

'That might just work.' Max's laughter became louder.

'What's so funny?' Bonnie stood at the door of the shop with her arms folded and out of breath.

'You really don't want to know,' Linda said. 'Kettle's just boiled if you want one.'

'I do, I'm parched.' She shot an exasperated look at Max. 'Fred's ranting about mice.'

'And have you found them?' Max asked.

Bonnie glanced at Linda. 'Not yet... no thanks to my workmate shirking in the back here.'

Linda grinned. 'I did the cockroaches last week, you're on your own for this little drama,' she called from the kitchenette as she flicked on the kettle to re-boil it.

'So, how's the world of Max?' Bonnie asked, tucking a stray hair behind her ear.

'I'm good,' Max said carefully.

'He has a girlfriend…' Linda cut in as she returned and handed Bonnie a mug. 'Her name's Sarah, if you want to know.'

Bonnie raised her eyebrows. The news that Max was finally dating was not a surprise, but the violent feelings it suddenly stirred in her were. 'And, where did you meet Sarah,' she asked, fighting to keep her tone neutral.

'At a wedding on Saturday night.' Max seemed as though he was also trying to play down any awkwardness.

Linda looked between the two of them, shook her head, and then went out to the shop with a mug of tea for Fred.

'She wasn't one of the bridesmaids, was she?' Bonnie asked, taking care to make her tone jovial.

'Actually, she was.'

'That old cliché, eh?'

'Yeah. If ever a man was a walking cliché, it's me.'

'I didn't mean that…' Bonnie's sentence trailed to nothing. There was a sudden tension in the air that she couldn't understand. Damn Max, why did he have to keep asking her out all these months, it was bound to end awkwardly. But Bonnie loved Max's easygoing manner – his visits in the mornings were one of the few bright spots of her working day and she didn't want to lose that for the sake of a difficult situation that would doubtless blow over if they didn't make a big deal of it. She shook away her negative thoughts.

'So, she's nice, this new lady?'

'She seems it,' Max replied. 'We went out last night and got on really well.'

'That's good,' Bonnie said. 'When are you seeing her again?'

'I thought Wednesday... that's not too soon, is it? Where do you think I should take her?'

'That sounds okay to me. As for where, I have absolutely no idea. The last time I went anywhere nice we had to hail a Hansom cab to get there.'

Max chuckled, seemingly more relaxed now.

'A meal out is always good, though,' Bonnie continued. 'Just take her somewhere quiet where you can talk.'

'We had a meal out for our first date. It wasn't exactly quiet, though, we were in that carvery just outside town and you wouldn't believe how loud toddlers can scream.'

'Try a fifteen-year-old,' Bonnie quipped.

'Paige still being awkward?'

'Nah... nothing out of the ordinary. She's just being Paige.'

'You want to share it?'

Bonnie shook her head. 'Thanks, Max, but I'd better get out to the shop before Freddie Starr out there blows a gasket.'

Max took his mug to the kitchenette and rinsed it before setting it down on the rusting draining board. 'I'd better get cracking too,' he said as he came back out. 'These carrots won't deliver themselves.'

Bonnie watched as he let himself out the back door. A strange feeling settled over her that, if she hadn't known better, she might have mistaken for regret.

*

Break time came and Bonnie sat on her own nursing a cup of tea, her blank sheet of flowery paper on the table before her, pen poised mid-air.

Dear Holden

My daughter won a competition to meet you and the other band members. Is that some sort of crazy karma or what? So it looks like I might get to meet you after all. I'll be honest: I'm not sure how I feel about that. I doubt I'll be any more special to you than the lady who makes your tea at the radio station. Being unnoticed by you, even though I'm right there in front of you, might be worse than you never knowing I exist at all. At least if you never know I exist, you'll never be able to reject me…

Bonnie tore the page in half and dropped it into the bin as she went back through to the shop.

*

Fighting against the wind to keep her scarf wrapped under her chin, Bonnie walked side by side with Linda.

'Not just a teensy bit bothered that Max has a girlfriend now?'

Bonnie threw Linda a withering sideways glance. 'He's had one date with her.'

'He seems keen,' Linda replied.

'Good for him. If he's happy, then that's one more happy person in the world.'

'What if it gets serious?'

'What if it does?'

'You won't care?'

'Linda, this is getting ridiculous now. Why should I care? Max was never serious about going out with me, he was just being Max. Cute in his own way, but just like every other man, he'd be willing to take it where he could find it. The fact that he just fell in with this Sarah woman proves it. If he was that crazy about me he wouldn't be asking other women out, even if they were dressed as pink meringues.'

'He didn't ask her out.'

'What?'

'Max didn't ask her out.'

'Of course he did.'

'He told me this morning when he was hauling the stock in that *she* asked *him* out.'

'That's very modern of her,' Bonnie replied in a scathing tone, but the fact had shocked her more than she cared to admit.

'You don't look at him properly,' Linda said. 'Sarah obviously saw what everyone but you sees – a really nice guy who is worth his weight in gold.'

'Well… then Sarah is lucky and I hope they're very happy together.'

Linda gave an impatient sigh. They lapsed into silence. The traffic roared past and the beginnings of fine rain spattered against their faces.

*

Five silent minutes later, Linda pushed open the door to The Bounty. 'Alright Stav?' she called as they walked in.

Stavros was handing a customer some change and his round face crinkled into a delighted smile at their entrance. 'Lovely ladies! How are you today?'

'Starving,' Linda said. 'You'd better have something extra gooey and nice for pudding too today, coz Bonnie here is in a foul mood and she needs sugar.'

'I am not!' Bonnie exclaimed.

'You are, you've been tetchy all morning.'

'Why are you only saying this now, in front of Stav?'

'Because I didn't dare while we were on our own,' Linda laughed. 'Stav will protect me if you decide to lamp me one.'

Stavros held up his hands in a gesture of surrender. 'Do not get me involved.'

Linda looked down the laminated menu on the wall. 'What are we having today, Bon?'

Bonnie shrugged as she perused the list alongside her friend. 'I'm not all that hungry, to be honest. Maybe I'll just have some soup to warm me up.'

'Yes,' Stavros agreed, 'the weather is getting cold quickly this year. Only three weeks ago we were all burning up, now look at us, scarves and soup.'

'I'll have a jacket, Stav, with beans and cheese,' Linda said.

Stavros nodded. 'And for beautiful Bonnie we have Moroccan spiced vegetable soup, very nice, put hairs on your chest.'

Bonnie smiled. 'Sounds lovely… apart from the hair bit. I'll have one of those.'

Stavros disappeared behind a curtain of coloured plastic strips for a moment. They could hear him shout in rapid Greek. Then he emerged again.

'How is Fred?' he asked conversationally. 'Business is good?'

'It depends who you ask,' Linda said. 'According to Fred we're headed for another Wall Street Crash. But me and Bonnie are up and down like prossie's knickers in that shop so it can't be all that desperate.'

Stavros broke into a huge belly laugh. 'The prossie's knickers. You are funny, Linda.'

'Don't you dare tell him I said that,' Linda warned, 'My life in that shop would be hell.'

Stavros grinned and lowered his voice. 'You know that you can have a job here. The offer I make is always good...'

'I don't think your mama would be too happy about that,' Linda replied.

Stavros grimaced. 'That ugly old goat. She gets more like a screeching harpy every day.'

'You're so mean to her,' Bonnie chided.

'Mean to *her*?' Stavros squeaked. 'She tortures me with her very existence! Always: *this is not right, that is not right, I'm so old I wish I could die.* I wish she could bloody die too! She will live forever!'

Linda chuckled. 'You don't mean that! You're all talk and you know it.'

As if on cue, a hunched old lady appeared through the plastic strips. She looked something like a prune on legs. Placing two parcels on the counter, she glared at Stavros and then gave the two women a good natured nod. '*Yia sas.*'

'How are you, Mama?' Linda asked. Not knowing her name, all the regulars at the Bounty just called her *Mama* like Stavros did.

The little woman threw her hands in the air and replied in an accent much stronger than her son's. 'Sick of being worked like a donkey in this shop by my disrespectful son.'

Linda laughed. 'You know he loves you really.'

Mama pulled a disbelieving face and then shuffled back to the kitchen.

'She's a little gem.' Linda took the parcels from the counter.

Stavros beamed with obvious pride but he didn't say a word. 'See you tomorrow, ladies.'

Linda waved a nonchalant hand as they left the shop.

*

Bonnie threw her coat over a chair as she walked into the living room. Paige was curled up under a duvet on the sofa watching TV and barely looked up.

'Good afternoon, Paige,' Bonnie said in a deliberate voice. 'Have you had a good day? *Why yes, thank you mother, for enquiring, did you have good day at work?*'

'Hey, Mum,' Paige looked up long enough to acknowledge the greeting but none of the rest of the comment.

Bonnie let it go. 'What do you fancy for tea?'

'I've eaten,' Paige said, not taking her eyes from the screen.

'You couldn't even wait? I thought we were going to start making an effort to eat together.'

'I called at Jeanie's on the way home from school, she fed me.'

'You called at Jeanie's?' Bonnie shook her head wonderingly. 'I mean, *your nan's*. How come?'

Paige shrugged vaguely. 'I was bored and I didn't want to sit on my own.'

Bonnie's eyebrows knitted together. 'You could have phoned to tell me you were there and I would have come to you.'

'I was going to, but Jeanie had some weird phone call. She disappeared into her bedroom for ages. So I got sick of waiting and came home.'

'Paige! She'll be worried to death about you!'

Paige rolled her eyes. 'Don't be ridiculous, Mum. She phoned here after and I told her I was okay. You stress too much.'

Bonnie perched on the edge of the sofa, frowning. 'What was the phone call about?'

Paige shrugged. 'No idea. She was speaking Spanish, though.'

Bonnie raised her eyebrows. '*Spanish*? Your nan doesn't speak Spanish.'

'She does a bit; she goes on her cigarette runs all the time.'

'Not enough for a phone conversation, though.'

'Oh yeah, well, she did speak some English too, after she said hello and asked how he was.'

'*He?*'

Paige shrugged again. 'It just sounded like a bloke, the way she was talking.'

'What was she saying?' Bonnie pressed.

Paige looked up from the TV. 'Mum… if you want to know, you'll have to ask her.'

Bonnie went to the kitchen, her mind turning over these new developments. As Paige wasn't eating, there didn't seem any point in cooking just for herself. She dragged a pack of ham from the fridge and buttered some bread while she wondered what on earth her mum was up to now.

Chapter Four

'Paige told me all about the competition already,' Jeanie said as she fastened her seatbelt.

'I thought so,' Bonnie said, throwing a knowing look at Paige on the back seat, noting again that particular shade of lipstick really was too bright for her daughter's complexion. It wasn't an argument you had with Paige, though, so she had kept her mouth firmly closed on the subject. 'That's why you went over after school out of the blue the other night.'

Paige grinned sheepishly.

'And I suppose you gave her some money for an outfit?' Bonnie arched an eyebrow at her mum.

It was Jeanie's turn to look sheepish.

Bonnie sighed as she started the engine. 'You did book this table, didn't you?' she asked Jeanie. 'You know what Blossom Palace is like on a Saturday night.'

'Yes, I booked. Stop stressing.'

Bonnie glanced across at her mum as she released the handbrake. 'You sound more and more like Paige every day.'

'She does not!' Paige put in from the back seat.

Jeanie grinned. 'Cool your jets, Paige, no one is taking your awesome crown from you.'

'Naaaaaan,' Paige groaned, 'don't talk that way, it makes you sound like an idiot.'

Bonnie laughed. 'It's your nan's birthday and she's having a mid-life crisis, so indulge her.'

'Cheeky cow!' Jeanie fired at Bonnie, whose laugh became louder still.

'Oh, I forgot, you've been having that since you were eighteen,' Bonnie quipped.

'You're not too old for a slap, you know,' Jeanie chided. Bonnie glanced across and caught the ghost of a smile.

'I tell you what,' she said, changing the subject, 'I'm starving. I haven't had Chinese in ages, I can't wait.'

'The buffet at Blossom Palace is awesome,' Paige said. 'Annabel goes all the time with her mum and dad,' she added with a slightly reproachful note in her voice. It didn't escape Bonnie.

'Annabel's mum is a nurse and her dad is a manager at a tyre plant. They can afford to eat at Blossom Palace a lot more than we can. I'm sorry that we don't go out enough for you.'

'I never said a word about that,' Paige replied defensively.

'No, but you were thinking it.'

'Let's not worry about money tonight,' Jeanie cut in, sensing an argument brewing. 'It's my birthday and it only comes round once a year, and who knows how many more I'll have…'

'Nothing like a bit of morbid melodrama to lighten the mood,' Bonnie said dryly.

'All I'm saying is let's enjoy ourselves tonight and worry about the rest of life tomorrow.'

'As it's your birthday, then I suppose you get to call the shots tonight.' Bonnie smiled and returned her attention to the road ahead.

*

Bonnie squeezed into the gap around the hotplate, Paige behind her. The restaurant interior was warm and fragrant with the smell of exotic spices and fruit and the food laid out before them glistened invitingly, the dishes and their sauces vibrant with colour. The thing that Bonnie loved about buffet evenings, like Paige and Jeanie had always agreed, was that you could try all sorts of new things and you didn't have to worry about taking ages to choose from the menu, wishing that you'd chosen something else after all when it finally arrived.

'Get me some of that prawn toast before it goes, Mum,' Paige squeaked impatiently.

'You can get it,' Bonnie replied, 'you're not that far off, it'll still be there when you get there.'

'Yeah, but you're nearer,' Paige insisted, 'and you know how much I like it.'

'If I put it on my plate then I have less room for what I want to eat. The idea of a buffet is that you can keep coming back up,' Bonnie said.

'You don't need as much as I do, I'm still growing.'

Bonnie sighed and reached for the tongs to pick up a small pile of prawn toast.

'Happy?' She turned to Paige.

Paige grinned and spooned a pile of fried rice onto her plate. Bonnie shuffled along in the line, pondering each compartment of food on offer. It had been a long time since she had been treated to a meal out, even if it was just a Chinese buffet with her mum and Paige, and she was going to make the most of it.

Once she and Paige had piled their plates high with various concoctions of rice, noodles, sauces and vegetables, they began to negotiate the busy restaurant back to Jeanie who was at the table, guarding their belongings and waiting for her turn. For a moment, Bonnie's attention wandered and she jumped back with a start, just about saving her plate from disaster as she narrowly avoided bumping into a red-haired woman.

'Oh, God, I'm so sorry,' Bonnie exclaimed.

The woman looked to be in her mid-twenties, clear skin and gentle grey eyes, an understated, willowy kind of beauty that Bonnie instantly felt envious of. 'It's really my fault.' She smiled apologetically. 'I wasn't watching where I was going; too excited about getting to the food.'

Paige had already left them exchanging apologies and was back at the table tucking into her meal. Bonnie looked across with a frown and was about to politely end their conversation and make her own way back when she heard a familiar voice. Max was now standing next to the red-haired woman.

'Bonnie!' He smiled. 'Fancy meeting you here!'

Bonnie fought the blush as she felt it rise from her neck. It wasn't that Max made her flustered usually; it was just the weirdness of seeing him here, of all places, that upset her for some reason. He slid an arm around the shoulder of the woman Bonnie had just been apologising to. Bonnie's heart seemed to miss a beat as she made the connection.

'I see you've met Sarah.' Max said.

'I sort of nearly tipped her dinner all over her,' Sarah said with a laugh that was so dainty and musical, Bonnie wondered if it could possibly be real.

'That's unfortunate,' Max said. He turned to Bonnie. 'So what brings you out? Celebrating something or just a lazy tea?'

Bonnie nodded her head in the direction of their table where Jeanie was just easing herself off her chair to make her own way to the hotplates. 'My Mum's birthday. Not a special one, but she wanted to treat me and Paige.'

'Oh, every birthday is special,' Sarah said warmly. 'I don't let a single year go by without marking it.'

Bonnie laughed self-consciously. 'It doesn't have the same appeal when you get older, or so my mum tells me.' She glanced down at her plate. 'I should probably get this to the table before I tip it over someone else.'

'Oh, of course,' Sarah said. 'It'll be stone cold and you wouldn't want that.'

Max nodded affably at Bonnie and took Sarah's arm protectively, ready to lead her to the hotplate. Something settled in Bonnie's gut as she noted the gesture, an emotion that she recognised but didn't understand in this context. Why now, of all times?

'It was lovely meeting you,' Sarah said in an earnest tone to Bonnie.

'You too,' Bonnie replied, 'Max has told us all about you, but at least now we know you're not a figment of his imagination.'

Sarah laughed. 'I hope not!' Then she added: 'Oh yes! Now I know, you're *Bonnie*, from Applejack's! Max told me all about you.'

Bonnie raised her eyebrows at Max, who simply grinned.

'All good I hope,' Bonnie said.

'Well…' he said with a playful look, 'Everything about Linda was good.'

'Cheeky!'

'Enjoy your meal,' Max said. 'And I'll see you on Monday morning bright and early.'

'Yeah…' Bonnie glanced at her dinner and then back at Sarah's slender shoulders. Suddenly she wished there wasn't quite so much food on her plate. She watched as they walked off together.

Her thoughts were interrupted by Jeanie's voice in her ear.

'Isn't that the delivery man for Applejack's?'

'Max, yeah, it is.'

'Is that his girlfriend with him?'

Bonnie nodded.

'She's very pretty.'

Bonnie ran her eyes over Sarah as she laughed lightly at something Max had said. She wore a flared, cream cheesecloth dress that virtually swept the floor, sleeveless with delicate floral designs embroidered into the neckline and hem. Bangles clacked along her wrists and she had a set of ethnic looking beads at her neck. Her make-up was subtle but chosen perfectly to accentuate the peachy tones of her skin and her auburn hair.

'That dress is a bit summery for this time of year,' Bonnie decided. Her gaze flicked down to her own jeans, and a pale blue smock top that, although it was an old favourite, was now a couple of seasons out of date. Jeanie was wearing her leather trousers and Paige had lipstick on that glowed so brightly planes would be able to land by it in the event of a blackout, but at least they had made an effort for tonight. Bonnie was beginning to wish that she had too.

'You'd better go and sit down,' Jeanie reminded her. 'Paige will be getting hit on if you leave her alone any longer in that outfit.'

Bonnie looked over to the table where Paige was sitting tucking into her dinner and staring at her phone intently, oblivious to anything going on around her. Bonnie frowned. Perhaps she should have said something about that top; now that she looked again, it was just a bit too revealing…

'I'll be back in a minute, just as soon as I get some of those noodles,' Jeanie added.

Bonnie nodded and went to join her daughter.

As she slid onto the seat beside her, Paige looked up from her phone. 'Wasn't that the delivery guy from your shop you were talking to?'

'It's not *my* shop,' Bonnie replied in a more irritated tone than she had meant.

'Whatever,' Paige said, glancing across to the food carts. 'Who is that with him, his wife?'

'No, a new girlfriend.'

Paige laughed. 'He managed to get a girl to go out with him?'

'What does that mean? Max is a nice bloke.'

'Yeah, but…' Paige raised her eyebrows meaningfully.

'But what?'

'Look at him.'

Bonnie followed her gaze. 'There's nothing wrong with him.'

'Those trousers? With that top? Jeez, Mum, you need a visit from the fashion police if you think he looks okay.'

Max was making his way back across the restaurant with Sarah now. Bonnie looked at what he was wearing: brown chinos with a white granddad shirt. She shrugged.

'He looks good.' As soon as she said it, she felt that heat spread from her neck again without knowing why.

As she watched, she saw Jeanie catch up with the couple, stopping them for a quick word. They pointed to a table by the window and Sarah did an elaborate mime to indicate that she was cold. The restaurant was busy, with every table taken, but Bonnie, Paige and Jeanie had a table that was plenty big enough for them and more besides. Bonnie watched the conversation with a sinking feeling as she realised what was about to happen. Jeanie, a naturally gregarious woman, was never one to stand on convention. Sure enough, she saw Max nod eagerly; then he and Sarah went over to their table and grabbed the few belongings they had left there before making their way over to follow Jeanie.

'What's going on?' Bonnie hissed at her mum.

'They're coming to sit with us,' Jeanie answered. 'That poor girl is freezing with the draft from that window and we have plenty of room.' She raised her eyebrows at Bonnie's look of consternation. 'You're always saying what a laugh Max is.'

Bonnie had no time to reply as Max and Sarah arrived at their table with slightly awkward smiles.

'It is okay if we join you, isn't it?' Max asked uncertainly.

Bonnie smoothed her expression into something as close to politeness as she could manage. 'Of course it is. Paige…' she nudged her daughter, who had barely looked up from her texting, 'budge up so that Max and Sarah can sit down.'

Paige pouted and looked as though she was going to complain, but then caught Bonnie's warning look and clearly thought better of it. Instead, she shuffled along the bench seat, Bonnie following. Max put down his plate and looked for a moment as though he would sit in the space next to Bonnie, but then quickly changed his mind, taking a seat next to Jeanie and leaving Sarah to squeeze in alongside Bonnie and Paige.

'Well,' Max said as he pulled his plate towards him and picked up his fork, 'this is cosy, isn't it?'

'The more the merrier, as far as I'm concerned.' Jeanie smiled as she picked up her own cutlery.

Paige's attention returned to her phone.

'So, it's your birthday?' Sarah asked Jeanie, who nodded.

'Don't ask me how old I am, though,' Jeanie quipped, 'or I'll be forced to kill you.'

Max chuckled. 'Whenever we meet, Jeanie, I see where Bonnie gets her sense of humour from.' He looked thoughtful. 'How long has it been since I last saw you?'

'Ooooh, last time I was in Applejack's at the same ungodly hour you get there was when Bonnie's car broke down and I had to run her into work until she got a new one.' She turned to Bonnie. 'How long have you had the car you've got now?'

Bonnie shrugged. 'About three years, I think.'

'That'll be it, then,' Jeanie said. 'Three years ago.'

'Bloody hell,' Max rubbed a hand across his chin. 'Time does fly. I'd only just taken on the business then from my dad.'

'I think you had,' Bonnie agreed. 'How is he, by the way?'

'He's brilliant. Early retirement was the best decision he ever made.'

'He went to France, didn't he?' Jeanie cut in.

Max nodded. 'He has a house in the Dordogne, loves it there.'

Paige's head shot up for a moment and she caught Bonnie in a measured gaze. But the reference to France that Paige and Jeanie had feared might send Bonnie into a dour mood seemed to pass without note. Bonnie was now too busy watching Sarah eat. Max's girlfriend seemed oblivious to the attention, and looked up from her plate with an unassuming smile.

'So, what do you do for a living?' Bonnie asked, trying to sound casual.

'I'm a mature student,' Sarah replied.

'Oh, what are you studying?' Jeanie asked, her interest clearly piqued.

'Fine art. I'm going into my second year now. I was a teaching assistant before, but I knew it wasn't for me. I'd always been interested in art, so I decided one day that life is too short and I should pursue my dream of becoming a professional artist.'

Bonnie tried to look suitably impressed. *Great, not only is she pretty but she's clever and talented too. Is there anything wrong with this woman?*

'She showed me some of her work when I went to pick her up tonight,' Max said, 'it's really good.' He added self-consciously, 'not that I know much about art. Potato prints, that's about my limit,' he laughed.

Sarah smiled affectionately at him. 'You are funny. You don't need to know about art to appreciate what you like. I always think that art is too elitist and should be more about people simply liking what they like.'

Oh dear God, Bonnie thought, *pretty, clever, talented and also nice beyond reason. How much more annoying could she be?*

*

'I've had a lovely evening.' Jeanie undid her seatbelt as they pulled up outside her house. 'It was nice to have Max and Sarah with us, livened things up a bit. I can almost pretend I had a real birthday party.'

'Thanks. Nice to know our company would have been so dull if they hadn't turned up,' Bonnie commented with a sideways glance.

'You know what I mean.'

'You could have invited your friends,' Bonnie said, 'nobody stopped you.'

'You don't like my friends,' Jeanie returned.

'I do.'

'As I recall, you called them a bunch of old crusties.'

There was a snigger from the back seat. 'Nice one, Mum.'

'I didn't mean anything by it,' Bonnie said to Jeanie, ignoring Paige.

'Anyway, I'm seeing them all tomorrow night. Pete and Tank have a special birthday performance lined up for me in Leathers.' Jeanie grinned, clearly excited by this prospect.

'That rock club at the edge of town? I thought you'd stopped going there.'

'What made you think that?'

Bonnie shrugged, suddenly feeling guilty. Had she really been so self-absorbed lately that she didn't know what happened in her mum's life when she wasn't there?

'I thought Sarah was boring,' Paige cut in from the back seat.

'Paige!' Jeanie chided.

'Max must have done too, because he spent all his time talking to Mum instead of his actual girlfriend,' Paige continued in a scathing tone.

'He didn't,' Bonnie said defensively. 'We do see each other almost every day so he knows me really well.'

'Exactly,' Paige insisted. 'You'd have thought he'd have nothing left to say to you and should be getting to know his date.'

'That's silly. It was just breaking the ice; he got the whole table talking. He's a natural chatterbox, is Max.'

'He's a natural something,' Paige fired back.

'I think he's lovely,' Jeanie said. 'Sarah is lovely too and I hope it works out for them.'

'They deserve each other,' Paige piped up, 'both as sad as one another.'

'Paige,' Jeanie snapped, turning around in her seat to hold her granddaughter in an icy stare, 'did anybody ask for your opinion?'

'But –'

'No buts,' Jeanie said, 'only to butt out.'

Paige fell into a sullen silence and Bonnie gave her mum a withering look.

'I'm in for a lovely evening now she's in a mood, thanks, Mum.'

'Don't lay the blame at my door. You don't tell her often enough when she's out of order.'

'Don't start, Mum…'

Jeanie held up a placatory hand. 'It's fine. I've had a lovely evening, despite what some people…' she inclined her head at Paige, 'think, and I don't want to ruin it by falling out with you.' She forced a smile. 'Do you want to come in for a quick cuppa before you go home?'

Bonnie shook her head. 'If you don't mind, I'm tired. I think I'll just climb into my PJs and call it a night.'

Jeanie paused for a moment, and then took a deep breath, almost as if she was screwing up the courage to say something important, something that she was afraid of. But then she smiled tightly and stretched over to kiss Bonnie on the cheek.

'Alright. Maybe I'll see you tomorrow?'

'Maybe. I'll see how late it is by the time I've cleaned the flat and done the shopping.'

'Night then. And you, Paige, sleep tight.'

Paige looked up and gave a sulky nod and Jeanie slipped out of the car and into the night.

*

Bonnie chewed on her lip as she ran her eyes over the instructions on the pack. Then she put the box back on the shelf and picked up a different shade. She pored over the photo on the front of the box, and then flipped it over to look at the result panel on the back. Caramel Cream… was that too dark? It looked dark over the blonde example on the box, though Bonnie's was a fairly dark blonde to start with. Did she want to go darker and more exotic, or blonder and bubblier? Her eyes caught another box: Copper Canyon. What about red? Maybe red could be a more exciting alternative? But could she really pull off red hair?

It had been a spontaneous decision to call in at the chemist on the way home from work that Friday night and Bonnie didn't even know what had made her do it. All she knew was every day that week had seen her mood become more and more impatient, and every day that she looked in the mirror, she was less satisfied by what she saw. Maybe a change was the answer?

But right now Paige would be on her own in the flat, waiting for Bonnie to get home. She glanced up and along the aisle where a girl with pink hair and a nose ring was picking up the same colour that was already on her head, clearly a refresher application. Bonnie hesitated for a moment, mesmerised by how young and trendy she was. Then she grabbed the red and marched to the tills.

*

'Oh my God, Mum, you look amazing!' Paige stared at Bonnie, who had gone into the bathroom after tea without a word to her daughter, applied the dye and then dried and smoothed her hair with rarely-used straighteners. The effect was dramatic, to say the least, and even Bonnie had been shocked at the sight of herself in the mirror. After a moment or two of wide-eyed contemplation, she began to bubble with excitement at the change, and Paige's reaction had reinforced that. Maybe this was all she needed to shake herself out of the rut her life had fallen into.

Paige flipped herself from the sofa and went over to Bonnie, picking up a lock of hair from her shoulders to examine. 'It's gorgeous.' She beamed. 'How come you decided to do this?'

Bonnie shrugged, trying to make light of the compliment, but the delight at Paige's comments evident in her smile. 'I just fancied a change.'

'The men will be fainting over you,' Paige said.

It was the first time Paige had ever talked so openly about the fact that Bonnie was single. Bonnie cautiously wondered whether to take it as a good sign. Perhaps Paige was finally coming to terms with the fact that her father was not coming back, and maybe she was coming around to the idea that Bonnie deserved a second chance at love… something Bonnie herself was finding it hard to do.

'I don't know about that.' Bonnie laughed lightly. 'I think it will take a lot more than a new hairdo. A year on the exercise bike to lift this saggy bum for a start.'

'Don't be daft. You look way prettier than loads of my mates' mums.'

Bonnie felt herself swell with pride. Was that how Paige really saw her? Maybe she was having some sort of personality crisis and being unusually kind. Either way, it gave Bonnie a feeling of warmth that she hadn't had for a long time.

*

Dear Holden

It's not long until we come and see you now, at least, until my daughter comes to see you. I suppose I'll be waiting in the flat here, or at the very best outside in the car trying not to embarrass Paige. I dyed my hair. I think it looks nice and Paige seems to like it. Henri would have hated it. I wonder what you'll think if I do get to meet you…

Bonnie ran a hand down her hair absently, still slightly surprised by the uncharacteristic sleekness of it. She read the letter through once more, then screwed up the page and threw it into the kitchen bin. The clock showed eleven-thirty and she had another Monday to look forward to again the following day. They came around so quickly she could barely keep up. In six hours she would be up again, yawning and arguing with Paige to get out of bed for school. With a deep sigh, she dumped her mug in the sink and went up to bed.

*

Linda wolf-whistled as Bonnie pulled back the wet hood of her coat. 'Wow, you look like one hot momma!'

Bonnie laughed lightly. 'Steady on.'

Fred put his head round the door to the stockroom to give them his usual morning reprimand. He stopped in his tracks with his mouth hanging open.

'Bloody hell...'

'Don't mince your words, Fred,' Linda said in a wry tone.

'What the hell have you done to your hair, lass?'

Bonnie frowned. 'Traditionally, this is where you compliment me on how nice and different I look.'

'I'll have to go home to get my sunglasses.' There was almost a grin, but not quite as he uttered his next sentence. 'Don't stand too close to the tomatoes today; we might not be able to find you again.'

'Cheeky bugger!' Bonnie exclaimed.

Linda cocked an incredulous eyebrow at her boss. 'I can't believe you, of all people, are making scathing comments about hair.'

Fred self-consciously ran a hand over his pate. 'I don't know what you mean,' he grumbled.

Linda shot a sideways glance at Bonnie, biting back laughter.

'Never mind that now,' Fred insisted, 'there's a shop that needs stocking out here. Get those fridges unlocked.'

With a quick grin at Linda, Bonnie went to get the keys from the kitchen. The usual early morning knock came from the back door and Linda shuffled over to answer it.

'Morning!' Max shook the rain from his coat. 'Kettle on?'

Linda stepped back to let him in. 'Not yet but give us a tick.'

'Alright, Max?' Bonnie stepped from the kitchen, immediately aware of Max's stare and suddenly feeling herself blush.

Max shook his head. 'Sorry... blimey...'

Linda laughed as she went to put the kettle on. 'Bonnie, you'd better not put make-up on tomorrow, the blokes round here might not be responsible for their actions.'

Bonnie slapped her arm playfully as she passed and squeezed into the kitchenette.

'You look...' Max's sentence trailed off again.

'Lovely? I'm sure that's the word you're looking for,' Linda called from the kitchen.

'I mean,' Max continued as if Linda hadn't spoken, 'not that you don't always look nice... it's just that...' He shook his head again.

Bonnie couldn't work out whether he approved or not. But then, she thought somewhat peevishly, it was her hair and she could do what she bloody well liked to it. Why should she be bothered that Max may not like it? Equally, what did it matter to her if he did?

Linda appeared at the kitchen doorway wiping her hands on a teacloth. 'Max, if that's your animal magnetism and easy going charm you're displaying there, it's a wonder Sarah didn't drop her knickers the minute she clapped eyes on you.' Max seemed to come back to himself and grinned widely. 'How's it going with Sarah, by the way?' she added as Bonnie sloped off to open the fridges.

'Good, thanks. I think we're coming up to our three-week anniversary.'

'Oooh, get you. Next we'll be talking weddings.'

Bonnie listened to the exchange as she stepped into the first walk-in fridge, her good humour dissipating. The cold never failed to surprise her no matter how many years it had been and, immediately, her skin prickled all over, her breath rising in a white plume. She dragged out a tray of Spanish plums and hauled them into the stockroom, glad to be back in the warm.

'When you've finished organising Max's love life, a little help here, Lind?' Bonnie snapped as she emerged from the fridge.

Linda shot a confused look at Max, who shrugged silently as Bonnie took the fruit out to the shop.

*

Try as she might, Bonnie hadn't quite managed to shake the dour mood that had settled over her that day at work, despite all the compliments and admiring looks from regular customers. By lunchtime, Linda had complained about her being less fun than a mass funeral, and stalked off to the Bounty to get lunch alone while Bonnie had sat in the kitchen of the shop nursing a cup-a-soup and a foul temper.

Linda's irritation only ever flared momentarily, so after her usual ten minutes of idle banter with Stavros, she was back to her old self. Busy all afternoon with customers, she hardly paid any more attention to Bonnie's dark mood and bid her a cheery farewell at home time.

As Bonnie had promised her mum she would call after work, she thought she'd better honour that promise. Jeanie had been less than enthusiastic about seeing her recently and Bonnie figured she'd somehow managed to upset her too.

*

Bonnie let herself in at Jeanie's house and shouted down the hallway. 'Hey, Mum, it's just me.'

Jeanie's head popped out from the kitchen doorway. 'Ooh, your hair looks nice! You didn't say you were going to colour it.'

'Thanks, Mum. I thought it was time for a change.'

'On your own tonight?'

'Paige is at Annabel's for tea. They're planning world domination, starting with the radio station next week. I've got to pick her up on the way home when she's created her masterplan.'

'Right.'

Jeanie's head disappeared again and Bonnie frowned. That wasn't the reaction to her joke she had been expecting. She entered the kitchen to find her mum sitting at the table with a magazine open and a cup of tea half drunk.

'What's that mag?' Bonnie asked.

Jeanie flicked the magazine shut and pushed it across the table to where Bonnie was sitting herself down. 'I've finished with it if you want to take it home with you.'

'Oooh, ta, Mum.' Bonnie pulled it over to look at the cover.

'Cup of tea?' Jeanie asked, pushing herself up from her seat. Bonnie watched her carefully as she went over to the kettle without waiting for Bonnie's reply.

'Are you feeling okay, Mum?'

'Hmmm?'

'You seem a bit… distracted.'

'No, no, I'm fine.' Jeanie flicked the switch to the kettle and reached for a mug from the cupboard.

'Mum, sit down.'

'I'll make your drink first…'

'Mum, the drink can wait. Just sit down and tell me what's wrong.'

'There's nothing wrong.'

'Something is bothering you.'

Jeanie paused, before exhaling loudly and then sitting down next to Bonnie at the table.

'I've been trying to tell you for ages…'

'Tell me what?'

'I've met someone.'

'What do you mean?' Bonnie knew perfectly well what her mother meant; but her brain couldn't compute the information for some reason.

'I've met a man…'

Bonnie stared at her mother.

'It's not that abnormal.'

'I know, but it's just so sudden.'

'Sudden? You're the one who's been telling me for the last five years I should find another fella.'

'It's just that…'

'It's just that you didn't really mean it even though you thought you did and now that there's someone on the scene it feels like a replacement for your dad, even though you know that nobody will ever replace your dad.' Jeanie smiled and pulled Bonnie into a hug. 'I knew how you'd feel about it, that's why I didn't want to tell you.'

'Okay,' Bonnie said quietly as she pulled away. 'You're right, just like you always are. How long has this been going on?'

'A couple of months.'

'A couple of months?' Bonnie thought back to the times that she could remember her mum being out over the past few weeks. 'But when? You're nearly always here.'

'He's been kind of hard to get hold of,' Jeanie replied awkwardly. 'There hasn't been much opportunity for us to see each other.'

Bonnie looked at her mum thoughtfully. 'So who is he?' she asked, rallying herself to cheeriness.

'He's named Juan.'

'Unusual name. Where's he live?'

'Costa del Sol.'

'What!'

'Spain.' Jeanie got up to fetch the biscuit tin from the cupboard.

'I know where it is,' Bonnie said. 'But how the hell are you going to sustain a relationship with a man in Spain?'

Jeanie shrugged as she popped the lid off the tin and nosed inside.

Bonnie sat at the table with a dazed expression. 'No wonder you've been on so many ciggie runs...'

Jeanie laughed. 'Sorry, love. I just didn't know how to tell you about him. But then after all that messing around and wondering how to put it, I realised that the best way was just to come out with it. After all, you're a big girl now.'

Bonnie paused. 'Spanish, eh?'

Jeanie nodded.

'We don't half have a thing for foreigners in our family.' Bonnie gave a faint smile.

'Let's hope we don't have a thing for deserters,' Jeanie replied darkly.

'It's pretty hard to desert someone when they live in another country already.'

Jeanie hesitated for a moment, holding her daughter in a carefully measured gaze and Bonnie felt her blood run cold. She'd seen that look a million times before and she knew she wasn't going to like what it meant.

'That's the thing,' Jeanie began slowly, 'I'm not sure we're going to be in separate countries for much longer.'

'Please tell me Juan is moving to England...'

Jeanie shook her head.

'Oh, God, Mum...'

'He's asked me to move to Spain, and I've said yes.'

'You hardly know the man!'

'That didn't stop you running off with Henri when you were eighteen,' Jeanie snapped.

'That was a three-month fling and then we moved back to England together, it was different, it was never meant to be permanent.'

'You didn't know that at the time.'

Bonnie sighed, fighting the tears that she knew were selfish. 'What will I do without you, Mum?'

Jeanie put down the tin and went back to the table. She took Bonnie's hand. 'It took me a long time to get over your dad, but lately I've come to realise something very important. I'm not getting any younger, despite the leather trousers that I know you think are unsuitable.' Jeanie laughed and Bonnie forced a smile. 'And life is too short to be so afraid that you let everything pass you by.'

'That means that you have to leap into risky moves across Europe with a man you hardly know?'

'Sometimes, yes, it does. Sometimes, you just have to take a chance. When you meet Juan I know you'll like him. He makes me feel more alive than I have done in years. He makes me complete, the way your dad used to. Can you be happy for me?'

'I'll worry to death about you,' Bonnie sniffed.

'You needn't. You have things more pressing than a silly old rocker to worry about.'

'I don't.'

'You have Paige, who is turning into a beautiful young woman before your eyes, who is smart and switched on in a way I've never seen in another girl of her age before. But she's also hurt and vulnerable. She needs you much more than I do.'

'We *both* need you,' Bonnie said.

Jeanie squeezed Bonnie's hand. 'You could always come.'

'With you? What would Juan say? That's gives a whole new slant on baggage.'

Jeanie laughed. 'It was just a thought. You'll be fine, and with budget airlines the journey out to me is quicker and cheaper than a train to London. You can come and visit as often as you like.'

'It'll be a bit of a bugger when Paige needs looking after during school holidays.'

'Paige won't want to come to me soon, and she's old enough to fend for herself while you're at work.'

'I suppose it will be quite nice having somewhere to take holidays,' Bonnie said. She tried to sound brave for her mum, but inside, she was cracking. Jeanie had been more than just her mum, she had been her rock, her best friend, someone who knew her better than anyone and kept her steady through life's storms. How could she even contemplate a life without her living just around the corner?

'Of course, and you'll be welcome any time,' Jeanie said, letting go of Bonnie's hand.

Bonnie's gaze dropped to the table and they fell silent for a moment, the sound of the kettle hissing as it boiled the only sound in the room. Then she swallowed and looked up.

'So this Juan... he has a nice house?'

'Gorgeous, a villa up in the mountains,' Jeanie said warmly.

'And he's a good man?'

'He's fantastic.'

'How did you meet him?'

'I decided to catch a bus from the coast to this little village in the mountains to have a look around. I missed the last bus back to the hotel as I couldn't work out where I went from and Juan found me sitting on a wall looking lost. At first I was just glad to come across someone who spoke good English, but he was so lovely and kind. He took me to a bar and sat me down while he checked on bus times, and when he realised that there wouldn't be one until the next day, he offered to drive me back.'

'And you went with him? He could have been a murderer or a rapist!'

'He could have been,' Jeanie conceded. 'But there was something about him, like goodness shining from inside him. I knew I'd be safe, and he was a perfect gentleman.' Jeanie's gaze was faraway for a moment, as if she was looking into the past. 'I sort of got the same feeling about him that I had with your dad when we first met. I haven't felt that since he passed on. It just so happens that I found it in Spain.'

It was Bonnie's turn to reach for her mum's hand across the table. 'Mum,' she said softly, 'if he makes you feel like that, then I can't be anything but happy for you... even though,' she added, 'I will still worry about you.'

'I'll worry about you and Paige too,' Jeanie replied. 'But you'll be fine and so will I.'

'I suppose we will. But I feel all at sea whenever you're not around.'

'You have Linda... and perhaps if you found yourself a nice man...'

'Don't start that, Mum,' Bonnie said wearily.

'I'm just saying. It would be good for you to have someone properly around to rely on, not just me. I'm not getting any younger and I won't always be here.'

'You certainly won't now,' Bonnie replied, the merest hint of bitterness creeping into her tone. 'Besides, I don't get the chance to meet men.'

'You don't even try.'

'If it means having to put myself on display in a nightclub like some going out-of-date meat then no thank you, I'd rather be single.'

'Nobody is saying that. But when a man *is* interested in you, you push them away.'

'I don't.'

'I've seen you do it, Bonnie. And I know why you do it, but you can't let what Henri did to you ruin the rest of your life.'

'It has nothing to do with Henri. We were never married, he has no claim over me and he can bugger off back to France whenever he wants. The reason I don't have a man is because there is no Mr Right for me. That soul mate that people talk of, *the one*, it's all a load of crap. Me and Paige get along just fine by ourselves. Besides, Paige might have something to say about someone coming home with me and she'd have a right to.'

'Paige wouldn't want to see you lonely. She might have reservations at first, but she'd come round.'

'Well, there's no need to worry about it either way, because as far as I can see, there's no Juan waiting to sweep me off my feet any time soon.'

Jeanie looked at her daughter sadly as she gulped down the last of her drink. Bonnie turned to her own mug and stared into it, unable to stand the pity in her mother's expression. She didn't want pity. Despite what she'd said, she just wanted a man in her life she could rely on. It wasn't too much to ask, was it?

Chapter Five

At lunch, Bonnie decided to forgo the usual trip to the Bounty and grab the opportunity for a quick look round the sale of Millrise's biggest department store. The radio station visit was less than a week away, and if there was the slightest chance of her actually meeting Holden Finn, then she wanted to look her best. Despite the previous Christmas now being almost ten months ago, she still had the vouchers that Jeanie had given her and now seemed as good a time as any to spend them.

'If you don't mind, I'll give it a miss,' Linda said darkly.

Bonnie laughed and rushed out into the drizzle to see if she could get anything in her meagre half an hour lunch break. If she got back late, well… she would just have to try and make it up to Fred somehow.

*

Once in the store, Bonnie marched towards the escalators. She had no idea what she was looking for and was fairly certain that half an hour was never going to be enough time to find it, try it on and pay for it. And if by some miracle she did, what was the betting that once she got home, she'd try it on again and either decide that it wasn't right after all, or Paige would make some sly comment that would put her off it for good?

Flicking through the clothing on the rails Bonnie frowned and muttered to herself.

Wrong colour... eeuuww colour... sequins ahoy!... too young... too tarty... too frumpy... too... what the hell is that supposed to be?

She looked up in despair and caught sight of a familiar shaggy blond head on the escalators. Not only that, but Max had Sarah on his arm. Bonnie let out an involuntary groan. Casting around, she could see that there was no way to make an escape. The only thing was to stay put and try to look as inconspicuous as possible.

Just as she thought she might have got away with it, Bonnie heard her name being called. Max came over, scarf draped casually around his neck and his hair wind-tousled so that it dropped cheekily over one eye. He pushed it back from his face and gave Bonnie a huge smile. Sarah huddled into him, her arm linked with his, and looking for all the world like she'd fall over if she wasn't leaning on him.

'I just said to Max,' Sarah squeaked excitedly, 'we seem to be seeing you everywhere at the moment.'

'Yes, you do, don't you,' Bonnie returned with as much enthusiasm as she could feign.

'And your hair looks amazing, did you colour it?' Sarah continued, almost without pausing for breath.

'Yeah. Thanks,' Bonnie replied.

'What are you up to?' Max asked with a good-natured smile. 'Treating yourself to something nice?'

'Hardly,' Bonnie said. 'You know Fred; he pays us in potatoes and time off for good behaviour.'

Sarah laughed. 'Max is always telling me how funny you and Linda are,' she said. 'He tells me it's his favourite stop in the morning.'

'Yes, you mentioned that at least four times at Blossom Palace,' Bonnie said tartly.

Max stared at her for a moment, a brief expression of surprise and annoyance crossing his genial features. But it quickly passed. Sarah didn't seem to notice anything untoward. Her gaze went to the dresses arranged behind Bonnie.

'Oooh, this one would suit you,' she said, pulling out a forest-green dress with bell sleeves.

Bonnie smiled and fought the irrational urge to shove Sarah head-first into the dress rack. 'Maybe I'll go and try it on then,' she said politely instead.

'You totally should, that colour would be fabulous with your hair now.' She stepped back for a moment and eyed Bonnie up. 'You know,' she said thoughtfully, 'we're about the same size. I have loads of dresses you could borrow if it's just for a one-off event. You don't want to pay the prices they charge in here.'

Bonnie smiled stiffly. 'That's very kind of you, but I couldn't possibly.' She decided there and then that she would rather go to the radio station wearing a bin bag (used and complete with bin juice) than wear anything of Sarah's. 'What are you two up to?' she asked, steering the conversation away from a subject that might just see her insult Sarah in a way she wouldn't be able to take back.

'We're window shopping for an hour,' Max said. 'We were going to the pictures but the film we wanted to see was sold out and we have to wait for the next showing.'

'Oh, what were you going to see?'

'*The Tempest*,' Sarah said, 'it's that new version with the guy who plays the vampire on that thing on telly.'

'Oh? I didn't have you down as the Shakespeare type,' Bonnie said to Max, barely keeping the conspiratorial smile from her face.

Max shrugged. 'I don't mind really. If I don't like it I can always have a quick nap.'

Sarah nudged him in the ribs. 'Don't you dare,' she laughed.

'I get up early, don't I?' he pleaded jokingly, looking to Bonnie for support.

'It's a hard life for him,' Bonnie said. 'We always say he looks like death warmed up when he comes in the morning.'

'Cheeky!' Max chuckled, 'I didn't mean that.'

Bonnie did a dramatic examination of her watch. 'Well, just look at that, lunchtime is nearly up so I really have to dash off.'

'That's a shame,' Sarah said earnestly, 'you could have grabbed a quick coffee with us.'

'Oh yes,' Bonnie said with as much fake sincerity as she could muster, 'that is such a shame. Maybe next time, eh?'

Max put his arm around Sarah again. 'See you tomorrow, Bon.'

'See you again soon, maybe,' Sarah said as she gave Bonnie the sweetest of smiles and a cheery wave.

Bonnie listened to Sarah's excited chattering fade as they walked away. She was such a lovely, guileless girl, and Bonnie knew that there was no rational reason to dislike her so intensely. But, Bonnie reflected wryly as she made her way back up the escalators, when did she ever need a rational reason for anything that she did?

*

Dear Holden,

Tomorrow I get to see you. Maybe. Annabel's mum and dad are away for the weekend and her older sister is at university. Annabel was supposed to come and stay with me and Paige anyway rather than be on her own so it seems that I'll be bringing them to the radio station after all. I can't believe that it's happening, even if it is just for Paige. She's a great kid, you'll really like her. Her mum is ok too, lol.

Argh, I can't believe I'm referring to myself in that way. I can't be the mum to a fifteen-year-old girl, God, what's attractive about that? You'd never look at me in a million years. And I can't believe I just wrote lol.

Bonnie tore the page from the pad and shoved it into the kitchen bin. Her gaze flicked to the paper on the table. The pad looked a lot thinner than it had a couple of weeks ago and not one of the letters she had written had gone anywhere other than the bin. If she wasn't careful, the whole lot would go that way. She sighed.

'MUM!' Paige's voice roared out from her bedroom. 'I can't find my curling tongs!'

'Have you looked in the drawer where they're normally kept?' Bonnie shouted back.

'Yeah, they're not in there.'

'It looks like straight hair for you tomorrow then.'

'Arrrgggggghhhh!'

Bonnie pushed herself up from the table and made her way to the source of the commotion. She stood at the bedroom door with her arms folded.

'Annabel…' Bonnie began, cocking her head at Paige and sharing a knowing smile with her daughter's friend – a pretty little doll of a girl now perched on the edge of Paige's bed and watching Paige fling the contents of her drawers around the room with a series of frustrated grunts. 'Is she this annoying and helpless all the time with you too?'

Annabel smiled politely. 'Um…'

'Don't worry,' Bonnie said, crossing the room and moving her daughter aside, 'you don't need to answer that.' Bonnie rummaged for a second or two before yanking on an electric flex; a moment later the rest of the curling tongs emerged from the murky depths of the drawer. 'Is this what you're looking for?' Bonnie handed them to Paige who gave a sheepish grin.

Bonnie's gaze was drawn to a dress hanging over the wardrobe door. 'Is that what you're wearing tomorrow?' she asked Paige.

Paige nodded.

'I hope you're wearing leggings or thick tights with it.'

'Why?' Paige frowned.

'It's a bit short.'

'It's not.'

'Trust me, it is.'

'Well I'm wearing it without anything and I don't care what you think.'

'That's good, because I think you'll look like a slapper.'

Paige folded her arms and fixed Bonnie with a confrontational stare.

Annabel watched the exchange, inching further down the bed in embarrassment. Bonnie threw her hands into the air.

'Whatever, Paige. You've got to sit in front of Every Which Way tomorrow, the one and only time you'll probably ever get the opportunity, and when you look back on that golden moment, you're the one that has to remember that you looked like a chav.'

'Don't be stupid, Mum,' Paige muttered, but she was blushing furiously and she glanced across at the dress, her expression now a little less resolute than it had been.

'Wear what you want,' Bonnie said as she marched out of the room.

As soon as she returned to the kitchen table, Bonnie regretted making a fool out of Paige in front of Annabel. What did it matter that her dress was a little on the short side? Bonnie would have been exactly the same at her age, wouldn't she? Hell, if she thought she had the legs to pull it off, maybe she'd be tempted by a dress like that now. Paige would look fantastic in it, she had no doubt. Perhaps, she thought glumly, that was part of the problem.

A few minutes later, Bonnie was back at the door of Paige's room holding two mugs of hot chocolate. Paige and Annabel were poring over a magazine, giggling at photos of the band members, a CD of them playing in the background.

'I thought you might like a warm drink,' Bonnie said in a tone that indicated she wanted to be friends again.

Annabel smiled up at her as she took her mug and Paige did a funny little wrinkle of her nose. Bonnie smiled. She knew the gesture well. It was Paige's way of saying she wanted to be friends again without actually appearing to back down or show forgiveness in any way.

'Is this going to help us to sleep?' Annabel asked as she took a sip.

'Nothing is going to help us to sleep tonight,' Paige said over the top of her mug. 'I bet we'll get an hour, just before dawn, and then have to get up straight away for the train.'

'It'll be a long day,' Bonnie put in. 'You should really try.'

'Oh, Mum, stop being such a…' Paige frowned.

'A mum?' Bonnie replied helpfully.

'Ha ha. You can't tell me you're not just a little bit excited too. After all, we are going to London.'

Bonnie couldn't deny it. The thought of the day to come made her insides dance, a strange mix of nerves and excited anticipation, and it wasn't hard for anyone else to see how jittery she was, even Paige.

'I haven't been to London for years,' Bonnie said. 'I am quite excited about that. Maybe I'll go off and explore for a bit while you have your meeting.'

'You're going to go and leave us?' Paige asked, looking almost panic-stricken.

'You'll be in safe hands, I'm sure.'

'I know but…well,' Paige floundered, 'I'm not that bothered, of course, but what about Annabel? You're responsible for her too.'

Bonnie smiled. 'If it worries you that much, I'll wait in the radio station for you. I'm sure there'll be a coffee machine or something that I can hang around next to trying to look sophisticated.'

'I didn't say it worried me, I just think you should be around, like, so that Annabel's mum and dad know she's okay.' Paige looked at her friend, who nodded uncertainly.

'Okay, I will.' Bonnie looked at Annabel. 'Do you have everything you need tonight?'

Annabel picked up a wash-bag from the bed and held it aloft with a grin.

'And what about your outfit?'

'Oh, that's here,' Paige cut in, removing her dress from the wardrobe door to reveal another outfit behind it. A tiny pink t-shirt and a pair of denim hot pants were draped over a hanger. Bonnie barely held back a groan.

'What are you wearing?' Annabel asked brightly, clearly unconcerned by the fact that Bonnie had made no comment at all on her choice of clothes.

'I haven't really decided,' Bonnie lied.

The truth was that she hadn't been able to find anything right with her leftover Christmas money, and right now, almost every item of clothing she owned was strewn across her bed.

'You should wear that little black lace dress, Mum, you'll look really nice in that with your red hair.'

Bonnie looked at Paige thoughtfully. 'Really? I thought that might be a bit dressy, what with me just running around London and hanging around waiting for you. If I'm only doing that and not really meeting anyone, perhaps I only need to wear my jeans.'

'No way.' Paige said. 'You can dress that down with a pair of opaque tights and your black boots, it'll look cool and not like you're trying too hard.'

'That's not a bad idea,' Bonnie mused.

Paige beamed at her. 'I know.' Draining the last of her chocolate, she dumped the mug on the windowsill, skipped over to the CD player and turned up the volume. Grabbing Bonnie by both hands, she pulled her into the room and started to jump up and down.

'Dance with me, Mum!'

Bonnie laughed and swayed self-consciously in time to the music.

'Come on, better than that!' Paige giggled. She reached for Annabel and pulled her up too.

All three of them began to laugh as they jumped up and down madly in time to the music. Holden sang to them…

Don't forget me babe
Don't ever say we're done
Tonight I wanna kiss you
Tonight I wanna love you
Tonight I wanna dance
While we wait for the sun

*

The train journey to Euston station had flown by as Paige and Annabel chatted incessantly about what might or might not happen when they finally met their heroes. Bonnie joined in occasionally, and at other times smiled indulgently as she listened, but every so often her stomach flipped with a small excitement of her own. She was so close to meeting Holden herself. And even if she didn't, she would be in the same building, breathing the same air, a stone's throw away, and that was closer than many people got.

London was dry and surprisingly mild for the time of year. It would have been a great day for sightseeing, had they not had something far more pressing to get to. Not wanting to risk missing their slot by getting lost on the tube, Bonnie had decided to hail a cab to get them to the venue on time, and at least this afforded a little landmark spotting. However, when the cabbie told her the fare as they arrived, she was hugely grateful that the radio station had agreed to reimburse their travelling expenses as part of the prize.

They pushed open the gleaming double doors to the radio station. The familiar lurid green and blue logo was emblazoned across the wall behind the reception desk and two glamorous looking receptionists juggled phone calls and guests with a practised and cool efficiency.

'We're the competition winners!' Paige announced before Bonnie even had a chance to open her mouth.

The receptionist nearest to Paige smiled patiently. 'Would that be the Every Which Way competition?'

'Who else?' Annabel squealed as she grabbed Paige's arm for the umpteenth time that morning. 'Seriously, there's nobody else in the world worth entering a competition for!'

'Well,' the receptionist said, reaching for a couple of clipboards and pens, 'we'll need to complete some paperwork before we do anything else.' She handed the girls a board each and indicated some sections with a scarlet-nailed finger. 'Just a few bits and pieces about you.' She looked up at Bonnie. 'Can you sign a disclaimer for them both?'

'A disclaimer?'

'You know, if they get injured or anything on the premises you won't sue us, that sort of thing.'

'Oh…' Bonnie glanced at Paige and Annabel as they huddled together over their forms, giggling. 'I suppose so, although Annabel is not my daughter.'

The woman waved away the excuse. 'That's fine. As long as we have a signature from a responsible adult.' She handed Bonnie a clipboard too and pointed to a box. 'If you can sign and date here, that would be great.'

Bonnie took the board and scribbled her name.

'Thanks.' The woman took the paperwork from Bonnie. She looked across at the girls. 'How are we doing? Almost finished?' Paige and Annabel handed back their papers with expectant faces. The woman looked them over. 'Great stuff. I'll call Raveena to take you through. The boys are just broadcasting at the moment, so you'll have to wait really quietly outside the studio while they finish, but then you can go in as soon as they're off air.'

Paige gave a stifled little squeal and Annabel gripped her friend's arm again.

'As I don't have a ticket, do I go and wait with them or stay out here?' Bonnie asked uncertainly.

'Ask Raveena when she gets down here,' the woman replied as she filed the paperwork in a drawer.

They hovered uncertainly for a moment, and then a baby-faced girl with an ID badge on a lanyard around her neck pushed open some double doors at the far end of the room. She looked across at Bonnie and the two girls with a bright smile.

'Are you guys here for the competition?'

'Yes!' Paige and Annabel squeaked in unison.

'Great. I'm Raveena. I'll be looking after you while you're with us.' She leaned over the reception desk. 'Paperwork in order, Rosemary?'

The woman who had checked them into the building nodded.

'Fantastic!' Raveena said. 'In that case, follow me.' She waved a hand to usher them through the double doors and into the working section of the station.

'Do you need me too?' Bonnie asked.

Raveena smiled warmly. 'Why not? The more the merrier. You can wait outside and watch through the studio window while the girls are interviewed with the band on air.'

'We're going on air?' Annabel squealed, practically hyperventilating as she did.

'We thought it would be nice for their fans to hear your meeting,' Raveena explained as they followed her. 'They're doing an acoustic set, a quick interview, and then we'll call you in and you can ask them some questions of your own.'

'OMG that will be so cool!' Paige said breathlessly.

'I hope so,' Raveena laughed.

They turned from the narrow corridor into a much wider one, lined with windows that looked into various studio spaces. Most were empty, but one contained an older man and a sound engineer. 'Newsreader,' Raveena said, sweeping a hand towards it. The next window along revealed a much larger studio. Bonnie felt her legs begin to buckle as she saw four fabulously dressed young men sitting on tall stools, singing and grinning at each other like loons.

'Oh my God!' Paige squealed.

Annabel just grabbed Paige's arm and stared.

'And I don't need to tell you who is in that studio.' Raveena smiled. 'They're on-air right now; once we get a chance between songs, we'll slip in and get comfy and you can have a quick word off-air.'

'Will we be able to hear them sing?' Paige asked.

'I'm sure they won't mind you listening in while they do their unplugged set.'

'Brilliant!' Paige sighed as Annabel shot her a huge grin.

They looked towards the booth, where it seemed the boys had stopped singing and were now relaxing on their seats. Raveena pushed open the studio door and the sound engineer waved her in.

'We're good to go, guys,' Raveena smiled. 'Are you ready to meet Every Which Way?'

Bonnie watched as Paige and Annabel were led through into the studio. Paige turned once with a huge grin and gave her mum a little wave. Bonnie smiled, ignoring the tiny tick of envy deep inside her. She couldn't remember the last time she had seen Paige look so elated. Bonnie stepped back towards a row of seats outside the studio. She saw one of the boys – Brad, as far as she could remember – nod in her direction and say something to Raveena.

Next thing, Raveena stuck her head out of the door again as Paige and Annabel turned to look at her. 'Would you like to come in?' Raveena asked. 'You'd have to sit and be quiet while the girls chat to the band on air, but you're more than welcome.'

Bonnie didn't realise her mouth had fallen open until she noticed how dry it had become. *Go in?* All this time she had been dreaming of meeting Holden, it had never seemed a real, actual possibility – even now as she stood outside a room he was inside. The thought terrified her and excited her all at the same time. What would he make of her? Would she look like a middle-aged idiot, sitting next to two beautiful and lively teenagers and drooling over a gorgeous international megastar?

This inner debate took a fraction of a second, and before she even knew what she was doing, Bonnie had followed Raveena's beckoning hand. The next moment, she found herself standing in the booth behind her daughter.

'This is Paige and Annabel,' Raveena said, indicating the girls in turn. Each boy – Holden, Nick, Brad and Jay – shook Paige and Annabel's hand. Every time they touched the girls almost collapsed in fits of breathless giggles. Raveena waved a hand towards Bonnie. 'This is Paige's mum…'

'Oh… I'm Bonnie,' Bonnie said, forgetting to offer her hand and just standing with her mouth slightly open as she gazed at Holden. He was dressed casually, but it seemed that the whole look – from the effortlessly styled hair to the seemingly relaxed wardrobe – had been carefully constructed for maximum sex appeal. The other boys, attractive as they were, seemed to melt into the background of his perfection.

'Bonnie?' Holden said, raising an immaculate eyebrow. 'That's an unusual name. Are you Scottish?'

Bonnie felt herself blush. She was just wondering whether to tell some romantic sounding story about her name when Paige cut in.

'Nah. My nan just totally loves Bonnie Tyler.'

Holden turned to her, looking confused now. 'Er, right.'

'You know, the eighties singer with huge hair?' Paige explained.

Holden looked to his band mates for help, but they all shrugged helplessly.

'I'm sure you're all far too young to remember Bonnie Tyler,' Bonnie explained, laughing nervously. 'I am too, come to think of it.'

'I've got some Bonnie Tyler somewhere,' the DJ cut in. 'I could play it for you on-air.'

'It really doesn't matter…'

'It'd be no bother,' he insisted.

'It's not me that's the fan…' Bonnie said, her sentence trailing off as she realised that the DJ was already scrolling down a tracklist on his monitor.

Then the engineer wagged a finger at them to indicate the countdown to being back on-air and they all fell silent, the boys watching the DJ expectantly and the girls grinning like maniacs.

'Right, that was your daily dose of Lily Allen, there,' the DJ purred into the mic in typically smooth DJ style, 'and we're back with the boys of Every Which Way, along with some VIP guests: the winners of our competition to meet the boys…' He looked down at his clipboard. 'Paige Cartwright and Annabel Frost.' He grinned at the girls, who both looked as though they might explode at any moment. The DJ continued, 'We're going to give Paige and Annabel the chance to ask the band some questions in a short while, but first, here's a song specially requested by Paige's mum, who is lurking in the background here in the studio and is a big Bonnie Tyler fan…'

Bonnie groaned inwardly as the opening bars to *Total Eclipse of the Heart* kicked in. Now she looked like a middle-aged saddo in front of the gorgeous, young, and very far from sad Holden Finn. The DJ gave a gormless thumbs-up to Bonnie as he turned the volume down and took off his headphones. She tried to smile back gratefully but even he must have been aware of just how forced it looked.

'Okay guys,' Raveena said to Paige and Annabel, sounding vaguely like a holiday camp entertainer. 'Have you got your questions ready, because it's nearly time.'

The girls nodded enthusiastically while the band looked on, every inch professional courtesy and indulgent smiles. They'd done this a million times before and it showed.

Bonnie suddenly wondered how they'd react to the question burning to escape her lips, the one that would be directed to a particular band member, and would, considering the circumstances, be highly inappropriate. Probably best to keep that one to herself, she decided with a wry inward smile.

*

The interview had gone well, with Paige and Annabel asking the same sorts of questions expected from the majority of Every Which Way fans: how did you get together (Nick had stumbled into the wrong audition), what's your favourite food (a mental note to make sure that one jar of peanut butter a week was sent to Holden's agent to pass on), who snores the loudest (Brad, by a mile). The answers had been given with a great deal of humorous banter, and the Q&A was then followed by another set of songs performed live by them. Bonnie was struck by how good they sounded together. She had always assumed that the snobbish belief held by Henri and countless others about 'manufactured' bands not being able to sing at all, their wailing only made palatable by studio tinkering, was true. But Every Which Way could *really* sing. And their harmonies were so achingly beautiful that they made the hairs on the back of her neck stand on end.

Once the set was over and the DJ put on his last record, there was a goodbye piece from the DJ to wrap up.

'So, girls… you've enjoyed your day?'

'Oh yes!' Paige and Annabel squeaked almost in unison.

'There's one more surprise for you,' Brad cut in with a broad smile crinkling his ice-blue eyes. 'We thought you might like VIP tickets to the first date on our sell-out arena tour next week.'

Raveena handed him a pile of what looked like slips of card and laminated passes and he gave one of each to the girls.

Bonnie thought that Paige might pass out, as she seemed to have forgotten how to breathe, and Annabel looked up at Brad with such love in her eyes there was a serious danger she was going to propose to him on-air.

'Those mean that you can come backstage afterwards, wherever you like. And make sure you come and say hi to us,' Holden said.

'Oh. My. God!' Annabel squealed. 'Thank you so much!'

Holden's gaze drifted over to Bonnie, who was sitting in the corner of the tiny studio, almost as breathless as Paige and Annabel. He turned to Raveena.

'Can we fix up another pass for Paige's lovely mum?' he asked with a winning smile.

Raveena had been the very epitome of professional charm and composure all afternoon, but at this request looked distinctly flustered. 'I'm sure we can,' she replied, looking about as unsure of whether they could as it was possible to look.

'There's really no need to worry about me,' Bonnie said quietly, her heart banging against her ribs.

'I insist,' Holden said. 'We'd love you to come with the girls. Besides,' he added with a chuckle, 'they do need someone to drive them there.'

Bonnie felt herself blush deeply. Perhaps it was something in the warmth of the gaze he held her in, or the fact that he had insisted she come, as if it mattered to him.

'Thank you,' she said, not knowing what else to say.

The DJ cut across their exchange. 'What a fantastic show we've had today. I'd like to thank all our guests: Brad, Holden, Jay and Nick, otherwise known as Every Which Way, and our competition winners Paige and Amelia…'

'Annabel!' Paige called over, but the DJ appeared not to hear as the band members shared a grin at the mistake.

Bonnie didn't hear the rest of his spiel. She was too busy being shell-shocked at the strange turn of events the day had thrown at her.

*

Feeling vaguely as though she was living some sort of surreal dream, Bonnie flagged a cab and watched the girls climb in before clambering after them and giving instructions for the train station. She had just been in the presence of Holden Finn. In her mind, even now, the memory of his image was being embellished; somehow his skin was more perfect, his hair more glossy, his eyes brighter and more playfully sexy. She found herself wondering whether it was possible to airbrush people in real life, because if it was, he must have had it done. He had touched her hand. He gave her VIP tickets and told her that he would *very much* like to see her backstage. Things like this didn't happen to Bonnie Cartwright. She opened her bag and stared at the slips of card, their foil embossing glinting as they caught the daylight.

The car roared into life, pulled cautiously from the kerb and began its stop-start journey through the London congestion back to Euston for their train.

Annabel giggled as she nudged Paige. 'Holden so totally fancied your mum,' she whispered.

Paige looked horrified. 'He did not!'

'He did,' she goaded. 'That's why he got an extra ticket for her and everything.'

'He was just being nice,' Paige pouted. 'Coz he is really nice. He's, like, the nicest one in the band.'

'He kept looking at her and smiling like crazy when she said anything,' Annabel insisted. 'He definitely liked her.'

'Yeah, he liked her like he thought she was a nice woman.'

'No, he *really liked* her.'

Paige grimaced. 'That's so gross. She's, like, loads older than him.'

'She doesn't look old, though,' Annabel reasoned.

Paige seemed to ponder this for a moment. 'I don't suppose,' she conceded.

'Ha ha,' Annabel giggled, 'can you imagine if Holden Finn was your new dad!'

'Oh my frickin' God, that's so disgusting!'

Annabel snorted and Bonnie looked at them with a vague smile.

'What on earth are you two laughing about?' she asked.

'Nothing.' Paige scowled. 'Annabel is being an idiot.'

Chapter Six

'Where's Max this morning?' Bonnie asked the gangly, spotty youth who knocked at the back door of the shop wearing overalls bearing the badge *Delaney's Fresh Produce*.

The youth gave a surly shrug. 'He's having a day off. Said I could open up the warehouse and go on delivery for a change.'

'But Max never has days off,' Bonnie said, forgetting, momentarily, to step back and let the boy into the stockroom.

The boy shrugged again. 'Everyone has days off.'

'Not Max, at least, hardly ever and he usually tells us beforehand.'

'Look, shall I go and get the stock in or what?'

Bonnie nodded uncertainly. 'So where is he?' she called after the youth, who was making his way to a blue transit van parked on double yellows in the entryway behind the shop.

'Off somewhere with his new woman,' he called back.

Bonnie left the door open and went back into the main stockroom. Linda was dragging a tray of kiwi fruit from a fridge.

'What's up?' she asked. 'Not still mooning over that concert you've been invited to at the weekend?'

'Max is having a day off,' Bonnie said.

Linda smiled with what looked like relief. Bonnie had talked of little except the concert since she had arrived in that Monday morning and

Linda was dangerously close to locking her in a fridge until she shut up. 'Everyone has days off, even Max.'

'Hardly ever.'

'Don't be daft. Anyway, what's the big deal? He'll be back in tomorrow, won't he?'

'I don't know.' Bonnie's attention was caught by the boy dropping a sack of carrots onto the floor in the middle of the stockroom, sending a cloud of dust up into the air. It seemed strange, this new and uncommunicative creature bringing their supplies in instead of Max's usual jovial presence. It wasn't right, somehow.

Linda whistled to the lad as he was leaving to get more bags, 'Oi, Slim Jim… is Max back tomorrow?'

'How should I know?' he asked sullenly. 'He's the boss, isn't he?' He broke into a sly grin. 'And if I was having it off with his missus, I'd be taking days off as well.'

Before either of them had a chance to reply, he was back through the door again. Bonnie looked at Linda with a grimace. 'Ugh, he's vile. I can't believe Max would let him go out to customers.'

'They do say love makes you do strange things,' Linda replied nonchalantly as she disappeared into the shop with the kiwis.

He's in love? The idea, as logical as it was, had never occurred to Bonnie. It made her feel strangely empty. Ridiculous, of course, she told herself, to even care. Max had been a single man and she had gone out of her way to make it clear that they could never be more than friends and that was what she firmly believed. Why should she begrudge his relationship with Sarah taking a more serious turn if she made him happy? Wasn't that what friends wanted for each other – happiness?

'They'll be getting engaged soon, you mark my words.' Linda's voice came from behind her, the note of glee in it just a little too grating for Bonnie's nerves. It seemed to say: *I told you so.*

'It's a bit soon for that sort of thing,' Bonnie replied irritably.

'He's at the settling down age,' Linda said carelessly as she went back into the fridge. She emerged a moment later with a box of deep purple plums. 'And she looks like a good breeding age to me too. They'll be thinking about it, no doubt.'

'You're disgusting,' Bonnie tried to laugh; 'you bring everything back to breeding.'

'Isn't that what it's all about, though?' Linda returned as she took the plums into the main shop.

Bonnie waited for her to come back through before picking up the discussion again. 'It's about love, surely?'

'Not when you're pushing thirty and you don't have a family it's not.'

'That's so old fashioned.'

'Max is old fashioned. In the nicest possible way, of course.' Linda stood with her hands on her hips and held Bonnie in a steady gaze. 'He wants to settle down, you can see it a mile off.' She raised her eyebrows at Bonnie. 'And I know you think I'm talking out of my arse, but I still say he wanted to settle down with you.' She shuffled off to the fridge again. 'It's not my fault you wouldn't have him and now it's too late.'

'Too late?' Bonnie asked as Linda emerged from the fridge again, this time staggering under the weight of a tray of mangoes. Bonnie lowered her voice, suddenly reminded that they were not alone by the thud of another sack of root vegetables being dropped onto the floor. 'What does that mean... *too late?*'

Linda halted for a moment and eyed her practically. 'You want him now you can't have him.'

Bonnie's mouth dropped open. Linda made her way out to the shop floor. Bonnie was just about to shout an outraged reply when Fred appeared from the toilet at the back, paper under his arm and still zipping up his flies.

'What are you staring at?' he snapped at Bonnie. 'You gone daft or something from all your gallivanting with pop stars? You may be rubbing shoulders with the rich and famous now, but we still have a shop to stock!' With that, he dropped his newspaper onto a bench and marched out into the shop to count the float for the till.

'You'd better take that stupid look off your face,' Linda said as she came back through, adjusting her tabard, 'or her royal Fredness in there will blow a fuse.'

Bonnie let her shoulders slump. She had come to work so full of life and excitement for good things to come, but now she felt like a deflated balloon. Linda stopped and touched her arm, her tone softer now.

'Don't be sad, Bon. You're gorgeous and there are plenty of men out there that would be happy to have you even look in their direction.'

Bonnie sniffed and tried to smile. 'How come you always know the right thing to say?'

'It comes from twenty years of being married to John. You can always get another tenner from his wallet if you know the right things to say…' She winked at Bonnie. 'Or the right things to *do*…'

Bonnie couldn't help but laugh as Linda went back to the fridges with a naughty grin. The thud of another sack of spuds hitting the ground made her spin round. She fired a hate-filled glare at the back of the delivery usurper and hoped that good old-fashioned, laugh-a-minute Max would be back tomorrow.

*

Dear Holden

It was amazing to finally meet you. Maybe I'm seriously deluded here, but I felt like there was something in your eyes when you looked at me, like some kind of chemistry between us. I know it sounds crazy and it would obviously never work, even if there was. But it was nice, you know, just to think that there might be. I can't wait to see you at the concert this weekend. You'll be busy, surrounded by tour people and fans and hangers-on, I know that, but I wonder, will that spark be there again when you look at me? I'm being daft, you won't even remember who I am. See you there anyway.

Bonnie (In case you don't remember, I'm the one who is not Scottish and not a Bonnie Tyler fan).

Bonnie gulped down the last of her lukewarm tea. She had just ripped up the page as Linda walked in for her break.

'What are you up to?' she asked, peering over at the now blank writing pad.

'Nothing,' Bonnie said quickly, shoving the pad in her handbag and taking the discarded page to the bin. 'Just doing some sums to figure out if I can pay the mortgage this month.'

'If you can afford to do that on posh paper, Fred must be paying you more than he pays me,' Linda laughed.

Bonnie smiled as she took her cup to the sink. 'Yeah, secretly I'm rolling in it. I only do this job for the company.'

'Bloody hell! I'll go and call the men in the loony van to come and collect you.'

Bonnie tipped her rinsed mug upside down on the draining board and gave Linda a grin.

'Don't let Fred hear you say that,' Linda added, as Bonnie left the kitchen to go back to work, 'he'll think he can stop paying you.'

*

Max turned up the next morning, but Bonnie couldn't help the absurd sense of irritation at the way his face lit up every time he mentioned Sarah's name. And if she had to hear one more time how brilliant Sarah's paintings were, or what a good cook she was, or how much fun they'd had at the cinema, she felt certain that she would clobber Max around the head with the first prize winning marrow she could lay her hands on.

But then, as the week flew by and the weekend drew nearer, bringing with it the promise of the Every Which Way concert, Bonnie found her daily irritation with Max gradually replaced by excitement and some trepidation for what the big night might hold. In the back of her mind, she wondered if the spark she had felt between her and Holden at the radio station might have the room to grow into something more, if only she could get close enough for long enough to make him see the real her. But then, what did the real Bonnie have to offer someone like him? Debt, a manky flat, a moody teenage daughter, the delicate beginnings of crow's feet and stretch marks – oh yeah, she was a real catch. But still, she convinced herself, there *had* been something there when he looked at her, she was sure of it. Stranger relationships had been made good. She couldn't think of any right then, but she was pretty sure she'd heard of some.

*

As Bonnie stepped out of the shower on the night before the concert, Paige came bursting into the bathroom.

'Paige! What the hell's the matter?' Bonnie shouted as she hurriedly wrapped a towel around her.

'Oh, Mum, Annabel's got flu!'

'She has?'

Paige nodded miserably. 'Her mum says she's running a fever and can't even get out of bed.'

'And you only just found this out?'

'Well…' Paige began, 'she wasn't in school today and texted me to say she wasn't well. I thought it was a twenty-four hour thing and she'd be alright, that's why I never said anything. But her mum has just phoned and said she's got worse through the day and now they have the emergency doctor coming out, so she must be bad, mustn't she?'

Bonnie nodded thoughtfully. 'I suppose she must. So she can't come tomorrow?'

'No. I can't believe she's going to miss it.'

'It does seem a shame. Do you want to give it a miss?'

'I don't know,' Paige said reluctantly. The internal struggle was clear as day to Bonnie. Paige obviously wouldn't want to miss out on the concert – opportunities like this came around once in a lifetime – but she would feel as though she had betrayed her friend if she went without her.

'What did her mum say?' Bonnie asked gently.

Paige shrugged. 'Her mum says that Annabel totally understands if I go and that if it was the other way around, I would tell Annabel to go too.'

'And you would, wouldn't you?' Bonnie prompted.

Paige nodded uncertainly. 'Yeah… yeah, of course I would.'

'Do you want to go?'

'I really do. But I'll feel so bad that she missed it.'

'She's already told you she doesn't mind.' Bonnie paused. 'What if we take a souvenir back for her? Like buy a tour t-shirt and get it signed or something? It wouldn't be anything like going, of course, but it would be something at least.'

'It's not much of a consolation,' Paige said doubtfully.

'No, it isn't. But there is nothing you can do to help Annabel whether you go or whether you don't. She'll feel guilty if you miss the concert because you don't want to go without her, so either way, one of you loses. But at least a gift like that will show that you appreciate her letting you go and that you thought about her while you were there.'

Paige considered for a moment and then nodded. 'Okay, you're right,' she sighed. 'So, what am I going to wear?'

Bonnie laughed lightly. 'That's what I like to see... practical as always.'

*

Bonnie slipped a pair of heels on with her skinny jeans and examined her reflection in the full-length mirror inside her wardrobe door. She'd piled her hair up in a stylishly messy bun, wore a neat vest top and fitted shirt casually unbuttoned, an understated diamond pendant at her neck. The heels made her legs look longer, but would she be able to stand them for the three or four hours that she'd be on her feet at the concert? She kicked off the shoes again and pulled on her ballet pumps, looking critically at her reflection. Comfy, practical and boringly safe, or sexy but at risk of looking like a bimbo and falling flat on her face at some point? It wouldn't matter, of course, if she was *just* going to see a concert. Steeling herself and knowing that in an hour or so she was going to regret her decision, she pulled the heels back on and went to see if Paige was ready.

Paige was in her room applying make-up. For once, she was wearing an outfit that Bonnie approved of. She had gone for a short, flared skirt with a wide belt pulling her waist in and a fitted top, but the top was high-necked and subtle and the skirt just the safe side of short with a pretty fifties vintage look about it that somehow made it look more respectable.

'You look lovely,' Bonnie said with obvious pride.

Paige grinned. 'You don't look so bad yourself. Like a yummy mummy.'

'I'm not too embarrassing then?'

'You'll do,' Paige said, turning back to the mirror to finish applying her mascara.

'Are you nearly ready? We need to leave soon.'

Paige screwed the lid back on the tube and turned to her mum, planting her hands on her hips in a model pose. 'Let's roll!'

*

Bonnie had wondered whether there would be someone to meet them at the arena, or at least a special door they would have to go through to make full use of their VIP passes, but as nobody had contacted them beforehand with any instructions, and none of the concert stewards on site knew what to do either, Bonnie and Paige ended up queuing impatiently at the main gates with the rest of the concert-goers.

They had arrived early, and it turned out to be a wise move, as even an hour before the show was due to start the arena was buzzing with excited teenage (and some not quite so teenage) girls. They decided to see how effective their passes actually were, and wandered around for a while, trying different official looking areas of the building to see if anyone stopped them from going in. What they had dubbed 'no man's land' (the area between the stage and the barriers separating it from the crowd), the side of the stage and a special drinks area all seemed to be okay. But Paige, having never been to a concert before, and being swept up in the soupy atmosphere of rampant teenage hormones, decided that she wanted to be right at the front in the crowd, so she could experience what she had assumed would be the best view of all.

'We can see that in front of the barrier,' Bonnie said, 'without getting squashed.'

'It's not the same, Mum, in front of the barrier. Everyone will be staring at us and I'll feel weird, like I'm not part of the concert.'

Bonnie laughed. 'There's no way you can be in this building and not be part of it.'

'You know what I mean,' Paige replied with a pout.

Bonnie sighed. 'Right then. If you really want to get in amongst it, I don't see we have a choice. But I'm telling you now that if it gets too rough, we'll be getting out over that barrier. I've been to enough rock gigs with your nan to know that these things can get scary.'

'You worry too much,' Paige returned sagely. 'This isn't one of nan's sweaty rocker gigs, this is proper organised stuff.'

Bonnie raised her eyebrows and bit back a wry smile. 'We'll see,' was all she said.

Half an hour before the concert was due to start, the engineers came on stage to check the equipment to a loud cheer. Even though there was a support band due on first, The Musketeers, who nobody particularly cared about, the crowd was already pushing forwards towards the front, everyone in a territorial bid to find the best spot and hold onto it ready for the main event. Even before the sound engineers had left the stage, Bonnie was feeling tense and claustrophobic, not to mention very hot. And she was pretty sure that rock crowds weren't that different from hordes of teenage girls (if anything, teenage girls were probably scarier) and that things were going to get a whole lot more uncomfortable before the night was out.

*

As it turned out, The Musketeers were actually quite good. Bonnie didn't know many of their songs, apart from their one big hit, but Paige knew them well and jumped up and down along with everyone else, mouthing the words to the songs she knew, pretending to mouth along with the ones she didn't, and the set flew by. They went off with a flurry and a roar of appreciation from the crowd, and then the stamping and clapping demands for Every Which Way began.

If the audience had been excited before, the departure of the support band and the imminent arrival of the one they had all really come to see sent them into a collective frenzy, so that it became not a room full of separate people, but one, huge, obsessive creature, hungrily baying for blood. Paige began stamping too, shouting, '*We want Holden, we want Brad, we want Jay, we want Nick...*' over and over again along with everyone else, her face alight with fervent hero worship. Bonnie could feel herself becoming seduced by it too, and she stamped and found herself wanting to shout and scream for the band to come on. The tension built and the stamping and shouting grew and grew in volume, and just as it reached a dangerous crescendo, the lights of the stadium went down and a great roar of anticipation erupted from the crowd.

There was a burst of fireworks from the stage, and in front of them, grinning madly and in various poses, stood the members of Every Which Way.

There was something about seeing them up there, backlit and awesome, that made them look strangely unreal; it was like looking at gods, not men. They wore different but complementary outfits, colour coordinated, and even the colour and styles of their hair seemed to work together to produce an overall effect.

And even as these brief thoughts ran through Bonnie's mind, she could feel the huge weight of the crowd behind her begin to push forwards and tensed herself to hold firm against it. She glanced warily at Paige, who seemed unconcerned, staring up, mesmerised, at the stage.

'ARE YOU READY TO HAVE A GOOD TIME?' Brad shouted, and a deafening wave of screams rolled across the arena.

'I SAID, ARE YOU READY TO HAVE A GOOD TIME?' he shouted again, holding a hand to his ear for effect.

The screams and shouts grew louder and the first bars of *Don't Forget Me* struck up, only to be drowned out in Bonnie's immediate vicinity by frantic squealing and not a small amount of yelled swearwords mixed with marriage proposals and offers of sex.

Slightly self-conscious at first, painfully aware of being the oldest person she could see up front, Bonnie got into the spirit of things. Paige was already swept up in the music and atmosphere, jumping up and down with her hands in the air, shouting along to the words of the song. And Bonnie couldn't help but get swept up too, so that three songs into the set, she started to jump with everyone else, and her arms went above her head and she shouted her undying love to Holden, because nobody would notice anyway, and it felt so good to let it out.

*

As things mellowed for a brief moment into a slower number towards the end of the set, Bonnie glanced across at Paige. Her daughter seemed quieter suddenly, staring up at the stage, though now she didn't seem to really be seeing it. Bonnie had become aware of the terrific heat being given off by the tightly-packed bodies, of the sweat running down her own back, and could see that Paige looked overheated too.

'Are you alright?' Bonnie shouted.

Paige looked across but didn't answer.

'Paige? Are you feeling okay?'

Then Bonnie saw Paige's eyes roll back in her head and she seemed to crumple. There was nowhere for her to fall, so she fell against the people next to her, limp and gradually sliding down to the ground. Bonnie felt her heart lurch in panic. If Paige fell to the floor, there was no way she would be able to get her up without the pair of them being trampled to death. She grabbed for Paige, pulling her up roughly under the arms and yanking her through the few layers of people right at the front with a strength she had no idea she possessed. Once at the barrier she waved frantically for the attention of one of the stewards. A woman came across to them, a quick glance enough for her to immediately understand the situation. She called across another couple of stewards, who hauled a now almost insensible Paige over the barrier, and then Bonnie too shortly afterwards. They took Paige to a chair at the side of the stage where a few other casualties stood and sat around about being tended to by first-aiders.

A cold sponge down the back of the shirt and a bottle of water seemed to bring Paige round just as the show was heading into its final song. Bonnie heaved a sigh of relief as Paige looked up at her with a faint smile.

'Sorry, Mum,' she said ruefully.

'Don't be silly.' Bonnie pulled her into a sweaty hug. 'I'm just sorry I didn't notice sooner that you weren't feeling well.'

Paige's attention was drawn to the stage where the band seemed to be saying their goodbyes. There would be an encore – there was always an encore – but their night was almost over.

'It's been amazing, hasn't it, Mum?' she said with a dreamy expression. 'I'm sorry Annabel didn't get to come, but I'm so glad that you did… you're like my other best friend.'

Bonnie looked at her beautiful daughter, wanting to hold her tight and never let go. Her eyes filled with tears and she sniffed them away. 'Silly,' she said, trying to underplay the emotion for fear of driving Paige back into her usual uncommunicative self. 'I've had a brilliant time too.'

*

After the madness of rescuing Paige from the surging crowds at the front of the stage, Bonnie was feeling a little delicate and in desperate need of a sit down in a cool, quiet room. She was pretty sure she wasn't looking her best either – burning cheeks, her fringe sweaty and slicked off her forehead and her clothes crumpled. But there was no way that Paige was going to miss the opportunity of mingling backstage, and once Bonnie had got out of the crowds and felt slightly better for the clearer air, the excitement began to build in her too.

They wandered for some minutes, completely lost amidst the confusing labyrinth of concrete-walled corridors away from the main arena, until they spotted a troupe of backing dancers heading towards a large set of red double doors.

'I could really do with a cold drink,' Bonnie said as they stood and looked. Now that she was faced with the doorway to goodness knew what, she wasn't sure she wanted to go in. Who was she kidding? She didn't belong to that world and never would, no matter what she wished for. They'd probably stand around in a corner all night looking like spare bits of furniture.

'I'm sure if we have VIP passes, we could get one in there,' Paige replied, something naively cocky in her tone.

'You think? I'm not so sure. It's one thing being backstage, another entirely to help ourselves to everything.'

'Mum, Holden is so nice, do you really think he'd let us sit there and not offer us a drink? He's probably got his own fridge full of cans and stuff and I'm sure he'd give us one.'

Bonnie glanced at Paige, whose eyes were bright with excitement. Okay, so even if she didn't want to go in anymore, Paige did. And goodness knew Paige deserved one special moment in her life, and Bonnie could never hope to ever give her a moment like this again. 'Okay,' she said, rallying herself. 'We'll go and see what they say. Even if they don't have spare drinks or anything, I'm sure we'll be able to bob out and get something when the crowds clear out in the arena.'

'Now you're thinking smart.' Paige grinned, looking across at Bonnie. 'Are you ready?'

'No,' Bonnie laughed.

'Me neither,' Paige giggled in return. 'But let's do it anyway!'

They pushed their way together through the double doors and found themselves in another concrete corridor, the noise from the arena outside instantly muffled by the heavy doors closing behind them.

'This is like a rabbit warren,' Bonnie said quietly, suddenly feeling the irrational urge to whisper.

'It stinks of dancer sweat,' Paige whispered back, 'so we must be close to the dressing rooms.'

Bonnie laughed softly. '*Dancer sweat?*'

'It does,' Paige giggled. She slipped her arm through Bonnie's. 'Come on, Mum, let's go and make the most of these babies…' She tapped the laminated bit of card that she had now hung around her neck on a lanyard, and they started to walk slowly down the corridor.

Bonnie pulled hers from a pocket and draped it around her neck too. 'We look like we work here now,' she laughed.

'I'll volunteer for costume change lady,' Paige giggled, 'I'd get to take Holden's trousers off.'

'Paige!' Bonnie squeaked, but Paige just laughed.

'I'm only kidding, Mum. Besides...' She shot a sly glance at Bonnie, 'don't tell me *you* wouldn't like to...'

Bonnie felt the heat rush to her cheeks. 'They're far too young for me, all of them.'

'Holden's twenty-three. That makes him...' Paige paused for a moment while she worked out the figures, 'twelve years younger than you. Not that bad really.'

Bonnie was trying to think of a suitable reply when she was saved the trouble by a door opening up ahead. A young woman staggered out under a load of clothes that looked suspiciously like some of the costumes the band had worn onstage. Paige looked at her mum and grinned. 'I think we've found the dressing room.'

They hurried over and tapped on the door. It was opened by another trendy looking woman. 'Can I help you?

'We have these,' Bonnie said, holding up her pass. 'We wondered whether we could come and say hello to the band... they did tell us we could...'

The woman held up a hand to stop Bonnie's rambling. 'They're already changed and in the Green Room,' she said, pointing down the corridor.

'The Green Room?'

'Where the after show party is.'

'Oh… okay, thanks…' Bonnie began, but the woman had already slammed the door shut before Bonnie's sentence had ended.

Bonnie and Paige looked at each other. Bonnie's insides were churning, and by the look on her daughter's face, she suspected hers were doing the same.

'Green Room then?' Bonnie asked.

Paige nodded, and they made their way up the corridor.

*

As they pushed the door open, Bonnie held Paige's arm protectively and peered in. The room didn't look remotely green, and although this fact vaguely registered, it wasn't uppermost in her mind. Beyond the crowd of sweaty dancers, Holden sat surrounded by his entourage like a king at court. Brad, Nick and Jay were sitting a little further away talking to a different, much smaller bunch of people. There was quite clearly a hierarchy at work here, one where Holden appeared to be top dog, despite the band's public image of the boys being all best mates together. It was something that had not been so apparent when they had been in the intimate confines of the radio station.

'He's there,' Paige squeaked, now taking Bonnie's arm and dragging her through the throng towards him. Bonnie didn't need to ask who *he* was. Although the rest of the band were lovely in their own way, there was only one member that either of them were really interested in.

A mountain of a man stepped in front of them, stopping Paige in her tracks.

'What are you doing in here?' he asked.

Bonnie looked up at him timidly. While he was undoubtedly the biggest, meanest looking man she had ever seen, there was no malice in his enquiry, and the ghost of a smile played about his lips.

'We have passes,' Paige said, shoving hers under his nose.

He peered at it. 'So you do.' Smiling, he stepped aside and let them go through.

They approached nervously and watched a few paces away for some moments as Holden chatted and laughed with his circle of admirers. He was clutching a beer bottle, and dressed casually in a checked shirt and jeans, his hair wet, as though he'd just stepped out of the shower. There was a slight blush to his cheeks and his eyes seemed to burn with feverish excitement. Looking at the rest of the band, Bonnie could see the same fire in their eyes too. Being on stage in front of thousands of screaming girls was obviously an exhilarating business. Holden conversed with exaggerated hand gestures, and every time he laughed, his devoted fans laughed with him.

Paige nudged Bonnie. 'If we don't go over, we're never going to get to speak to him.'

'I know,' Bonnie replied quietly, 'but he seems sort of preoccupied.'

'Oh, Mum, you're far too polite.' Paige held up her pass and waved it at Bonnie. 'He gave us these and said we should go backstage and talk to him. So let's go talk to him, he won't mind, he's really nice.'

Bonnie took a deep breath. 'Okay.'

They nudged forwards together, moving close enough so that they could see him, but trying not to get in anyone's way. For a while, he carried on talking, and both Bonnie and Paige tried vainly to catch his eye without actually having to call him purposely to speak, but he seemed oblivious to their presence. Eventually, Bonnie decided that she wasn't going to make the end of Paige's special night (and hers too, though it was harder to admit to herself just how much this evening meant to her) a complete wash-out. She cleared her throat, and as a natural break in the conversation came, she spoke.

'Hi Holden... remember us?'

He looked at her, for a moment no recognition in his eyes, and then he smiled.

'Yeah, I think...'

'The radio station last week?' Bonnie finished for him helpfully.

'Of course! How are you doing?'

'Brilliant!' Paige cut in. 'You were amazing tonight,' she added breathlessly.

'Yeah?' he asked, raising an immaculate eyebrow, clearly already aware that he had been amazing.

'Yeah, totally. I mean, I nearly fainted because you were so good.'

He laughed.

'Actually,' Bonnie said, 'I think that might have been something to do with the fact that we were squashed up at the front of the stage with about ten thousand people behind us trying to get where we were.'

'Okay, give a compliment in one hand and then take it away with the other,' Holden laughed and everyone else laughed too. Bonnie felt herself colour again.

He caught her eye and he seemed to hold her gaze for just a moment more than was appropriate before turning to Paige again. Bonnie felt her heart beat so hard she was certain everyone would hear it. She barely noticed what Paige was saying to him.

'Right, Mum?' Paige asked.

'Hmmm?' Bonnie replied vaguely.

'I said, it was the best night of our entire lives,' Paige repeated.

'Yeah,' Bonnie said, trying, but failing, to pull her gaze away from Holden's eyes, that seemed to be locked hungrily onto her now.

Brad turned from a momentary lapse in the conversation he had been having and noticed Bonnie and Paige.

'Hey!' he greeted, swinging his chair around. 'It's Paige, isn't it?'

Paige lit up at the mention of her name, clearly thrilled that he had remembered it.

Bonnie smiled as Paige skipped over to talk to him. Holden left his chair and took Bonnie gently by the arm, slightly away from the rest of his little crowd.

'You want a drink?' he asked, reaching across her for a bottle of beer on a tray just behind. She felt his breath on her neck and her heart began to pound erratically again. She nodded mutely and he handed her a bottle. 'Here,' he said, grabbing an opener and wrenching the cap off. 'So… how long have you been Paige's mum?'

Bonnie laughed. 'Um…'

'Terrible joke, right?'

'A bit,' Bonnie admitted.

'You enjoyed the concert?'

Bonnie nodded vigorously.

'You don't say much, do you?' He raised a questioning eyebrow.

'I just… yes, I've had a great night,' she replied, hardly able to take her eyes off him.

'Good,' he said, gently taking her beer from her and putting it to one side with his own. 'It could be about to get a whole lot better.'

He spun around and his gaze rested on a trendy twenty-something blonde.

'Kate…' He beckoned her over. 'Why don't we take…' He waved his hand at Bonnie.

'Bonnie,' Bonnie said helpfully.

'Yeah,' he continued, 'Bonnie and Paige for the guided tour?'

Kate tripped over to where Paige was chatting to the other band members while Holden fixed Bonnie with a smouldering look that she thought might make her spontaneously ignite. A few wordless moments later, Kate arrived back with Paige in tow.

'What's up?' Paige asked eagerly.

'We thought you might like to see the inner workings of a pop tour,' Holden said smoothly.

'Cool!' Paige squeaked, clearly so enamoured of Holden that if he had suggested a tour of a working Victorian sewer she would have said they were her absolute favourite things on the planet.

'Okay.' Holden looked at Kate. 'Shall we do the costumes and dressing rooms first?'

Paige glanced across at the other band members, who were still talking and laughing with various members of the tour entourage. 'Is anyone else coming?'

'Let them chill for a bit, and maybe they'll be in the mood to sing you a song later?' Holden suggested.

'But you don't mind interrupting your break to show us around?' Paige said. 'You're the best!'

Kate smiled and nudged Holden. 'Shall we get started?'

He nodded, then gallantly ushered Bonnie and Paige from the room to wait in the corridor, he and Kate following on.

'I wish Annabel could have been here for all this,' Paige said to Bonnie. 'She would have loved it.'

'Annabel? Was that your friend who won the competition with you?' Holden asked as Kate closed the door to the Green Room behind them.

'Yeah,' Paige replied. 'She's got flu so she couldn't come. We got her this…' She opened her bag to reveal a carefully folded up t-shirt. 'We were going to ask you to sign it for her before we went home. Not much of a consolation, but we figured it was better than nothing, didn't we, Mum?'

Bonnie nodded.

Holden thought for a moment. 'Maybe we can do better than that. Kate…' He looked at his assistant. 'I know the merch stand will be packing up now, but they should still be knocking around. How about you take Paige down to pick out some more stuff for her friend, anything she likes, and the tour will pick up the tab.' He paused. 'Take as long as you like,' he added in a deliberate tone. 'Make sure she looks through everything properly. Then maybe buy her some food or something, I heard her saying earlier that she was hungry.'

'I never,' Paige protested.

'Really? I thought you did. But I bet you are,' Holden said encouragingly. 'And maybe your mum is?' He turned to Bonnie.

'I could eat something,' Bonnie replied, 'but I'm sure we can stop off at a MacDonald's or something on the way home.'

'No way. You're our guests, Kate will get something for you, won't you Kate?' Holden turned to his assistant, who nodded.

'Come on then,' Kate said to Paige, 'otherwise everything will be packed up.'

'Should we go down with them?' Bonnie asked as they turned to go.

'Pointless us all going down. Besides,' Holden added in a dark voice, 'if there are still fans hanging around down there it'll be like world war three if I turn up.'

'Oh, yeah, of course,' Bonnie agreed.

'We can carry on our tour and they can catch us up later.'

Bonnie turned to say goodbye to Paige but she and Kate had already disappeared through a set of doors.

'Shall we?' Holden gestured along the corridor in the opposite direction.

Bonnie followed him until they came to the first doors they had knocked on when they got backstage to look for the band: the dressing rooms.

'This is where we all get naked.' Holden grinned as he held the door open for Bonnie, who felt herself blush despite her best efforts not to. She looked up at him, his eyes still unnaturally bright, that flush still on his cheeks, his hair now drying into thick waves, his skin, the most flawless and smooth skin she had ever seen on a man… Peering in through the door, she nodded. 'It looks… cosy,' she commented, and then stepped back out into the hallway again.

'Let's go in and look around,' Holden said, nudging her back through the doorway again.

'I've seen it.'

'You haven't seen it all,' Holden insisted.

Bonnie suddenly found herself inside. Holden shut the door behind them.

'Nice, huh?' he asked.

She glanced around. It was nothing spectacular – plain walls, mirror-topped dressing tables; it seemed that the wardrobe team had already emptied out as there was very little tour paraphernalia left anywhere.

'It's great,' Bonnie said, unconvinced, but her heart suddenly banging against her ribs as she realised that they were alone together in the tiny space. In all her wildest dreams, she couldn't have imagined this. This was a moment that would live long in her memory. It was something to treasure. She looked up at him expectantly.

But instead of saying anything, he simply pushed her up against the wall, holding her in an intense gaze with his body pressed against hers.

'What are you doing?' Bonnie asked, her pulse racing.

'What do you think?' He leaned to kiss her.

Shocked at first, she stiffened, but then the softness of his lips melted her into submission and she began to kiss him back, tentatively, and then harder and hungrier with him. *I'm kissing Holden Finn!* This was like some mad fairy tale where the prince notices Cinderella and, against all odds, chooses her over every noblewoman and princess in the land. This was amazing, this sort of thing didn't happen to women like her, it was too good to be true...

But then his kisses became rougher, his hands all over her, she could taste the sourness of beer on his breath. There was the sound of a zipper tearing open and then fumbling fingers at the button of her jeans too.

Bonnie pushed him off in blind panic. 'What the hell are you doing?'

'I thought you liked me,' he said, looking confused.

'I thought you liked *me*!' Bonnie replied.

'I do, that's why I'm trying to get your jeans undone, so if you wouldn't mind helping me out...'

Bonnie glanced around the tiny dressing room. Now that it was empty, it was more like a dusty store cupboard with posh mirrors. The stockroom at Applejack's looked more glamorous. 'You're trying to get my jeans undone in here?'

He shrugged. 'Well... yeah. Where else do you suggest?'

Bonnie suddenly felt sick. Her mind went back to Paige, even now happily choosing a gift for Annabel, oblivious to the seedy drama unfolding in her absence. 'You sent my daughter away so you could have a quick shag?'

'You don't want her watching, do you?' He grinned.

Bonnie was overwhelmed by anger. She raised a hand to slap him but something stopped her. The image of Paige in the crowd having the time of her life was the one thing that would make the memory of this night bearable. If she slapped him now, who would security believe? She and Paige would be thrown out, shamed, and Bonnie would have to tell Paige the sad truth about the man she idolised. She didn't think she could live with being the one responsible for waking that cynicism in her daughter, the same cynicism and distrust that stopped Bonnie from finding happiness herself, that made her pine for some image of perfection which was, when the real and dirty truth was laid before her, a lot less perfect than all the choices she had been faced with before.

In that same second, she dropped her hand and raised herself to her full height, looking him squarely in the eye, all fear and worship gone. 'If you don't mind, I'll go and get my daughter and leave.'

Holden's mouth dropped open comically. 'You're going?'

'Of course I am. Why would that be such a shock to you? Did you really think you were that irresistible?'

'You're the one who's been drooling all night; I've watched you, dying to get in my pants. I thought you'd be happy I chose you. I could have had any of those younger women at the party!'

'Is that so?' Bonnie said calmly as she straightened her top. 'Help yourself... And I hope you get Chlamydia.'

Chapter Seven

Looking back on that night, Bonnie would never know how she held it together for long enough to avoid Paige becoming suspicious that something was wrong. She mumbled some excuse about the party packing up because they had plans to move on for the next date and Holden, thankfully, said nothing to the contrary. The other band members, oozing professional charm, posed happily for photos and signed armfuls of official merchandise that they had gifted to Paige, oblivious to the mayhem that their band mate had caused; Holden played along with as little participation as he could get away with. But Bonnie had to be thankful for small mercies; he could have made things a great deal more awkward had he chosen to. Holden's only retaliation for her rejection and humiliation was an icy glare as Bonnie was leaving.

Paige fell asleep on the journey home, leaving Bonnie to drive back in silence, the dark, empty roads stretching out before her as if mirroring her dark and empty life. How could she have been so stupid? As if someone like him would ever have valued her as anything more than another sexual conquest, just one more in a long line of women desperate to catch his attention in whatever form it took.

Finally arriving home in the early hours of Sunday morning and seeing Paige to bed, she slipped beneath her own covers. But sleep wouldn't come. Instead there were hot tears and bitter thoughts and the knowledge that she would never trust another man again.

*

When Bonnie arrived for her weekly catch up after work one night, Jeanie was in her spare bedroom surrounded by half-packed boxes and dusty belongings organised loosely into piles around the floor.

'Here you are!' Bonnie said, peering around the doorway. She cast a critical glance at the debris littering the floor. 'What are you doing?'

'Sorting out,' Jeanie said, dropping a duster onto of a set of drawers. 'I thought it was about time I started.'

Bonnie was gripped by a horrible realisation. 'Started for what, exactly?'

'For when I move out,' Jeanie said, forcing an airy smile.

'You're really doing this?'

Jeanie nodded. 'You knew I was.'

'I know…' Bonnie faltered. 'I suppose I thought you might change your mind.'

'No,' Jeanie said softly. 'I'm not going to change my mind.'

Bonnie picked up a faded rag doll from the floor, threads hanging from a grubby dress. 'Sally Raggy. I didn't know you'd kept this,' she said sadly.

'Of course. It was the only thing that would get you to sleep for the first three years of your life. I remember the time we left her in the caravan in Wales; what a nightmare that was, I thought your dad was going to blow a gasket when we told him he'd got to go back.'

Bonnie smiled. 'That's one of my first proper memories, that holiday.'

'Take Sally Raggy with you, if you want.'

Bonnie put the doll down on a pile of books and folded her arms across her chest in a defensive stance.

'Despite what you think, you'll be okay, you know,' Jeanie said. 'Come down to the kitchen and I'll get the kettle on. There's something I want to talk to you about.'

*

'I know you've always been adamant that you don't want money from me, so I've stood by and watched you struggle since Henri left and it's killed me,' Jeanie said. Bonnie made to argue but Jeanie held up a hand to stop her. 'Listen, for once.' Bonnie closed her mouth with a frown and Jeanie continued. 'Juan has a gorgeous big house in Spain which he owns outright, and he doesn't expect me to pay anything into it. Your dad made sure that I would be looked after too, if anything happened to him. So I've been thinking. What's the use of me selling this house? What if things don't work out with Juan and I want to come back? Besides, this is the house you were born in and I love it, I don't want to see some strange family in here.'

'You could rent it,' Bonnie cut in.

'I'm getting to that, Bon, just shush for a minute, will you.'

Bonnie dragged her tea across the table and took a sip.

'So, I could rent it out but that would mean trusting my tenants not to trash it. And again, what if I wanted to come back? I'd then have to get them out and it doesn't seem fair.'

'What can you do then?'

'I want you and Paige to have the house.'

Bonnie put her tea down and stared at her mum. 'I can't afford the rent on this place.'

'I don't want rent.'

'What...'

'I want you to have it, live here for free. I mean...' Jeanie added quickly, sensing a fresh line of argument, 'it would come to you anyway when I die, so why not have it now?'

'Because it's yours and you need the income, or at least the stability of knowing it's there for you if you want to come home.'

'I don't need the income. And I want to see you have some stability while I'm around to appreciate it, not when I'm six feet under. And as for knowing it's there if I want to come home, would you turn me away if I came back with my suitcase and a box of tissues?'

'Of course not,' Bonnie said, 'you know I'd never do that.'

'Exactly. This way, everybody is happy.'

'Not me.'

'Think about someone else for a change,' Jeanie snapped. She paused for a moment and then softened her tone. 'Don't be so stubborn all the time when it serves no purpose. Think how good this would be for Paige. And how much more settled I'd be knowing that you have this rock solid roof over your head, no rent to worry about, no threats of eviction...'

Bonnie looked at her thoughtfully as she took another sip of her drink. 'What about legal stuff?'

'I'd sign it over; there's no point in messing about.'

'I wouldn't want you to do that.'

'I know you wouldn't... which is why I've already looked into the legal side of things and there are clauses you can have written in that will protect me and make you feel better.' Jeanie smiled encouragingly, sensing that Bonnie was beginning to come round to the idea.

'Have you decided when you're going?'

'Just as soon as I have this sorted. There doesn't seem any point in putting it off. I love Juan, crazy as that might sound to you, and I want to spend what years I have left with him.'

'In a gorgeous Spanish villa surrounded by orange trees and sparkling mountains and year round sunshine,' Bonnie pointed out with a faint smile.

'Exactly. And you know that you are welcome whenever you want, you and Paige. And now that you won't have a pokey flat to worry about paying for, you'll have a little spare cash for the air fare.'

'I never said that I would take the house on.'

'No,' Jeanie said, 'but you will.'

Bonnie sighed. 'I'll have to talk to Paige about it.'

'As if she's going to say no.'

'It might mean her moving schools,' Bonnie replied practically.

'You're making excuses. She has a year left, less in fact, and I'm not going straight away. You can certainly manage for that long.

*

Try as she might, Bonnie couldn't help but smile when she thought of the future that could now be hers. Alone, other than Paige, but at least the burden of keeping a roof over their head would be lifted and they could maybe live a little – take some of those trips they had often discussed, buy that new dress when she fancied it, go out for that impromptu tea after work instead of scraping the freezer for unidentifiable leftovers. Maybe she could even cut her hours at work – she would have to see how things went first but the idea turned her smile into a grin that seemed like it would never stop spreading.

Paige had been upset when she first found out about Jeanie's move, but when she learned that they would be taking on the house and would also be welcome for holidays at any time in Spain, she had acted in a typically Paige way and promptly forgot to be annoyed with her nan and her mum. In fact, she had taken herself off to her bedroom to begin packing, despite the warning that nothing was set in stone just yet and there was no practical timescale to work to. Bonnie didn't see the point in stopping her; why not let her enjoy the excitement of the moment? And after the few weeks Bonnie had endured, maybe it was time she enjoyed a bit of good fortune too, instead of feeling guilty about it.

With Paige in her room busily organising her belongings Bonnie remembered that she hadn't yet opened the post that had been lying on the mat when she got home. A quick shuffle through revealed a handful of bills and junk… apart from a thick, parchment-coloured envelope, handwritten and addressed to her. Dropping the rest of the letters onto the table, she opened it quickly. Inside was a hastily scribbled note on the same paper.

Dear Bonnie

I got your address from Capital Sounds. My PA did, anyway. I know it sounds weird, but will you meet me? Let my PA know your decision, the number is on the letterhead up top, and she'll sort out a venue.

Holden Finn

Dazed, Bonnie wandered into the living room and dropped onto the sofa. She read the letter again. It had to be some kind of joke, some sort of sick revenge for what she'd done to him. Or was it one of Paige's friends? It had to be something more than it seemed to be.

'Mum…' Paige called from her bedroom.

Bonnie hastily stuffed the letter into her pocket and went to see what she wanted.

'Do you think we could put these toys on Ebay?' Paige asked, holding up a box of what could only be described as filthy, malformed plastic lumps.

'What are they?' Bonnie asked in a bewildered voice.

Paige peered into the box. 'Um… I can't remember.'

'In that case, probably not,' Bonnie said. 'How would you write the product description?'

'Modern art?' Paige grinned. 'Okay, I'll bin them.'

'They should have been binned years ago,' Bonnie commented. 'Where did you find them?'

'Under my bed.'

'Hmmm.' Bonnie looked around the room thoughtfully. If there was that much junk hidden away, maybe Paige's enthusiasm to get started early wasn't such a waste after all. They might have to spend the next year clearing the flat out.

Paige tossed another couple of bits of unrecognisable plastic into the box and stretched. 'I think I'll call it a night.'

Bonnie glanced at the chaos in her daughter's room. It wasn't so much sorting, as simply moving the rubbish around. 'Maybe you want to move this stuff before you go to bed. A trip to A&E at midnight because you've fallen over Harry Potter's wand while getting up for a drink of water is not my idea of a good night out.'

Bonnie left Paige to clear up while she went into her own bedroom. Sitting on the bed, she pulled the crumpled letter from her pocket and read it again. She looked at the number on the top for the supposed

PA. Was that even real? There was only one way to find out, but she would have to wait until her lunch break the following day to call.

*

'You're not coming to the Bounty?' Linda asked.

'I'm not that hungry today,' Bonnie assured her. 'I'll grab a cup-a-soup. I've got to make a quick phone call too, and it has to be office hours.'

Linda's expression darkened. 'Not money trouble again? I've told you that me and John can lend you some –'

Bonnie shook her head vigorously. 'No, nothing like that. Don't worry, Lind, everything will work out with my finances soon.' Bonnie hadn't yet told her friend about Jeanie's offer to let her and Paige have the house. There was a small part of her that still thought it was too good to be true, or that to say it out loud would be to somehow jinx it. She had given Linda a clue that things might be about to change in her fortunes, but that was as much as she dared hint at, and Linda had asked no more, content to wait for Bonnie to share her news when she was ready.

Linda shrugged. 'I'll bring you a carrot cake back; you're bound to want a sugar rush this afternoon.'

Bonnie smiled. 'Thanks, Lind.'

Linda pulled on her coat. Bonnie watched her leave the tiny kitchen and gave her a minute before closing the door and pulling her phone from her bag, along with the letter.

She dialled the number and waited.

'Hello... I've been given this number for...' Bonnie paused. If this was a huge wind up, then telling the person on the end of the phone line that she was ringing because Holden Finn had written to her would sound truly idiotic. 'I had a note through the post to phone this number and arrange a meeting,' she said instead, hoping it would be enough information to see her through any eventuality.

'What's your name?' the woman on the other end of the line asked.

'Bonnie Cartwright.'

'Hmmm. Holden is free next Tuesday if you are. He did say that he could travel to see you if you needed, as the tour is in your area for a few nights.'

'I can't do weekdays,' Bonnie said, not thinking about how unhelpful this might be and simply bewildered by the information that this letter seemed to be genuine after all.

'Tuesday evening?' the woman asked. 'He could fit you in around five thirty, just before he has to be at the venue. He would have to be quick, though.'

Bonnie's mind wandered back to the night of the concert, and their disastrous tryst in the dressing room. It seemed Holden Finn was too busy and important to do anything other than quickly.

'I don't know,' Bonnie replied hesitantly, 'I don't finish work until five.'

'I have Sunday afternoon otherwise; there's no performance on Sunday,' the woman said, 'then the tour goes to Scotland… unless you can travel to Scotland?' she asked in a haughty tone.

Sunday… Paige would want to know where Bonnie was going. What could she use as an excuse? She quickly made a decision.

'I suppose I could do Sunday. Where do I need to go?'

'Hang on the line, let me google some suitable venues. You do realise that the utmost discretion is required here?'

Bonnie grimaced. *Oh yeah, like I'm going to run a newspaper ad.* Then again, part of her thought that if she did invite half of Paige's school

Holden shook his head. 'I think we're just going to have a drink. Unless…' He looked at Bonnie. It was weird, but Bonnie could swear that it was almost a hopeful look. 'Unless you want to eat?' he asked.

'I'm not hungry,' Bonnie said. 'A drink is fine with me. Can I just have a mineral water, I'm driving.'

'Sure,' Holden said. 'I'll have the same,' he told the waitress, who nodded, giving Holden a curious look as she went.

He looked at Bonnie expectantly as they were left alone again. When she didn't speak, he filled the silence instead. 'I bet you're wondering why I asked you to come.'

'You could say that,' Bonnie replied dryly.

'What happened…' He hesitated, seemingly unsure how to broach the subject.

'When you thought you'd try out the older woman theory?' Bonnie offered icily.

'I was drunk. And I was post-show. I can't explain it, but after a show like that you feel… well, kind of invincible, like you rule the world or something. It makes you weird and it makes you do weird things. I just needed to let off some steam.'

'Okay,' Bonnie said in a level voice. 'I get it. You're sorry. Don't worry, I won't be selling my story or blackmailing you or anything else that you've been losing sleep over. And I haven't told a soul.'

His expression relaxed. 'I know you won't. You're not like the other girls I meet. You're older, I know, but you're just different. You don't care about all that showbiz stuff and what you did… you know, you wouldn't let me do what I wanted with you…'

Bonnie waited patiently for him to finish but he seemed at a loss for words. The waitress appeared and left their drinks with a warm smile. Then Holden continued.

'I've never met anyone like you. I was angry the other night at the gig, sure I was. But then afterwards I couldn't stop thinking about you. And look at you today…' He smiled, his eyes now full of affection as he gazed appreciatively at her from under the brim of his cap. 'You don't care, just throw your jeans on even though you're meeting Holden Finn and you look… amazing.'

Bonnie's glass stopped halfway to her mouth and she stared at him. 'You are joking me, right? This is some sort of revenge where you pretend to like me and then humiliate me?'

'No, Bonnie, I swear it's not like that.' He shook his head earnestly. 'I fancy you like mad. I can't understand it myself. Not that you're not attractive,' he added quickly, 'but we shouldn't be right for each other. I keep telling myself that but I can't get you out of my head.'

'What makes you think that I would still like you after what happened?' Bonnie asked slowly.

'You liked me before that, didn't you?' he asked, the ghost of a cocky smile about his lips.

'That night changed everything.'

'Scrub that. I wasn't being myself. Let's pretend it never happened and maybe try a date or something.'

'Now I know you're taking the piss.'

'I'm not. I really mean it.'

Bonnie put her drink down and held him in a frank gaze. 'Holden… explain to me how this works.'

He shot her a puzzled frown.

'Even if what you're telling me isn't a wind up, I don't see how it can happen. You're on tour all the time,' she elaborated, 'you have young girls throwing themselves at you. You're mobbed everywhere you go and every single move you make is reported and examined. How do you see a relationship with a thirty-five-year-old mother of one who works in a greengrocer's and drives a battered Toyota Yaris being successful?'

'We don't have to tell anyone.'

'Great, so I'd get to be your dirty little secret.'

'I didn't mean that, I just meant so you wouldn't get loads of unwanted attention.'

Bonnie sighed. 'It's mental. Whatever bee is in your bonnet, you need to get rid of it. If this is a joke, then you've had your laugh. Otherwise, it's a ridiculous idea.'

He grabbed her hand across the table and pulled her into an impulsive kiss. Shocked, she responded without thought, melting into it as their lips met. She felt the heat rise in her, the smell of him invading her senses and removing any grain of rational thinking. His words had seemed so earnest, what he had promised something she had dreamed of more times than she could count. It would be so easy to let him in.

After feverish moments, she broke off and gazed sadly at him.

'It won't work,' she said, gathering her coat and sliding across the seat of the booth to leave.

'What…'

'Forget it. There's no way this is happening.'

'I won't give up,' she heard him call as she walked out the door. 'I won't stop until I get you!'

Chapter Eight

'Bloody hell, Bonnie, you look like death warmed up,' Linda observed as Bonnie shuffled into the back room of Applejack's for the start of another week. 'In fact, death warmed up would look like it had been given a Boots' makeover standing next to you.'

'Cheers,' Bonnie grunted as she took her coat off.

'Bad weekend?'

'Try bad life.'

'It can't be that serious?'

Bonnie sighed. It wasn't, not really. Her mum was practically giving her a house and Holden Finn was allegedly in love with her. She ought to be feeling like the luckiest woman alive. But she had tossed and turned in bed all night trying to figure out why she felt so wretched about it all. Perhaps it was the way each of those supposed gifts came with a condition – like every up had to come with a down to balance out the yin and yang of the world. Her mum was giving her a house, but was also moving thousands of miles away to live with a bloke she hardly knew, and as for Holden... well, she didn't know what to make of that.

The usual morning knock came at the back door of the shop and Linda went to open it as Bonnie hung her coat and bag on the peg.

'God, Max,' Linda said as she stepped aside to let him in, 'did you go to the same beauty salon as Bonnie? I didn't think it was possible for anyone to look more knackered than her but you've managed it.'

Max flashed a weary grin. 'Thanks, you really know how to flatter a man.'

'Hey, Max,' Bonnie said as she came through into the stockroom.

'So, what's ailing you?' he asked her.

'What do you mean?'

'Linda says you're not well this morning.'

'Oh, I'm okay, just didn't sleep much.'

'Something on your mind?'

'Something like that,' Bonnie said. She looked him over critically. 'How about you? Something on *your* mind?'

'Something like that.' Max smiled faintly.

'I'll put the kettle on,' Linda cut in, 'and then you two miserable sods can spill the beans.'

Bonnie exchanged a concerned look with Max. Whatever it was that was on their minds, it didn't seem like either of them wanted to share it.

Fred poked his head around the door of the stockroom. 'Oh, it's you,' he said, giving Max a brusque nod. He switched his attention to Bonnie. 'Are you coming to restock these apples or what?'

Bonnie sighed. 'I'm on my way, give me a minute to get in the door, will you?'

Fred disappeared back into the main shop and Bonnie shrugged apologetically at Max, who was frowning as he watched Fred go.

'Bonnie,' Max began slowly, 'is it me or has Fred got even more miserable these days?'

Bonnie chuckled softly as she fastened her tabard and went to stack the apples.

Linda came back through from the kitchen with two mugs of tea. She handed one to Max. 'Where's Bon?' she asked.

Max angled his head at the shop doorway. 'Fred called her in to fill up the apples.'

'Right,' she said briskly. 'Are you going to tell me what's up with you?'

'Nothing,' Max replied, taking a sip of his tea.

'Yeah, that's what Bonnie says when I ask her.'

He laughed. 'Well, her misery is definitely nothing to do with me, that's the one thing I know for certain.'

'Okay. So what is it you *don't* know for certain?'

He sighed. 'Whether I've done the right thing,' he said simply.

*

'He's dumped her?' Bonnie asked as she and Linda walked side by side to the Bounty for their daily deli fix.

'I think the word *dumped* is a bit harsh, but yeah, they're not together any more,' Linda said.

'Why?'

Linda shrugged. 'He says he doesn't even know why. It just didn't feel right.'

'I thought they were love's young dream.'

'So did I. But it seems not.'

'I'll never understand men as long as I live,' Bonnie said wearily.

Linda threw her a sideways glance. 'I can think of one who might say that exact thing about you.'

'Not that again.'

'It's obvious to anyone who has eyes why he's dumped Sarah.'

'That's ridiculous.'

'He's mad about you, always has been.'

'He's Max.'

'And he's lovely. Why don't you just go on one date with him, see how it goes?'

Bonnie mulled over the idea for a moment as she walked. 'No,' she said finally. 'And before you say anything, I can think of a million reasons why not. He's only just finished with Sarah, and I'm nobody's rebound. It's also Max – he's my mate. Not only that but we have to see him every day. Can you imagine the atmosphere every time he walked in here if it didn't work out between us? We have a laugh now, and I'm not about to ruin things. Besides, Paige has made it quite clear what she thinks of him.'

'Paige wouldn't be going out with him; it's none of her business.'

'Of course it is. Paige has to like anyone I bring home or it's doomed before it's begun.'

'She hasn't had to do much rejection then because you never take anyone home, as far as I can tell,' Linda replied tartly.

'I appreciate your concern, Lind, I really do, but this has nothing to do with you either.'

'You're my mate, and so is Max. Neither of you seems to be happy separately so why not give it a go with each other?'

'I can't understand why he would just finish it with her,' Bonnie mused, ignoring Linda's last question. 'They were practically engaged last week.'

Linda shrugged. 'Who knows? It's kinder than stringing the poor girl along if his heart wasn't in it, though, so good for him.'

'But his heart did seem in it,' Bonnie insisted. 'He seemed so keen on her.'

'Maybe he was trying to convince himself that he she was Miss Right and now he's come to his senses.'

'Maybe I should start to look around for him. If he really wants to settle down, perhaps we should find Miss Right for him? We know loads of the girls who work in the shops nearby; we could try to fix him up.'

Linda burst into a hearty laugh. 'You are mental! Stav's mama is single; perhaps we should fix him up with her!'

Bonnie frowned. 'I'm serious. We know him really well – what sorts of things he likes and what he doesn't, where he likes to go, his sense of humour. We could match him up and do a really good job.'

Linda stopped laughing and fixed her friend with a warning look. 'You can try, but you're playing with fire, honey.'

*

When Bonnie arrived at work the following day, she had a huge grin on her face. 'You look a lot happier than you did yesterday,' Linda commented as Bonnie took her coat off. 'You won the lottery or something?'

Bonnie rolled her eyes. 'Do you think I'd be in here lugging spuds if I had?' She hung her bag on her peg and turned to Linda, barely able to contain her excitement. 'I think I've just got Max a date.'

'What!'

'Kerry, in the shoe shop. She just split with her boyfriend. She says she's seen Max come in and out and she thinks he's really cute. I asked her what she thought about going on a date with him and she said she was willing to give anything a whirl.'

Linda folded her arms and gave Bonnie a stern look. 'I'm telling you, this will end badly.'

'It won't, Lind. I'm going to sort Max out. I hate to see him miserable.'

'Then you go out with him.'

'Kerry is perfect. She's pretty, down-to-earth and a good laugh. She doesn't have kids either, so no baggage.'

'Max isn't the sort of bloke to be worried by baggage.'

'Still makes things easier, though,' Bonnie called as she went through to the kitchen to put the kettle on.

Linda followed, shaking her head. 'I'm having nothing to do with this, Bon.'

'Oh?' Bonnie turned around, drying the mug she had just rinsed. 'You're normally the first one to pitch in with a fun scheme.'

'This is not a fun scheme. I've told you what I think.'

'It'll be fine. My life is complicated enough, so I can at least sort one of my mates out.'

'I don't see what's so complicated about your life, other than the fact that you sit on your own night after night while Paige goes out with her friends.'

Bonnie bit back a wry smile. She hated that there were some things – massive things – going on in her life that she had to keep from her friend. But right now she wasn't in a place in her head where she could share them. While she was thinking about a tactful reply, the morning knock came at the door. Linda went to get it and a moment later, Max came in.

'You still look terrible,' Linda said.

Max didn't even bother with his usual witty response. He just shrugged. 'Another bad night,' he replied carefully, glancing at Bonnie.

'It's okay, I told Bonnie about Sarah,' Linda reassured him.

Max heaved a sigh of relief. 'Not that I wouldn't have told you, Bonnie,' he said.

'It's okay.'

'Anyway,' Max continued, 'Sarah turned up at mine last night. She wasn't very happy and we had a long talk.'

'Please tell me you didn't get back with her,' Linda cut in.

'No. I was tempted, though. I just felt like I'd been such a bastard to her. But there's no point, it would only make things worse, and they're bad enough already,' he concluded miserably.

'Maybe my news will make things seem better?' Bonnie offered.

Max seemed to perk up suddenly. 'Oh?'

Linda threw her hands into the air and blew out a puff of exasperation. 'I'm going to make that brew,' she said as she stalked off into the kitchenette.

'I got you a date,' Bonnie said, proud of her handiwork.

'You did what!'

'I got you a date,' Bonnie repeated patiently. 'With a girl who works in the shoe shop down the road. Her name is Kerry, she's twenty-six, she's –'

'Whoa, whoa…' Max held up a hand to silence Bonnie. 'You're fixing me up on a blind date?'

'Well… yeah… I mean, no. You can go and talk to her first if you like, she's only a few shops away.'

'You think I should just walk into her shop and announce myself as her new boyfriend?' Max asked, his voice rising with incredulity.

'Of course not. Just go and talk to her.'

'I can't do that.'

'Yes you can, it's easy.'

Max was silent for a moment. 'If it's so easy,' he said slowly, 'then how come you're still single?'

Bonnie's forehead wrinkled into a frown. 'It's not the same.'

'Sorry, Bonnie, I know you mean well but I'm not going to do that.'

'But I fixed it up with her now!'

'Then you'll have to unfix it.'

'But...'

Max folded his arms resolutely. He didn't look angry, but he did seem determined to stand his ground.

'Look, Bon. I've just finished with Sarah. It was messy and I'm not sure I want to get into another situation like that, at least, not yet. You understand, don't you?'

'You wouldn't get into a situation like that with Kerry; she's much more suited to you than Sarah was.'

'I can only take your word for that. But I'm not going to find out.'

Linda came back through to the stockroom balancing four teas on a tray. Max and Bonnie both took one.

'You told him your little scheme?' Linda asked, looking at Bonnie, whose expression could leave no doubt what Max's answer had been. 'And you said no,' Linda added, looking at Max, who simply nodded. 'Good. I told her it was a stupid idea. Now that's sorted, I'd better take this tea into Fred and get the stock out before the stress makes what little hair he has left come out.'

Linda left Bonnie and Max eyeing each other awkwardly. Bonnie was suddenly aware that he looked hurt, a hurt so deep that it ran right through the whole of him.

'Your break up with Sarah really got to you?' Bonnie asked gently.

He shook his head. 'It was tough, but I can deal with it.'

'There's something else bothering you then?'

He paused, appeared poised to say something meaningful as he gazed at her, but then seemed to change his mind. 'I'm old Bounce-Back-Max. You know me, I'm always fine.'

Bonnie took a sip of her tea. She was about to reply when Max put his cup down on the bench and, without another word, headed out of the back door to his delivery van.

*

Dear Bonnie,

I know our last meeting didn't go well. Maybe I didn't explain myself properly, or kissed you when I shouldn't have done, but give me another chance. I forget my dance moves, or the words to songs, and the others are wondering what the hell is wrong with me. It's you that's doing it, Bonnie; I can't stop thinking about how much I want you. I'm stuck in Scotland right now with the tour and I feel so far away from you. Call my PA, she can arrange flights to Glasgow and I'll meet you.

   Please do it.

Holden. X

It was the fourth time she'd read the note since it had arrived in the Saturday post. The boy was clearly in need of help. What on earth could she offer him that was so good he'd go to these lengths? She was beginning to wonder whether it wasn't Bonnie that he was pining for, but the victory of winning her. It seemed a far more likely explanation.

Her thoughts were interrupted by the shuffling of socked feet. Bonnie glanced up at the kitchen door with a guilty look as Paige came in yawning and scraping her hair straight with her fingers.

'What have you got there?' Paige asked, nodding at the letter, written on thick cream paper, which Bonnie was screwing up.

'It's nothing. A stupid hairdresser gimmick, that place up the road trying to drum up business.' Bonnie dropped the letter in the bin. She stared as it sat on top of the rubbish for a moment, then hastily covered it with some old potato peelings before closing the lid on it.

Paige dropped into a chair at the table. 'So what's the plan for today?'

'I thought we might go shopping. It's Linda's fiftieth birthday party next week and I need to get her a present. I could do with a dress too, if I can find one cheap enough.'

'You want to go into Manchester?'

'There's enough open on the retail park here for what I need,' Bonnie replied, dropping some bread in the toaster.

'Do I have to come to Linda's party?'

Bonnie turned to Paige, hands on hips. 'It would be polite. Linda never misses your birthday.'

'Yeah, she gets me a card and stuff, but I don't make her come to my parties.'

'That's completely different and you know it. She's an old friend and someone I value.'

'Yeah, she's your mate; she won't care if I'm there or not. It's only in her house anyway.'

The toaster popped and Bonnie pulled the slices from it, sliding them onto a plate, which she dumped in front of Paige with the butter dish. 'We'll see. Don't think it'll be your cue to fill our flat full of teenagers for a party of your own if I do go to Linda's without you.'

Paige grinned up at her mum as she reached for her toast. 'As if!'

'In fact…' Bonnie continued thoughtfully, 'you should probably sleep over at your nan's.'

Paige's grin faded. 'Do I have to? Can I go and stay with Annabel?'

'Your nan's not going to be in England for much longer. Perhaps you ought to make the most of the time you have left before she's hundreds of miles and an airplane ride away?'

'I suppose so,' Paige conceded, slumping in her chair.

'You'll miss her when she's gone, even though you don't think so now.'

'I know that.'

'Then make the most of her while you still have her.'

*

By the time Bonnie had arrived at the double gates of Linda's house, the noise from the party could be heard from the street. It had taken her a frustrating half hour to find Paige's phone and Paige had stubbornly refused to go anywhere without it. Eventually, it had turned up in the laundry basket, and then the taxi had arrived late, so that far from being relaxed and ready to celebrate when she arrived at her friend's house, Bonnie was feeling distinctly stressed and a little bit sweaty. She looked up at the house as she tottered down the drive in heels that were far too high for her, yanking at the hem of a midnight blue dress that clung deliciously to her curves – at least, she had thought so when she'd tried it on in the shop. Now it felt far too short and far too tight and Bonnie feared that if she had to suck her stomach in all night the way she was right now, she was in serious danger of passing out.

Bonnie had always thought that Linda's house was gorgeous – it was a mock Tudor detached and set in a sweeping corner plot with impressive looking double gates leading onto a long gravel driveway. It was one of the best houses on the estate. Linda was on the same pay as Bonnie, but her husband, John certainly wasn't. Bonnie often wondered why Linda worked at all, especially putting up with Fred's moody demands as she did, when John could comfortably keep her.

But that was Linda all over; she would never be dependent on someone else for her upkeep, no matter how much money he earned.

Bonnie paused at the door and held a hand to the bell, but it was opened before she had a chance to press, Linda pulling her into a bone-crushing hug.

'I didn't think you were coming,' she squealed, already sounding distinctly tipsy despite the fact that it was only just after nine o'clock.

'Yeah, sorry about that. The usual trouble with Paige.'

'Never mind, I'm just glad you're here.' Linda pulled Bonnie into the house and dragged the wrap from around her shoulders, slinging it into a pile of coats behind a doorway in the hall, and then leading her down to the kitchen where most of the noise seemed to be coming from.

In the kitchen there were about twenty people. Many of them Bonnie had met at previous parties at Linda's house; two she had never seen before and were introduced as work colleagues of John's. They were so unremarkable that almost as soon as they'd been introduced, Bonnie had forgotten their names. John bounded forward and gave Bonnie a hug, and then shoved a glass of wine into her hand, making her giggle.

'Not trying to get me drunk, I hope?' she asked.

'Absolutely. If I don't succeed, Linda will kill me.'

Bonnie laughed. She had always liked John. He and Linda were cut from the same cloth – down-to-earth, good-humoured, generous and kind. Ten years older than Linda, he had been handsome once, though a heart attack at forty-five followed by a subsequent battle with throat cancer had taken their toll on his looks. He made the most of life, though, and his eyes were permanently crinkled into a smile.

Bonnie scanned the small crowd, nodding recognition and greeting people as she did, and then her gaze settled on Max, propped up against the kitchen counter with a bottle of beer. He smiled warmly as he caught her attention and she made a beeline straight for him.

'Thank God you've come,' he whispered. 'I thought I was going to be the only person here who had come alone. Awkward much?'

Bonnie laughed. 'I'm used to it by now. Henri wasn't much for going out, even when we lived together.'

'Well,' he said as he looked her up and down approvingly, 'if it was me, I wouldn't let you go to any parties alone. You look gorgeous and I'd be terrified that some other bloke was going to run off with you.'

Bonnie felt herself blush and fiddled with her hair self-consciously. 'I bet you say that to all the girls.'

'Only when I have my beer goggles on.'

'Like now?'

'No,' he said. 'Right now I'm stone cold sober.'

Bonnie coloured even more under his intense gaze. Embarrassed, she smacked him on the arm playfully. 'You're such an idiot.'

He suddenly seemed to shake himself. 'Thanks,' he grinned.

Bonnie glanced across and saw that Linda was hovering, watching them closely. Seeming to sense that she'd been rumbled, she came over.

'Thanks so much for the gorgeous flowers, by the way, they arrived this morning,' Linda said, kissing Bonnie on the cheek. 'I told you not to get anything though.'

'I'm hard up but not a skinflint,' she laughed.

'I put them in the living room, next to Max's.' Linda smiled at Max, who put on a look of mock innocence.

'I didn't send flowers, Lind. It must be your secret admirer.'

Bonnie laughed. 'I bet it was Stavros.'

'It's funny, because the card said Max,' Linda frowned, playing along.

'It must be another Max,' he said. 'I got you a sack of parsnips; they're in the car right now.'

Bonnie giggled but Linda looked with disapproval at Bonnie's wine glass. 'You don't seem to be doing much damage to that. Get it down you so I can fill you up.'

'Why is everyone determined to get me drunk tonight?' Bonnie asked, rolling her eyes.

'Because nobody leaves one of my parties sober, you know that.'

Bonnie took a large gulp of her wine.

'All of it,' Linda chided.

'You'll be carrying me home at this rate,' Bonnie said.

'No carrying anyone home tonight. I have a perfectly good spare bed for you and… *anyone else* who might be in need of it,' Linda replied mischievously with a quick glance at Max.

'Don't look at me,' Max said. 'I turn into a pumpkin at midnight so I have to be home.'

'Everybody must be steaming drunk tonight, so drunk that they wake on my floor in the morning with no recollection of their own name, let alone where they live, otherwise I will consider my birthday party a complete failure,' Linda said sternly. 'So no rushing home at midnight for either of you.'

Bonnie was about to reply when the stereo was whacked up to a volume loud enough to loosen the roof tiles of houses across the estate, the first bars of *Disco Inferno* blasting out.

'Lucky we invited the neighbours,' Linda shouted over the music, 'that way they can't complain. Good eh?' She gave Max a cheeky wink and he grinned.

'I knew there was a reason I liked you, Lind.'

Linda grabbed a nearby opened bottle of wine and tipped some into Bonnie's glass. 'Get that down you, girl.'

*

An hour later, Linda was wearing neon legwarmers, star-shaped glittery deely boppers and a satin basque over her dress. John had a pink wig gradually sliding down his bald head and sunglasses, and the whole party had done the conga at least twice around Linda's garden, resulting in Bonnie getting a heel stuck in the flowerbed, Max gallantly yanking her leg out as she giggled drunkenly, and carrying her back to the house.

Inside, Bonnie flopped down on the bottom stair as the rest of the guests continued their outdoor celebrations. Max grinned down at her as she kicked off her muddy shoes.

'I'm so glad you came tonight,' Bonnie said, looking up at him. 'I didn't think you would. I love Linda to bits, but she'd be too busy playing hostess and I would have been sat like a right lemon by myself.'

'Nah,' Max said, nudging her over and squeezing next to her. 'Linda would never have let that happen, she cares too much about you.'

Bonnie nodded in agreement and they both became quiet. Sitting so close together in their companionable silence, Bonnie was now acutely aware of how good he smelt, of the heat of his body pressed against hers. Whether it was the drink, or whether she just wasn't thinking straight after her very weird few weeks, she couldn't tell, but it stirred something. She suddenly wanted to grab him and kiss him until her lips bled. Fighting the urge, she let her head rest on his shoulder. He reached over to absently stroke a hair from her forehead and his gentle touch set her nerve ends on fire.

'Bonnie,' he said quietly.

'Hmmm?'

'I need to say something. If I don't say it now, I'll kick myself every time I think about this moment and how I wasted it.'

'Don't…'

'You don't know what it is,' he replied, a note of surprise in his voice.

'I do. Because I'm thinking the same thing. It's the drink talking, Max, and we'll regret it tomorrow.'

'I'm not drunk.'

'I am.'

He swung an arm around her and rubbed his thumb gently across her shoulder as he pulled her in to nestle against him. 'You look amazing tonight, better than I've ever seen you look.'

'That's because you only ever see me in my tabard,' she said, forcing a self-conscious laugh.

They were silent again. The muffled sounds of shouting and singing reached them from outside in the back garden. Someone mentioned fireworks.

'Do you still love Henri?' Max asked suddenly.

Bonnie didn't reply straight away. Finally, she shrugged. 'I think I do.'

Max took his arm from around her. 'Sorry,' he said, standing up.

'For what?' Bonnie asked, confusion colouring her features.

'You're right, I'm drunk and this is a bad idea.' He ran a hand through his hair and smiled awkwardly. 'We'll miss those fireworks if we don't go back out.'

*

When Bonnie woke, she was in Linda's spare bed, just as Linda had predicted. The winter sun washed the room in a pale light through Linda's pastel curtains. She had absolutely no idea what time it was, or who else had stayed over that night. There were flashbacks, snippets of conversations that made her cheeks burn as she recalled them. While she had been very drunk, she hadn't been so plastered to have forgotten one particular bit of the night. She only hoped that Max had been.

Pushing herself up, she got out of bed and went downstairs to find out.

The sofa was taken up by a snoring John, who didn't appear to have even made it up to bed. Linda was nowhere to be seen so Bonnie presumed she had. Balloons, streamers, bits of fancy dress, food and half-empty glasses littered the living room and kitchen, the sour smell of old alcohol turning Bonnie's already delicate stomach as she crept around trying to find her shoes and see who else was still there.

Other than John, the rest of the ground floor was empty. Being unsuccessful at locating her shoes, she went back upstairs to look for them. Putting her head around Linda's bedroom door, she saw Linda stir slightly as she slept on top of the bedclothes, still in her party outfit too. A female guest that Bonnie vaguely recognised as one of Linda's old school friends was wrapped in a blanket on the floor beside the bed, her husband a few feet away with his mouth hanging open making a curious clicking noise as he slept. Bonnie couldn't help a quick grin. This sort of thing was not unusual at one of Linda's dos – there were few teenage parties that could compete with them, despite the fact that Linda's guests were much older. On reflection, it was a very good job that Bonnie hadn't made Paige come after all.

A search of the rest of the top floor revealed Bonnie's shoes in an airing cupboard (she had no idea how they had got there) but no Max. So, he had gone home. Bonnie wondered when – she couldn't remember him saying goodbye. Had he stayed over and snuck out early, or had he left last night?

As she crept along the landing, she met Linda coming out of her bedroom.

'Morning,' Linda said blearily.

Bonnie grinned. 'How's your head?'

'Like it's got an illegal rave going on in there. How's yours?'

'Pretty much the same.'

'Good night, though, wasn't it?'

'It was. We're going to pay for it today, though.'

Linda waved a hand vaguely. 'That's why Sundays were invented.'

Bonnie followed her downstairs and into the kitchen, pulling up a high stool at the breakfast bar and hauling herself onto it.

'Want a coffee?' Linda asked, going to fill the kettle.

Bonnie nodded. 'And a paracetamol if you have one.'

'Hair of the dog works much better,' Linda said, sloshing the dregs of wine in a bottle.

'Ugh,' Bonnie said, 'coffee is just fine.'

Linda grinned and dropped the bottle into her recycling tub. 'You and Max seemed cosy last night,' she said carelessly.

'We were the only singletons at the party.'

'Seemed like more than that from where I was standing.'

'When were you standing?' Bonnie quipped. 'I can only remember you crawling and falling down quite a lot.'

'Don't change the subject, lady.'

'I'm not. There's nothing to tell.'

Linda threw her hands in the air. 'That's it! I despair of you two!'

'Then stop trying to pair us off. There will never be a Max and me, and the sooner you get that into your head, the better.'

'Okay, okay. Consider last night my swan song. I officially retire as Bonnie Cartwright's chief matchmaker.'

'Good. Now where's that coffee?'

*

Dear Bonnie,

As you didn't phone my PA, I decided to get her to book tickets anyway. I know you work in the week, so I got a Sunday flight with a same day return. They should be enclosed with this note.

You have to meet me; I'm going crazy without you.

Holden x

Bonnie let out a frustrated little squeal as she ripped up the letter, along with the plane tickets. What the hell had she seen in that man? He was nothing but a spoilt kid who was throwing his toys out of his cot because he couldn't get what he wanted.

Bonnie tossed her coat over the back of a chair and put the kettle on. What was it about her that attracted the most disastrous relationships? She didn't want money, or a posh house, or wardrobes full of clothes, or to be worshipped… she just wanted a man who would treat her as an equal, someone with whom she could enjoy life, someone she could rely on. Instead, she had Henri, missing somewhere or other until he 'sorted his head out', an obsessive pop star, and Max… what, exactly, was Max?

He had turned up as usual this morning at the shop acting as if nothing had happened between them over the weekend, full of jokes about the various drunken states of Linda's other guests. Even the bluntest of hints from Linda seemed to pass him by. He hadn't seemed that drunk to Bonnie, despite the fact that she'd been in a pretty bad state herself. Did he really have no recollection of the things he had whispered in hot breaths in her ear, or the way he had stroked his hand across the bare skin of her shoulder, how he had gently lifted the hair from her face? Bonnie should have been relieved to be off the hook – it meant no awkward moments at work, of course – but something about it made her feel empty.

Paige interrupted her thoughts as she wandered into the kitchen.

'What's for tea?'

'Hello to you too, Paige.'

'Whatever. You still have a hangover?'

Bonnie rolled her eyes. 'How to win friends and influence people. Does your charm know no bounds?'

'What?'

'Never mind. Sausages for tea. Let me get a drink first, it's been a hell of a day.'

'All you've done is shove apples in bags for old ladies,' Paige said carelessly as she went to the cupboard to rifle through the snacks.

'Is that so?' Bonnie fired back. 'In that case you can do my shift tomorrow.'

'I would, but you won't let me get a job.'

'I've never stopped you.'

'You put me off.'

'If only you were so easy to put off with everything else.'

'Ooooh,' Paige tore the wrapper from a chocolate biscuit, 'someone's hormonal today.'

'For God's sake, Paige, just once in your life, show something that approaches respect for me. I'm your mother, not some girl at school that you think it's okay to gang up on!'

Paige's mouth dropped open comically.

'You know what?' Bonnie added, grabbing her coat from the chair, 'you can get your own tea, I'm going out for a walk.'

'A walk?' Paige repeated stupidly. 'Where?'

'I have no idea. Anywhere away from you!'

*

As soon as Bonnie had reached the grey, damp street, she regretted losing her temper with Paige. But it was too late to go back inside; she had to be missing for a little while if Paige wasn't going to think she was a complete pushover. As she walked quickly around the block, the streets darkening and the lamps flickering on in their first dull light, she ran over all the things that had been happening to her lately. Her life was getting weirder by the minute and she was almost convinced that she would wake one morning to find it had all been a strange dream.

Eventually, she decided that Paige had stewed long enough, or, at least, she had been missing long enough to give her daughter some food for thought, and headed back.

As Bonnie opened the front door of the flat, she smelt the aroma of cooking sausages. Layered beneath it was the smell of burning, but she tried not to think of that as she hurried into the kitchen.

'Hey,' Paige smiled sheepishly as she pulled a pan from the stove.

'What are you doing?' Bonnie asked, her eyes wide.

'What does it look like?'

'You're... *cooking*?'

Paige frowned as she shared out the sausages between two plates. 'I have done food tech at school, you know.'

'You might have done but you don't do it at home.'

'Ha ha.'

Bonnie took her coat off and hung it over a chair as Paige dragged a tray of chips from the oven. She gave a grateful smile as Paige brought the plates to the table and placed one in front of her, a moment later plonking down condiments and a glass of orange juice.

'Thanks, Paige.'

Her daughter shrugged. She would never say sorry; this meal was as close as Bonnie would ever get to an apology from her. It didn't matter. She looked down at her plate. Something that resembled charcoal briquettes sat against the sausages. Bonnie surmised that they had once been oven chips.

'This looks… lovely.'

'Sorry, the chips are a bit burnt. I had trouble getting everything to be ready at the same time and then I didn't know what time you would be back.' Paige grinned. 'It's a good job you didn't go for a long walk, you might have come back to a flat full of firemen.'

'Oh, I don't think that would necessarily have been a bad thing.' Bonnie smiled impishly.

'MUM!' Paige groaned.

'Well, I am hormonal.'

'Yeah… about that…'

'Forget it, eh? I had a bad day and this lovely tea has made it a whole lot better. Let's keep it that way.'

*

Despite the working week stretching ahead endlessly on Mondays, Fridays always seemed to come around so quickly that the days of Bonnie's life appeared to melt into one indistinguishable mass of time; before she knew it, retirement would be upon her. Not that she was prone to fits of melancholic brooding, but as she pulled on her tabard to get ready for work on that particular Friday, she reflected that the way her life was going, her imminent retirement was set to be a gloomy and lonely affair.

At least there had been no more letters from Holden, and Max had slipped back into the old familiar friend that she knew and loved

– wise-cracking and full of good humour – all awkwardness between them apparently forgotten. Linda had stopped her interference in Bonnie's love life too and had even mentioned helping with Bonnie's newly-resurrected quest to find Max the perfect girlfriend.

And so all was back to normal – or, at least, Bonnie had thought so. She arrived to find that Linda had opened up and Fred was nowhere to be seen.

'Where's Fred?' Bonnie asked as she walked through the main shop, shrugging off her coat.

Linda shot her a sideways glance as she took the tarpaulin cover off the apple display.

'He's going to be in late again today.'

'Really?' Bonnie asked, stopping in her tracks. 'He normally asks me to open up when he's going to be late.'

'He couldn't get through to your phone…'

Bonnie frowned. She hadn't thought to check her mobile this morning. Pulling it out of her pocket, her stomach lurched. She knew that the bill had been due a couple of weeks previously, and that she would have to be late paying it, but from the looks of things as she studied the display and saw that there was no network showing at all, the phone company had got tired of waiting and suspended her account. She wracked her brains for a solution, angry with herself for letting things get this bad.

Linda watched her closely. 'If you need some help with that…' she said gently, guessing what the situation was.

Bonnie forced a bright smile. 'I forgot to pay the bill, silly me. I'll sort it out later.'

Linda paused for a moment, before she nodded and returned to her task.

'You want a cup of tea?' Bonnie called as she went through into the back of the shop.

'That's the best offer I've had all day,' Linda called back.

As Bonnie filled the kettle, the usual morning knock came at the back door. Bonnie went to open it, moving aside to let Max in before returning to the kitchen to put out an extra mug. 'You're just in time for a brew,' she said from the tiny sink.

'Ah, that's because I have my tea radar on,' he replied, rubbing the cold from his hands. 'I can hear the kettle clicking on from three streets away.'

Bonnie came back through to the storeroom. 'Got any plans for the weekend?'

'Not really,' he replied carefully, though Bonnie suddenly detected a change in his demeanour, as if there was something he didn't want to say.

'I'll be here for most of it, of course,' Bonnie added, trying to make light of his discomfort and change the subject. 'Bloody shop work, I must be mad. A one day weekend is rubbish.'

'Yeah,' Max agreed, 'there are some things to be said for being your own boss. At least I get to choose not to deliver on Saturdays.'

'Yeah, Fred hates that, he's always moaning about how he can't have fresh stuff on Saturdays… just so you know.'

'I know he does. Unless he wants to get his stuff for twice the price at Countywide, he'll just have to put up with it.' He glanced through the doorway to the main shop. 'Where is the old goat anyway?'

'We don't know,' Linda said, coming back through from the shop and catching the turn of the conversation. She turned to Max. 'So what's this thing you're not really doing at the weekend?'

'Bloody hell, Lind, you must have ears like a bat!' Max exclaimed.

'You've got to get up early in the morning to get anything past me. So spill.'

Max glanced uncomfortably at Bonnie, hesitating for a few moments before he finally spoke. 'I'm going to see Sarah.'

'You're what!' Linda spluttered.

Max shrugged helplessly. 'She called and said she wanted to talk. What else could I do?'

'She wants to talk you into giving it another go, you know that, don't you?' Linda warned.

'Probably. But I suppose I owe her the courtesy of hearing her out at least.'

'You owe her nothing. If saving the girl a broken heart further down the line is wrong, then I don't think you want to be right.' Linda glanced at Bonnie, whose expression had become suddenly uptight.

'I'll go and make that tea,' Bonnie said quietly, slinking away to the kitchenette.

'This is madness,' Linda continued to Max, lowering her voice. She sighed. 'The sooner you and Bonnie realise that you were made for each other, the better.'

'Bonnie doesn't want me.'

'Of course she does. Weren't you looking a minute ago when she sloped off to make the tea? Her face said it all – she's gutted about you getting back with Sarah.'

'I never said we were getting back together. I'm going to see her, that's all.'

'Hmph.'

'I promise, Lind, I'm just going to talk to her.'

'Where are you meeting?'

'Blossom Palace.'

Linda arched a cynical eyebrow. 'Kind of public and date-like to be a serious talk about why you can't get back together.'

'Her idea.'

'I'll bet it was.'

Bonnie came back through with three mugs on a tray. Linda and Max both took one and Bonnie removed hers, putting the tray to one side. She took a silent sip, looking from one to the other before putting her cup down on a bench and announcing that she was going to start getting the cold stock from the fridges before Fred came in. Linda had a curious look on her face as she watched her go.

'I'd better get cracking too,' Max decided as he left his cup next to Bonnie's.

'Actually…' Linda said slowly, 'I could do with you looking at this tray of kiwis.'

'Kiwis?' Max said in a bemused voice.

'Yeah, we had some complaints that there was some kind of worm in the ones we sold yesterday. I kept them in the fridge so I could show you.'

Max followed Linda to the huge, open fridge doors. Bonnie was in there rotating the stock on the shelves.

'Just in the corner,' Linda said, ushering Max in. 'Oh, and you two…' she added with a sly grin, 'I am really sorry about this, but you'll thank me one day…'

'Huh?' Bonnie looked up.

Linda's grin widened. 'I'm not letting you out until you agree to go on a date with each other.'

And she slammed the door before either of them had a chance to get to it, trapping Max and Bonnie inside.

Max spun around as the fridge was plunged into gloom. 'What the hell…'

'Oh my God, Linda!' Bonnie squealed, tripping over a tray of tomatoes that sent her sprawling across the floor to land at Max's feet. She felt a strong pair of hands pull her gently up to stand.

'Are you okay?' Max's concerned voice cut through the darkness.

'Yeah, nothing broken. What the bloody hell is Linda doing now?'

Max chuckled softly. 'I always knew she was a bit of a loose cannon but this is off the scale.' He thumped a hand on the door. 'LINDA!'

'She probably can't hear through this thick wall, and even if she can she's not going to give up that easily,' Bonnie said. 'Hang on…' She was silent for a moment as she felt along the wall. A strip light flickered into life and she could see Max's part-quizzical, part-annoyed, part-amused expression. It looked a lot like the one she was sure she had too.

'She's joking, right?' Max asked. 'She won't make us stay in here?'

Bonnie bit her lip. 'I wouldn't put it past her.'

'But Fred will be back soon, surely? She's got to let us out before then.'

'Fred doesn't scare Linda. She's got this mad idea in her head and she won't let go of it.'

'About you and me?' Max gave her a sheepish grin.

Bonnie nodded.

'So the only way we get out of here is if we agree to go out on a date? Doesn't seem like such a hardship when you put it like that.'

There was no escape this time. Bonnie couldn't change the subject or make excuses and scuttle off like she usually did. Linda knew what she was doing locking them in together, because faced with telling Max like this, Bonnie wouldn't be able to do it. She flopped down onto a sack of carrots and looked up at Max, who came over to sit next to her.

'It's pretty cold in here,' he said, the breath unfurling from his mouth in a soft plume to reinforce the fact even as he spoke. 'Let me know if you need warming up.'

Bonnie shot him a sideways glance. His face was poker straight but there was an impish humour dancing in his blue eyes.

'We'll both be frozen stiff if we don't get out of here soon.'

'That's a bit melodramatic,' Max chortled.

'We might suffocate then.'

'More likely.'

'Bloody Linda. Wait till I get out of here.'

'*If* you get out of here.'

'I thought I was the melodramatic one?'

'But just imagine,' Max began, putting on a spooky voice, 'Linda is kidnapped right now and driven away in the boot of a car and nobody knows we're here until it's too late…'

Bonnie smacked him on the arm and he grinned broadly.

'So, what are we going to do then?'

'We can tell Linda we've agreed to it,' Max said.

Bonnie shook her head. 'She's not that stupid.'

'There's only one thing we can do then,' Max replied.

'One drink,' Bonnie warned. 'And there's nothing in it but mates going out together.'

'One drink. I knew you'd see sense eventually…'

Bonnie was thoughtful for a moment, hugging herself against the cold that was now beginning to bite through her clothes. Max leaned across and rubbed her arms to try to warm her.

'What about Sarah?' she suddenly asked.

Max's arms dropped to his sides again. 'I still have to meet her. I said I would.'

'Does that mean you want to try again?'

'I don't think so. I don't know, if I'm honest.'

'What would she say if she found out about us?'

Max held her in a penetrating gaze for a moment before he replied. 'There is no *us*, is there? It's just a drink, like you said.'

'Yeah,' Bonnie said, something like disappointment creeping into her expression. 'Just a drink. Of course it is.'

The door opened and they both looked to see Linda grinning from the doorway. She held a mop out at them threateningly. 'Don't think you can rush me and get out. Have you sorted it yet?'

Bonnie and Max shared a loaded glance.

'Yeah,' Bonnie said. 'We have.'

'And?' Linda asked.

'We'll do it. One date and then you leave us alone.'

Linda stepped back and let them out of the fridge.

'Bloody hell, Linda, it's cold in there. I need another brew now to thaw out,' Max said as he stepped back into the cool, but at least a little warmer, stockroom.

Before Linda had time to reply, Fred's furious, bright red face appeared at the doorway of the stockroom. 'Industrial action is it this morning?'

Bonnie gave him a confused frown.

'Well, don't just stand there; we have a shop to open. What the bloody hell have you been doing all morning?'

Bonnie glared at Linda, but she simply burst into laughter and went to put the mop away.

Chapter Nine

'You're going out?' Paige asked with more than a hint of suspicion in her tone. 'Where?'

'I do go out, you know,' Bonnie said as she looked at her via the mirror, fastening an earring.

'I know but…'

'Twice in one month?' Bonnie raised an eyebrow. 'Is that what you were going to say?'

'Course not. It's just weird.' She folded her arms across her chest. 'Do I have to go to Jeanie's? Why can't I have Annabel here? Why do I have to sleep at Jeanie's? You won't be that late, will you?'

'I don't know how late I'll be. There's no harm in seeing your nan, she'll be happy to have the company.'

'She'll make me watch rubbish films.'

'Take a book or something.'

Paige frowned.

'Alright, take your iPad then.'

'Can't I stay here? Tina and Mike are just next door if I need anything.'

Bonnie turned around. 'You can't go knocking for Tina and Mike every five minutes. They have lives of their own, you know.'

'Yeah, but they don't mind. Tina's dead nice; she's said loads of times that they always wanted kids so they like having me around.'

'For the occasional five minutes at the end of a school day, not in the evening when they're trying to relax.'

Paige scuffed her shoe against the doorframe with an irritated pout. Bonnie looked up from rummaging in an old stained make-up bag for the right lipstick.

'Surely the prospect of going to your nan's can't be that bad.'

'It's not that…'

'What then?'

Paige shrugged silently.

'If I didn't know you better, Paige Cartwright, I'd say the reason you want to stay here is to check that I come home tonight.'

'MUM!' Paige groaned.

'I'm right then?'

Paige paused for a moment. 'Okay,' she said finally. 'Who is he?'

'He?'

Paige looked her up and down meaningfully. 'Usually, if it's a drink with a mate – which you never do, by the way – you wear your jeans; you don't dress up like that unless it's a special occasion. You're going on a date, right?'

Bonnie sighed as she straightened her dress. In the end, she had gone for a forest green lace number with a fitted bodice and flared skirt. It had a vintage look about it and Bonnie had always felt that it was one of her most useful dresses, one that she could wear tarted up, or dressed down, as she had done tonight by keeping the accessories to simple silver jewellery. 'Does it matter if it is a date?' she asked.

'Depends who it is.'

'I think that's my business.'

'Not if you're thinking of moving him in.'

'Of course I'm not thinking of moving him in,' Bonnie replied wearily.

'So you admit that you're going on a date then?'

'One date. Just to see how it goes, and I very much doubt there will be a second one to be honest.'

Bonnie thought about the meeting that Max had scheduled in with Sarah for the following evening. In the end, she and Max had decided that there was no point in beating about the bush, and they had made their date for the Saturday night, so that Max could arrange to see Sarah on the Sunday. Bonnie wasn't sure how she felt about this arrangement. On the one hand, they had both agreed that this date was purely to appease Linda. At least, that was Bonnie's reasoning behind it. She still felt slightly uneasy about how Max seemed a little too keen on the whole thing. Bonnie had been furious about the fridge stunt, while Max seemed faintly amused. But his insistence that he was still going to see Sarah afterwards rankled with Bonnie more than it ought to. He had made it clear that he was not meeting Sarah for any reason other than that she had asked him to, and to draw a line under their relationship once and for all. But still... what if Sarah persuaded him to take her back?

Bonnie shook her negative thoughts away. What did it matter? She had been trying to get Max a girlfriend anyway, so what if Sarah was the perfect one after all and he just couldn't see it?

'Whatever,' Paige said, and disappeared into the living room.

A moment later, Bonnie went to find her. She was sitting on the sofa with a sheepish grin.

'Okay, what have you done?' Bonnie asked, narrowing her eyes.

'There's been a slight change of plan...'

Bonnie's hands went to her hips. 'What?'

'Jeanie says she'll come over here.'

'You phoned her and told her to come here?' Bonnie's frown deepened.

'What does it matter where she looks after me as long as she does?'

'Because… it means dragging her out on a cold night, it's not fair.' Bonnie didn't add the real reason she wanted them both out of the way safely at Jeanie's house. Max had offered to pick her up and she didn't want either of them to start asking awkward questions when they saw who her date was with. If she could have them both tucked away at her mum's house before Max arrived, that would be perfect.

'Phone her and tell her to stay put,' Bonnie said, checking her watch. 'I'll run you across there now.'

'She's already got a taxi,' Paige said.

'How can she…' Bonnie glared at Paige. 'You phoned her ages ago! I specifically told you what the plans were and you went behind my back!'

'Like you're doing with me?' Paige fired back.

'How do you work that out?'

'Secret dates, trying to get me out of the way so I don't know anything about it. If this guy is going to be my new dad, I have a right to meet him first.'

'For the last time, he is not going to be your new dad!'

'So I can meet him anyway?'

'So you can cock it up?'

'Ha! You said it was one date, now you admit that you *are* thinking of moving him in!'

'Paige!'

'Next thing you'll be telling me it's that loser of a delivery man that comes to your shop. He's always drooling over you.'

'Max does not drool and it is only one date to shut Linda up!'

Paige's eyes opened wide. 'Oh my God, tell me it isn't him...'

'I don't have to tell you anything.' Bonnie swallowed the lump in her throat. It was her life, how dare Paige make her answer for everything she did. 'Go to your room and wait for your nan to arrive.'

'Make me...'

'So help me, Paige, if you don't get out of my sight I won't be responsible for my actions!'

Paige leapt up from the sofa, glowering at Bonnie. 'Alright, keep your knickers on.'

She threw a last mutinous glare back at her mum as she slouched to her bedroom and slammed the door.

Bonnie drew a huge breath and collected herself. Now she knew for certain that there could only ever be one date with Max. But she was sure as hell going to enjoy it, if only to teach Paige a lesson.

*

Jeanie kissed Bonnie lightly before shrugging her coat off.

'I'm so sorry that Paige dragged you over here,' Bonnie said as they walked through into the living room.

'It doesn't matter,' Jeanie said briskly. 'If she's not well then it doesn't seem fair to drag her out on a night like this.'

Bonnie's eyes narrowed. 'She told you she wasn't well? Little sod.'

'Oh,' Jeanie replied with a half-smile. 'Not entirely true, then?'

'About as true as me being related to the Pope.'

'Well...'

Bonnie's forehead creased into a frown. 'Not even in jest, Mum.'

Jeanie grinned and settled on the sofa.

'You know where everything is, Mum. Paige is in her room – long story – and my lift will be here any minute –'

'Is this an actual date?' Jeanie cut in.

'Mum…' Bonnie began slowly. 'When you see who is picking me up, don't get any funny ideas about it being a date. It's just a drink together, a one off, that's all. Okay?'

Jeanie nodded with fake solemnity. 'So who is this mystery man?'

Bonnie paused. 'Max Delaney,' she said quickly before shoving her head down to root earnestly in her bag.

'Max? Delivery Max?'

'Mmm,' Bonnie said.

'I thought he was going out with that Sarah?'

'He was… is… I don't know. But we're not going on a date so it doesn't matter who he is or isn't going out with.'

'I think it does. What does Sarah think about this non-date?'

'I have no idea.'

'But he's going to tell her?'

'It has nothing to do with her. It's not a date and he's not seeing her anymore anyway.'

'You just said he was.'

'He's not.'

'You don't sound so sure.'

Bonnie held up a hand to quiet her mum. She was just about to reply when there was a knock at the door.

'That'll be him now.' Bonnie grimaced. 'Please don't give him the Spanish inquisition when he comes in.'

'My lips are sealed.'

Bonnie threw her a warning look and went to get the door.

Max stepped in. 'You look great, Bon,' he said cheerfully, kissing Bonnie lightly on both cheeks.

'I'll just get my jacket,' she said, flushing with pleasure.

'No problem.' Max followed Bonnie to the living room, stopping in the doorway as he saw Jeanie on the sofa.

'Oh, hello…' he said awkwardly, sticking his hands deep in his pockets as though, if he put them in far enough, they could somehow swallow the rest of him too.

'I'm babysitting while you go out on your friendly drink,' Jeanie said carelessly. 'How's Sarah, by the way?'

Max blushed. 'She's good… We're not together, actually,' he added quickly. 'Just friends now.'

Jeanie nodded slowly. 'Just friends. Like you are with Bonnie?'

'Mum…' Bonnie cut in, 'can you just come into the kitchen so I can show you what Paige is having for supper?' She raised her eyebrows and nodded her head towards the door in an exaggerated gesture. Jeanie gave Max a saccharine smile and got up to follow her.

As they stepped into the kitchen, Bonnie closed the door behind them.

'What are you doing?' Bonnie hissed. 'I asked you not to grill him.'

'I don't see what he has to hide.'

'Nothing! He has nothing to hide but you're making him feel uncomfortable.'

'Because I don't want you hurt again.'

Bonnie waved a hand at her. 'You were the one that said I should start dating again!'

'You said this wasn't a date,' Jeanie shot back.

Bonnie sighed. 'We're going for a drink, that's it. There's no need to worry.'

'But I do. If he's already led Sarah a merry dance, then who's to say he won't do that with you? I won't be here soon to pick up the pieces if you get messed around by another man.' Jeanie reached out and smoothed a stray lock of hair behind Bonnie's ear. 'All I'm saying, in my own ham-fisted way, is that you should be careful.'

'I know, Mum. And I will be. There is absolutely no danger of me and Max becoming an item, so put your mind at rest now… okay?'

Jeanie arched an eyebrow and looked Bonnie up and down meaningfully. 'For someone who is treating this as a simple friendly drink, you've made quite an effort.'

'This old dress?' Bonnie said, trying to play down Jeanie's observation. 'I just got it out to get the moths drunk.' She leaned over to kiss Jeanie on the cheek. 'I won't be late. Don't let Paige give you too much grief.'

*

'I thought we were just going for a drink?' Bonnie said as Max pulled up on the car park of the *La Bella Roma* restaurant.

'We are,' Max said, yanking the handbrake on. 'We might just get some pasta with that drink.'

'It's expensive here.' Bonnie frowned, glancing through the car window at the brightly lit building.

'It's on me.'

'I can't let you do that…'

Max held up a hand. 'I said I wanted to take you out and I'm happy to pay. If this is the only chance I'm going to get then we might as well make it good.'

'I don't feel right not paying my half,' Bonnie pressed.

'We'll share a plate if you're worried.' Max turned to her with his most charming grin. Something fluttered inside Bonnie but she swallowed the feeling down.

'Cheapskate,' she quipped.

Max clambered out of the car and sped around to the passenger door, opening it for Bonnie with a low bow. '*Madame…*'

Bonnie giggled. 'Wow, if I had known how charming you were out of your delivery overalls I'd have gone out with you years ago.'

'I'm like the Hulk, only in reverse,' he grinned, 'by day a grumpy Neanderthal, by night a sophisticated man-about-town.' He offered Bonnie an arm. She took it. Max noticed her shiver slightly. 'You're cold?' he asked.

She nodded. 'A little bit. But it's hardly very far and it's my fault I came out in a stupid dress and a tiny cotton coat.'

'Here…' He whipped off his jacket and hung it around her shoulders. 'Better?'

Bonnie looked up at him gratefully. He had made an effort to muss his hair stylishly and wore a suit cut from expensive looking wool, teamed with a charcoal grey granddad shirt that complimented his blonde hair and created an air of casual, effortless elegance. Bonnie sniffed a little at his jacket. It smelled amazing and the scent of his woody aftershave filled her head, setting off that butterfly in her stomach again.

'I am actually quite hungry,' she said, trying to take her mind off the naughty little creature that was plaguing her. 'Which makes me quite a pig as I had something to eat when I got in from work.'

'That's over three hours ago,' Max said gallantly, looking at his watch. 'They say the best way to eat is a little every couple of hours or so.'

'Who says that?' Bonnie laughed as they made their way across the car park to where the restaurant's wide glass windows revealed the plush interior and well-dressed diners already tucking into their meals. 'Clearly people who have backsides the size of Manchester.'

Max laughed out loud. 'I think it might be some very well respected scientist, actually. But I like your version better.' He opened the door for Bonnie and she stepped in.

'I've never been in here before,' she whispered as they waited for someone to greet them.

'Me neither,' Max whispered back. 'But I'm told it's very nice.'

Bonnie pondered this information for a moment. So he had never brought Sarah here? It seemed strange, considering how keen he had appeared to be on her. This seemed like a much more obvious choice than Blossom Palace for a romantic rendezvous, nice as that place was. Romance was definitely off the menu tonight though. He felt sorry for Bonnie, obviously, because he knew how broke she always was; he wanted to do something nice for her because he was Max and that was the sort of thing Max would do. To imagine there was anything more to it than that was silly.

A waiter approached them with a warm smile.

'You have reservations?' he asked with the merest hint of an Italian accent.

'Yes,' Max replied. 'Do you think this shirt works with these trousers?'

The waiter stared at them uncomprehendingly as Bonnie stifled a giggle. 'Sorry, ignore me,' Max continued, looking a little more awkward now. 'I've booked in the name of Delaney.'

The man consulted a folder on a desk near the door and then nodded. 'This way please,' he said smoothly as he led them to a cosy table with two seats near a window that overlooked a grove of trees strung with fairy lights.

'Sense of humour malfunction there, eh? I thought it was funny anyway,' Bonnie said, inclining her head at the waiter. Max gave her a grateful smile.

Once they were seated, the waiter handed them a menu each. Bonnie beamed as she looked around. 'It's gorgeous in here. I could get used to this sort of luxury.'

'Salmon paste sarnies will seem a bit of a disappointment tomorrow.'

'They will,' Bonnie laughed. 'Just like my Pot Noodle.'

'You could come again if you like it tonight,' Max said.

'On my wages?'

'I'd love to bring you again.'

Bonnie's eyebrows knitted together, but she couldn't help the smile that played at the corners of her mouth.

'Oh yeah,' Max said with a sheepish smile, 'just one date to shut Linda up.'

Bonnie put the menu up to her face so that he couldn't see her and grinned broadly. When she dropped it again, her face was stony straight but Max was grinning at her instead. 'Can you see that menu okay?'

'Yeah, but it's all in foreign, see?' Bonnie said, putting on her best squeaky bimbo voice.

'Why don't we live dangerously and order something at random?'

Bonnie pulled her face. 'What if we get squid or something?'

'That's part of the fun. You should take risks once in a while; you might find yourself pleasantly surprised.' As Max said this, he looked at her suddenly as if his whole life depended on her answer.

Bonnie felt herself colour. 'Sometimes you get nasty shocks too.'

Their moment of clarity seemed to disappear as quickly as it had come, and the conversation returned to their easy banter.

'Perhaps you should get one of the waiters to translate then, I'd hate to see you struggle with a fried octopus leg,' Max laughed.

'Hmmm,' Bonnie replied. 'Easier to manage than one of Fred's tempers.'

'Or being locked in a fridge,' Max added.

The waiter approached their table. 'Would you care to order drinks now?'

Max looked at Bonnie. 'I'm driving so it will have to be mineral water for me. How about you?'

Bonnie thought about the last time she had been steaming drunk in Max's presence, how very near she had been to saying or doing something she would have regretted afterwards. 'Perhaps I should stick to orange juice, as Paige will be waiting with a rolling pin and a breathalyser when I get home.'

'One or two won't hurt,' Max said, looking up at the waiter with a mischievous twinkle in his eye. 'Do you have a nice champagne?'

'Max, no –'

'One date – you promised, remember? If this is the first and last, let me enjoy it by treating you.'

Bonnie relaxed. 'How can I argue with that?' She smiled. 'There's an extra biscuit with your tea on Monday, that's for sure.'

Max returned his attention to the waiter who then took his cue to rattle off a list of their champagnes along with the price of each bottle.

Bonnie frowned slightly at Max. 'If you insist on buying some, please humour me and don't get the most expensive.'

'Which do you recommend?' Max asked the waiter, ignoring her.

The waiter hesitated for a moment, glancing between the two of them, clearly torn. 'The *Mumm Cordon Rouge* is very good and excellent value for money.'

'We'll have that one,' Bonnie said before Max had time to reply.

The waiter nodded. 'Would you like a little longer with the menu?'

'How about the waiter recommends something for us?' Max cut in gallantly. 'What do you fancy?'

'Maybe chicken? Not too creamy with the sauce.'

'Would madam perhaps enjoy *chicken a al cacciatore*?' the waiter asked. 'It is a tomato based dish, with a little piquancy.'

Bonnie looked at Max enquiringly.

'You like a bit of spice, don't you?' Max grinned.

'Shut up,' Bonnie said, biting back a grin of her own. 'It sounds lovely, I'll order that.'

'Would madam care for a starter?'

'Bonnie shook her head. 'I don't think so.'

'Yes she would,' Max cut in. 'We'll have the sharing bruschetta platter.'

'I thought you said you hadn't been here before,' Bonnie said, arching an eyebrow.

'I haven't. I just checked the menu online before I came to pick you up. I wanted to be sure it was classy enough.' He glanced up at the waiter. 'No offence, mate.'

The waiter nodded. 'None taken, sir.'

Max turned his attention back to the menu. 'I'll have the seafood linguine. As long as it doesn't include any live octopus…'

The waiter gave them a confused look and then smiled knowingly. 'There is no octopus on the menu tonight. Chef lost a wrestling match with one and it refused to go into the pot.'

Max burst out laughing. 'That's a relief then!'

The waiter took their menus and glided away.

'Looks like he found his sense of humour after all,' said Bonnie. She added in a whisper, 'This is going to cost you a small fortune.'

'I know,' Max said. 'I'll have to add it to Fred's bill next week.'

'He'd love that, he says you're dear enough already.'

'Actually, I wanted to take you somewhere more expensive than this, but I knew you wouldn't let me. I've been waiting long enough.'

'Don't be daft,' Bonnie laughed lightly, digging her phone out of her bag in case Paige or her mum needed her.

'I mean it.'

Bonnie narrowed her eyes. 'It wasn't you that put Linda up to the fridge stunt?'

Max gave her a look of mock affront. 'Of course not! How could you suggest such a thing?'

'Don't bull me, Max.'

Max put his hand on his chest. 'I swear it was nothing to do with me. But Linda did me a huge favour.'

'Hmmm, I'll believe you, even though thousands wouldn't.'

The waiter returned with the champagne and opened it with a flourish. He poured a glass for Bonnie before leaving them. She took a sip.

'Wow! That's amazing.'

'That's good,' Max took the bottle from the ice bucket and gave it a swish, 'because you have to drink all this.'

'Ruddy hell, you'll be carrying me to the car.'

'Don't worry; I'm used to lugging huge weights around.'

'Cheeky bugger!' Bonnie slapped his arm and her phone pinged. She picked it up with a frown.

'Everything okay?' Max asked.

'Yeah…' Bonnie said distractedly as she opened the message. 'I just don't recognise the number.' She was silent for a moment as she read it. The silence continued as she processed it.

You haven't replied to my letters. Why not?
H

Bonnie felt the blood drain from her face.

'You're sure you're okay?' Max asked, his face now a mask of concern as he watched her put the phone back on the table without tapping out a reply.

Bonnie shook herself and tried to smile. 'Something and nothing.'

'Is it something I can help with?'

Unless you can offer a blow job to a teen heart throb in my place, then probably not. 'I don't think so,' she replied.

'You want to go home?' Max asked earnestly. 'I can take you if there's trouble.'

Bonnie reached across the table and squeezed his hand. 'Thanks, Max, but I'm finishing this champagne if it's the last thing I do.' She drew her hand away and lifted the glass to her lips, determined not to let Holden bloody Finn ruin her one and only date night with her mate Max.

*

The food at *La Bella Roma* was incredible, as it turned out, and Bonnie couldn't remember a time when she had laughed so much. The champagne had helped, of course, the warm effervescence seeming to make the roots of her hair tingle deliciously. As the evening wore on, Bonnie pushed all worries about Holden to the back of her mind, and concentrated on having a good time. Max had gone to so much trouble to make this a special treat for her, she at least owed him that.

Max himself became somehow more and more attractive the longer she spent in his company, and no matter how much Bonnie tried, she could think about little else. When the bill arrived, she watched Max settle it with a stab of regret that the night was almost over.

She wobbled slightly as he led her with a protective arm to the car. She hadn't managed all the champagne, sadly, and had considered asking if she could take it home. It seemed like such a shame to leave it behind and it wasn't likely that she'd ever drink something that good again, but in the end she hadn't wanted to embarrass Max. She glanced at him as they walked the length of the car park. Usually she thought his height and his messy blonde hair made him look gangly, but tonight they gave him the air of a Byronic hero. It was the champagne, of course, but she felt a stirring; not like the infatuation she had felt for Holden Finn, but something like real, honest desire, something she hadn't felt in a long time.

After Max had opened the car door and helped her in with a wry smile as she hiccuped, they began a quiet journey home, the joviality of the evening now replaced by weariness as the car and the alcohol lulled Bonnie to a half-sleep.

*

Max shook her gently.

'I wasn't asleep,' Bonnie mumbled as she came to and found that the car had pulled up outside the apartment block where she lived.

'Of course you weren't.' Max grinned.

'I was resting my eyes.'

'Booze does make your eyes very heavy.'

'I'm not drunk… much,' Bonnie giggled.

'That's a shame,' Max said slyly. 'I consider our date a failure then.'

Bonnie stretched herself awake. 'I had a great time. I'm kind of glad Linda locked us in the fridge.'

Max laughed. 'Me too.' He paused for a moment. 'You do realise that there is one more part of the deal you have to honour before I let you go in?'

Bonnie frowned. 'Deal?'

'Traditionally, when a man and a woman go on a date, at the end of the night, this happens…'

Before she had time to react, he leaned across and kissed her. She didn't fight it. She knew that there was no point in trying to; she couldn't fight the rush of desire that coursed through her and she didn't want to.

'Friends don't do that with each other,' she murmured as his lips left hers.

He smiled. 'Clearly you have the right sort of friends then.'

'Except you,' she said.

'Except me. I'm a bad, bad friend…' he whispered as he moved closer, his lips grazing hers again. 'Can you forgive me? You just look so kissable.'

Bonnie was about to reply when they were both startled by a frantic hammering on the window of the car. They turned in unison to see Paige staring in at them, her face contorted in a look of horror.

'That's so gross!' she wailed.

Chapter Ten

Bonnie slammed the front door as she followed Paige in.

'I can't believe you were spying on me!'

Paige wheeled around in the hallway. 'I can't believe you were kissing that loser!' She wrinkled her nose. 'And you stink of booze. I bet you're drunk, that's the only reason you could have been kissing him.'

'It's none of your business!'

Jeanie came from the living room rubbing her eyes. 'What's going on?'

'Ask her!' Paige shouted, flinging an arm in Bonnie's direction as she stomped away to her bedroom.

Jeanie threw Bonnie a questioning look.

'Paige just caught me kissing Max. And before you say anything, it was nothing, a goodnight kiss, that's all.'

'Why would I say anything? You told me before that you know what you're doing, so you go and give goodnight kisses to anyone you want.'

'Ha ha.' Bonnie kicked her heels into the corner of the hallway and squeezed past Jeanie.

In the kitchen, Bonnie flicked on the kettle and spooned some instant coffee into a mug. 'Do you want one?' she asked as Jeanie joined her and sat at the table.

'Go on then.'

Bonnie's tipsiness had dissipated like the rush of air from a popped balloon, so that her thoughts were crystal clear again. Why did Paige have to go and see her kiss Max? More importantly, why couldn't she get the taste of his lips out of her mind?

Then another worrying thought came back to her. When was Holden going to get the message that she wasn't interested?

Jeanie sat at the table yawning in silence. Bonnie stood at the worktop, tapping her thumb on her mobile as she waited for the kettle to boil. They both jumped slightly as the phone pinged in Bonnie's hand. With her heart beating wildly, Bonnie read the text.

> *Once isn't enough. How about we get Linda to lock us in the fridge again?*

Bonnie smiled as relief washed through her. Another date with Max... maybe that wouldn't be such a hardship after all.

She looked up as Paige came into the kitchen wearing a scowl.

'Aren't you tired?' Bonnie asked. 'It's late.'

'I'm not five, Mum. I can stay up if I want to.'

'Suit yourself. I'm knackered.' Bonnie glanced at Jeanie. 'Your nan looks exhausted too.'

'I fell asleep on the sofa for a while,' Jeanie admitted sheepishly.

'For a while?' Paige scoffed. 'More like three hours.'

'It's been a long day,' Jeanie replied defensively. 'I've cleared the garage out all by myself. My granddaughter had said she was going to help me...'

'Yeah, about that...' Paige began.

Jeanie waved away the excuse. 'I know, you were busy. It doesn't matter, I'm just telling you why I was asleep for three hours.'

'We'll get this coffee and I'll fetch the fold-up bed out,' Bonnie said to her. 'You can have my bed tonight, it's far too late and you're far too tired to make your way back home.'

Jeanie smiled gratefully.

'Spectacular,' Paige grimaced. 'I get to listen to Jeanie snore all night.'

'You can always sleep in the car,' Bonnie shot back.

'Whatever,' Paige huffed, and shuffled from the room again.

'You really should tell her when she speaks to you like that,' Jeanie chided gently.

Bonnie shrugged as she poured boiling water over the coffee granules. 'Right now, I'm just glad that she seems to have dropped the whole me kissing Max business.'

Jeanie stifled a yawn as Bonnie handed her a cup. 'She'll be all guns blazing in the morning, you know that, don't you? Right now, she's planning her angle, that's why she's quiet about it.'

'I know,' Bonnie said with a heavy sigh as she took a seat at the table.

'So…' Jeanie said, dropping her voice and leaning towards Bonnie. 'Did it go well? Are you seeing him again? What did he say about Sarah?'

Bonnie's forehead creased. She had forgotten, somehow, about Sarah. Max had barely mentioned their imminent meeting all night, and Bonnie had been so wrapped up in the excitement of the date and their easy banter, and occasionally worried thoughts about Holden, that the problem of Sarah hadn't really crossed her mind.

'I think he's going to put Sarah straight tomorrow, once and for all,' Bonnie said with more conviction than she felt.

'So you're going to see him again?'

Bonnie paused as she took a sip of her coffee. 'I don't know,' she said slowly. 'Maybe.'

'You like him, then?'

Bonnie pondered the question. It was hard to deny that she did like Max. The fear was that she liked him a little too much.

*

Jeanie went home early next morning, and Paige's interrogations about the state of Bonnie's relationship with Max began shortly afterwards. Whenever Paige took a break from the grilling, it left a quiet space in Bonnie's thoughts to worry about what was happening between Max and Sarah, or where Holden's stalking would end. It was too bizarre that only a couple of months before she had been mooning over posters of this guy, only to have the tables turned so completely that he now mooned over her while she desperately tried to repel his unwanted advances. Because the more she thought about it, the more she realised that she didn't like Holden much at all. Who would believe this crazy story if they heard it? She could only hope that if she continued to ignore him, he would give up and leave her to get on with her life in peace.

Around lunchtime Bonnie's phone pinged. Her anxious frown turned into a smile as she read the message from Max.

You still haven't told me if I'm going to get another date or not.

She was about to reply, when a sudden thought made her change her mind. She was beginning to realise that her feelings for Max were bigger than a furtive text and the odd quick drink, no matter how much she fought them. But there was still the shadow of Sarah, looming over them. She had to be sure about his feelings for her first; she'd been hurt too many times before. And Sarah wasn't the only barrier to happiness – there was Henri too.

Bonnie had considered many possibilities since Henri had left, including the fact that he might even be dead, although the French police had assured her that he wasn't, without being able to tell her where he actually was. The nights she had spent crying over him, the days she had spent on autopilot trying to keep everything as normal as possible for Paige, even though her soul felt like it was cracking into thousands of pieces – she didn't think she had the strength left in her to do that again with another man. She had finally accepted that Henri wasn't coming back and, more importantly, Paige had too. But before she trusted another man, she had to be certain he wasn't going to be the one to finally finish her off. And she had to be sure that Paige would be happy, above all else.

Putting the phone in her dressing gown pocket, Bonnie wandered into the living room deep in thought. 'Are you in a better mood?' she asked Paige, who was busy with her iPad.

Paige looked up. 'There was nothing wrong with me. I wasn't the one kissing loser Max in the car. You want your head looking at, you do.'

'Paige…' Bonnie sat down with a heavy sigh. 'I don't know what I think about Max. It probably isn't going anywhere. But you are wrong about him, he's really a great guy and whoever ends up with him will be lucky.'

'I bet that Sarah thought it was her till he dumped her to go out with you.'

'He didn't dump her for me.'

'Of course he did. Any idiot could see that he was drooling over you all night when we sat with them at Blossom Palace.'

'He was lovely to Sarah. They just weren't right for each other.'

Paige raised her eyebrows. 'And you are?'

'I like him, he's a laugh. If you're worried that I'm going to move a new daddy in for you, you needn't be. Is that what you wanted to hear?'

Paige pouted as she looked at her screen.

'So I have your blessing to see him again?' Bonnie asked.

'You don't need my blessing,' Paige replied without looking up, 'as you so often remind me, you can do whatever you like. But I'll never be happy about it, so don't think you're going to change my mind.'

Abandoning an argument she knew she couldn't win, Bonnie rubbed a hand through her hair.

'I'm going to get showered and dressed,' she announced, pushing herself up from the sofa.

*

Feeling fresher and more awake, Bonnie wound up the flex of the hairdryer and looked approvingly in the mirror. The red in her hair was gradually fading, but if she was truthful, it was a relief. Somehow, her own ash blonde felt safer, more like the real Bonnie.

Pulling a sweatshirt over her t-shirt, she wandered into the living room. Paige was in exactly the same spot still glued to her iPad.

'Don't you have homework?' Bonnie asked.

'Nope,' Paige replied without looking up.

'You want to do something together then?'

'Like what?'

Bonnie shrugged. 'I don't know. Go for a walk or something?'

Paige glanced up at the window, where a grey sky pressed down on the streets below. 'Not especially. Looks like rain anyway.'

Bonnie sighed and went to retrieve her phone. The new text message icon flashed at her.

'Did my phone go off when I was in the shower?'

'Yeah,' Paige said. 'I forgot.'
Bonnie unlocked the phone.

You can't keep avoiding me.
H

What the hell was wrong with him? Didn't he have enough willing groupies to keep him busy? Her fingers moved rapidly over the keypad.

I'm ignoring you because I have a boyfriend.

Bonnie barely had a chance to put it back in her pocket when it pinged again.

You have a boyfriend that is better than me??????

Bonnie almost burst out laughing. He really was more clueless, arrogant, or deranged, than she had given him credit for.

Yes.

Moments later another text arrived.

You never said before.

Bonnie tapped out a reply:

It's none of your business.

I love you.

Bonnie stared at the new message. Things were getting ridiculous now, like the plot of a mad film.

You don't even know me.

Bonnie locked her phone and glanced up to find Paige watching her carefully.

'Who are you texting?' she asked.

'Nobody.' Bonnie felt the colour rush to her cheeks.

'It's got to be Max,' Paige said in a scathing tone, 'that's the longest text conversation I've ever seen you have.'

'It's not Max, and it's my business,' Bonnie shot back, taking the phone into the kitchen.

She flicked the kettle on and sat down. The phone pinged and she hardly dared look.

Get your coat, you've pulled.

Bonnie smiled with relief to see it was Max and quickly sent a reply.

What do you mean?

Seconds later another message arrived.

I'm outside your flats now. Fancy a drink?

Thanking her lucky stars that she was looking a lot better than she had done an hour before, she ran to the window in the living room. Separating the slats of the blinds, she peered down onto the road. Max was leaning against his car, presumably waiting for her. She sent him a quick reply.

On my way down.

'You reckon you'll be okay for an hour or so?' she asked Paige.

Her daughter looked up from her iPad with an expression somewhere between surprise and annoyance. 'Why, where are you going?'

'I just need to pop out.'

'I thought we were going out together.'

'You said you didn't want to.'

'Maybe I changed my mind.'

'Bloody hell! Why do you have to be so awkward? I'll be an hour. I'll lock the door behind me and I'm on the end of the phone if you need me. Okay?'

Paige didn't reply and Bonnie grabbed her keys and jacket and headed for the door.

*

Max set a glass down in front of Bonnie. He had taken her to a lovely old pub down by the canal, a favourite with the narrow-boaters who cruised through. She was sitting in a cosy spot by the open fire on a plump armchair worked with rich, antique looking tapestry.

'Spritzer,' Max said. 'You sure you don't want a proper drink?'

'This *is* a proper drink. It just has a little something mixed in so that my liver can recover from last night.'

Max reached for his half of bitter and took a satisfied gulp. 'I know I'm driving, but you can't come here without having at least a little taste of the Old Speckled Hen.' He put his glass down and his expression became serious. 'So, what do you think about what I said in the car?'

'It's over with Sarah?'

Max nodded. 'Yes, she's okay with it now.'

'But she doesn't know about us?'

'I didn't think there was any need to tell her. Besides, I wasn't sure there was an *us*.' He gave her his most appealing look. 'Is there?'

'I had a great time last night, Max, I can't lie. I just don't know what to think.'

'Bon… if you had a good time and I had a good time, and we always enjoy each other's company… And you know I think you're gorgeous…' He paused, but Bonnie said nothing. 'Well,' he continued less certainly, 'I don't know what there is to think about. It's a no-brainer. We'd be great together, you know we would.'

'It's not just about us, though, is it?'

'Why not?'

'There's Paige too. And daft as it sounds, it's about Applejack's as well. You deliver every morning and if this ended badly, we'd have to see each other every day. Imagine how awkward that would be. Right now we both have lovely memories of a fun night out and we're still mates. We could ruin all that.'

'It wouldn't end badly,' Max said, reaching for her hand. 'It'd be great.

She looked up at him. He was hanging, waiting for her to say the right words, the ones he so clearly wanted to hear. There was so much hope in his eyes and she wished she could share his faith that their relationship was meant to be. Against her better judgement, she leaned over and kissed him.

'I just know I'm going to regret this, but what the hell…'

'You won't,' he said, smiling broadly as she pulled away. 'I promise you won't regret it at all.'

＊

'What is the news of the day, lovely ladies?' Stavros beamed as Linda and Bonnie walked into the Bounty. The day was bright and sunlight bounced off the white marble counter-top that Stavros leaned on with an open newspaper in front of him.

Linda shot a wicked grin at Bonnie.

'Don't you dare!' Bonnie warned.

'Bonnie has a new boyfriend,' Linda said, and then poked her tongue out at her friend.

Stav widened his eyes. 'Praise to the heavens! Who is this wonder man who can catch the eye of our beautiful Bonnie?'

Bonnie laughed. 'Stav, you're such a tease. It's nobody; it was just a date that Linda forced me to go on.'

'Yeah,' Linda fired back, 'but no one forced you to see him the day after as well. And no one is forcing you to see him again this week…'

'Thanks, Lind, just spread my business around the whole of the town.'

'Why keep it a secret?' Stav cut in, spreading his arms wide, 'true love *should* be spread around the town!'

'I'd hardly call it true love,' Bonnie said, laughing.

'But it could be,' Linda replied, nudging her.

'Don't be daft,' Bonnie said. 'A few dates, that's all. We're just two single people who happen to get along quite well and decided to go out together.'

'But that's just it,' Stavros said. 'All the best marriages are based on two people who get along well.'

'I'm not going to marry him!' Bonnie laughed.

'Bon,' Linda said, becoming serious, 'if ever I saw a couple perfect for each other, it's you and Max. Never say never.'

'Max?' Stavros asked. 'Not Max Delaney?'

Linda nodded, grinning.

'Oh! He is a perfect match for you, Bonnie!' Stavros exclaimed. 'A very nice man, good business, nobody else's children for you to look after…'

Bonnie grimaced. 'I'm more worried about what my child will make of him when he tries to get acquainted with her.'

'Have you told her about him yet?' Stavros asked.

'Oh, I didn't need to,' Bonnie replied ruefully, 'she caught us kissing goodbye in the car. She wasn't very impressed.'

'She'll come round,' Linda said. 'Just give her time.'

'I hope so,' Bonnie sighed. 'Otherwise this is going to be over before it's begun.'

*

'Hey Mum!' Bonnie called into the hallway as she took her coat off. It had been a hectic day at work and she was ready for a quiet cup of tea and a catch-up. She could hear the radio on in the living room, but went through to find it was empty. 'Mum?' she shouted.

A faint voice replied. 'I'm up here!'

Climbing the stairs, Bonnie could see that the loft hatch was open and the ladder down. 'What are you doing up there?' Bonnie called into the opening.

Jeanie's face appeared. 'Grab this…' she said, handing down a box.

Bonnie climbed a couple of steps and took it from her. It weighed a ton. She peered inside to see that it was full of old seven inch records.

'Whitesnake…' Bonnie said, smiling to herself at the bottom of the ladder as she thumbed through them. 'Bon Jovi, Def Leppard… wow,' she said to Jeanie as she watched her carefully descend moments later, 'I haven't heard these in years.'

'I know,' Jeanie said, wiping her hands down her old track suit trousers. I'd forgotten I had them. There might be some valuable ones in there – I bought picture discs and coloured vinyl and all sorts back in the day.'

'You're not going to sell them, are you?'

Jeanie shrugged and took the box from Bonnie. 'I won't be able to take them to Spain, and I don't play them anymore. I can't imagine you'd want them…'

Bonnie wrinkled her nose in reply.

'So,' Jeanie laughed, 'I might as well. If I do get a bit of cash from that secondhand record shop on the edge of town, it'll help with the moving costs.'

Jeanie took the box through to the kitchen and dumped it on the table.

'Want me to get the kettle on?' Bonnie asked.

'Oh, yes, if you don't mind.' Jeanie went to the under-sink cupboard and fetched out a duster. She went back to the box and carefully removed the records, a few at a time, laying them out on the table. Grabbing the top one, she proceeded to remove the disc from its cover and gently clean it.

'Have you got a date yet?' Bonnie asked as she fetched cups from a high cupboard. 'For moving, I mean.'

Jeanie paused. 'Juan says I can go and join him whenever I'm ready really. I thought I'd just get straight here, however long it takes, and then book my flights. I think about two months should do it now that

I don't have to sell the house. I suppose it would be alright to leave you my furniture too?'

Bonnie nodded slowly. 'Although it will mean that I'll have some doubling up, as I have a sofa and stuff of my own. I'll have to figure that out. But I won't get rid of yours, even if it means renting some storage – at least, not until you know you're settled and staying over there for good.'

'I'm staying. Whatever it takes I'm making this work. I really like Juan; I think we'll be very happy together.'

'I still think you're mad,' Bonnie replied.

'Sometimes, in life, you need to make a leap of faith,' Jeanie said gently. 'And that's what I'm doing.'

Bonnie sniffed. 'More like a bloody suicide jump.'

'Could you not just be happy for me, instead of tainting everything with your negativity?' Jeanie frowned.

'I'm just being realistic. One of us has to have some common sense.'

'Like you do over your mess of a love life?'

'This is not about me.'

'I think it is, more than you realise.'

Bonnie frowned. She opened her mouth to argue but then stopped herself. 'Let's not fall out, Mum. I've only got an hour or so tonight and then I'd better get back. Paige is due back from Annabel's house and I dread to think what she'll get up to with me not there, the mood she's in lately.'

'She's still annoyed about Max?'

Bonnie nodded. 'She was even more annoyed after he called to take me out for another drink yesterday.'

Jeanie's eyes widened. 'That's keen.'

Bonnie couldn't fight the smile that now spread across her face. 'I daren't say it, but I think I like him, Mum.'

'He's a nice man.'

'No… I mean I *really like* him.'

'What about Sarah?'

'He says that's all over now.'

'And you're certain it is?'

Bonnie shrugged slightly. 'I have to believe him, don't I?'

'I don't think you *have* to do anything, I think you *want* to.'

Bonnie nodded thoughtfully. 'Maybe I do.'

Jeanie sat down and Bonnie put a mug of tea in front of her before taking a seat with her own.

'I hope *you* know what you're doing,' Jeanie said.

Bonnie laughed. 'Listen to us. Eighty-odd years between us and no more clue about men than we had when we were teenagers.'

'I think I was more clued up when I was in my teens. The biggest worry about a date was whether my lippy would last. Life certainly seemed a lot simpler back then.'

'It did,' Bonnie agreed. 'But then a certain Frenchman had to turn me into a gibbering wreck.'

'He's gone now,' Jeanie said, 'and you finally have a new man. However things turn out with him, perhaps this is your moment to take a leap of faith?'

Bonnie was silent for a moment. 'Perhaps you're right.' She raised her mug with a wry half-smile. 'To leaps of faith.'

*

As she drove home from her mum's, Bonnie felt more positive than she had in years. She had made up her mind. As soon as she got home she would phone Max and ask him to come and meet Paige properly, as someone that her daughter needed to accept as part of Bonnie's life now. The more she thought about it, the more she realised she really did care for Max. Jeanie might have seemed mad for packing up and moving to Spain with Juan, but at least she was doing something that made her happy. The decision made Bonnie's insides flutter. She didn't know if it was the right one, but making it was more exciting than she could say.

*

Bonnie opened the door of the flat, her mind still teeming with the thoughts that had raced around it on the journey home, the conversation she would have with Paige carefully constructed in her head. But then she stopped dead in the hallway. Something wasn't right. A tatty black holdall lay abandoned on the floor a few feet away from the front door. A smell hit her, something familiar, something that she hadn't smelt for a long time. A rush of memories overwhelmed her, the blood drained from her face and the world around her began to spin.

Paige burst into the hallway from the living room. 'Mum!' she squealed in a state of manic excitement. 'Daddy's home!'

Chapter Eleven

When Bonnie opened her eyes, Paige was fanning her face frantically with a newspaper. She found herself lying on the sofa, without knowing quite why. As the room came into focus, she saw another figure standing behind her daughter. And then everything came back to her: the holdall, the smell of his aftershave, Paige running to greet her. But it couldn't be true. For what seemed like a long time, Bonnie didn't speak, she just stared at him as though he was a ghost.

Finally, in a croaky voice, Bonnie said, 'You complete bastard.'

'Hello Bonnie,' Henri replied with a wry smile, '*ça va?*'

'Isn't it brilliant?' Paige said. 'He's home.'

'Have you asked him where he's been for the past two years?' Bonnie replied, not looking at Paige but staring at Henri as though her anger alone had the power to disintegrate him.

'Does it matter?' Paige said.

'Of course it bloody matters,' Bonnie spat. 'He abandons us and suddenly he's back and that's alright? What about all the nights you cried over him and blamed yourself for him leaving? Don't they mean anything to you now, Paige? Are they all forgotten?'

Paige's face fell. 'I never did those things.'

'What!' Bonnie pushed herself up. 'Why are you protecting him? I should be the one you protect, not him!'

'Bonnie…' Henri cut in, 'I should go and check into a hotel tonight while you discuss things with Paige…'

'No way, Dad,' Paige said firmly.

'Great idea,' Bonnie said, glaring at Paige.

'Oh, you complete cow!' Paige replied. 'I bet this is all because of Max –'

'Max?' Henri interrupted. 'Who is Max?'

'It has nothing to do with you,' Bonnie shot back.

'It's her new boyfriend,' Paige sneered.

'You have a boyfriend?' Henri shouted.

'YOU LEFT US!' Bonnie cried. She struggled to regain control of her temper but her next words were coated with ice. 'You left us. We didn't know if you were alive or dead. We had no idea why you went. You expected me to sit around and wait for you?'

'Yeah, Mum –'

'Paige…' Bonnie massaged her temples and looked at her daughter imploringly. 'Please, just let me talk to your dad for five minutes alone.'

Paige looked as though she would argue, but Henri gave her an encouraging nod.

'We will be only five minutes,' he agreed. 'And then you can tell me all your news about things I have missed.'

Reluctantly, Paige headed for her bedroom. Bonnie turned to Henri, her voice low and hard.

'How could you do this to us?'

'Bonnie, I am truly sorry…'

'Don't!' Bonnie held up a hand to silence him. 'If it's going to be the same old crap, I don't want to hear it.'

'You know that I was ill,' Henri said defensively.

'Okay. But what is this all about now? You think it's okay to just waltz back in? What about a phone call, some kind of warning? A request even? What made you so certain we wanted you back?'

'Paige does.'

'And that's why you came back without warning when you knew she'd be here,' Bonnie growled. 'You knew if you got round her first the rest would be easy.' Tears were burning her eyes, but there was no way she was going to let them fall, not for Henri, not after everything he had put them through.

'I hadn't planned to come back. I didn't know I was coming until I was on the Eurostar. I had an urge to see you again and the next thing, I was here.'

Bonnie stared at him. Before he'd left them he'd looked pale and tired. But it seemed that home had treated him well – he had put on some weight, although he was still on the slim side, he was tanned and, despite the tension in the air between them now, he looked relaxed. He watched for her reaction, his dark gaze imploring, begging for forgiveness. She was reminded, in that instant, of what she had fallen for when she'd first met him. Even as she told herself not to give in, she felt her resolve begin to crumble.

'Where the hell were you?'

He shrugged. 'I needed to think.'

'You needed to think? You could have nipped into the toilet to take a dump and had a think in there while you were at it, you didn't need to go back to France.'

He smiled ruefully. 'Same old Bonnie.'

'Don't give me that. Where were you?'

'I spent some time in Grasse, St Tropez, Cannes, Toulon… lots of places, mostly in the sun, doing odd jobs to pay my way. I travelled and saw my country a little, the same as I had always planned to before we met.'

'You didn't go back to your parents' place at Reims?'

'For a while I visited. But it became awkward.'

'When I kept phoning them to find out where you were because I was frantic with worry?' Bonnie said in a low voice.

He shifted awkwardly. 'Yes. They told me I had to come back and make things right with you.'

'Clearly you take a lot of notice of them then.'

'Don't be angry, Bonnie, please. I don't know what to say to you.'

'How about we start with *sorry?*'

Henri dropped to his knees on the floor beside her and took her hands in his. 'You know I am.'

Bonnie wriggled from his grip. 'I need a drink. You can stay for an hour to talk to Paige, but then I want you to go and find a hotel.'

'You don't want me to stay?' he asked reproachfully.

'You said you would give me time to discuss things with Paige. Besides, you don't live here anymore.'

'But…'

'It was never your flat,' Bonnie said in a harder voice than she felt truly capable of. 'But we let you live here. When you left, you forfeited any right you had to call it home.'

'Very well.' He stood up, a formal stiffness in his demeanour now. 'Can I speak to my daughter?'

'I can't stop you,' Bonnie said wearily. 'But don't go putting stupid ideas into her head, or I'll have you out of here quicker than you can say *court order.*'

Henri didn't reply but made his way to Paige's bedroom to find her. Bonnie lay back on the sofa and let out a deep sigh. How could this be happening? Why was her life always destined to be such a monumental disaster? As these bitter thoughts ran through her head, the mobile in her coat pocket bleeped the arrival of a text message. For a moment, Bonnie ignored it as she listened to Paige's excited chatter through the walls, and Henri's deeper tones every so often in answer. But then she pulled the phone from her pocket and unlocked it to make sure it wasn't Jeanie, or more awkward still, Max on his way over for another impromptu visit.

Please stop ignoring me. I can't stand it. I need you to love me like I love you.

Bonnie let out a tiny squeal of frustration. Along with the new boyfriend and the returned deserter, she had a crazy popstar stalker to contend with. As if things weren't complicated enough.

Bonnie made her weary way to Paige's room. Henri and Paige were sitting on the edge of her bed chatting animatedly as if he had never been away. Of all the scenarios Bonnie had imagined, she could never have envisaged this. Paige was always so sullen, so difficult to engage with – what did Henri have that made her so different with him, even after everything he had put her through? It was as if she had wiped every bitter memory from her head, or simply refused to acknowledge them in the presence of the dad she now seemed to idolise. Daddy's girl syndrome, Bonnie supposed; there was no other explanation for it.

'Maybe we should sit around the table and discuss this properly over a drink, all three of us together,' Bonnie interrupted.

'You're not going to freak out again, are you, Mum?' Paige asked warily.

'No, I'm not,' Bonnie replied coldly. 'You have to understand, though, that seeing your dad here when I wasn't expecting to was a shock, especially after all this time.'

Henri nodded. 'I understand that.'

'You were just feeling guilty in case your boyfriend turned up, that's more like it,' Paige snapped.

'Who is this boyfriend?' Henri cut in, narrowing his eyes at Bonnie. 'Is it serious?'

'I don't know. Does it matter?' Bonnie stammered. She felt guilty, as though she was betraying Henri – but why? 'It has nothing to do with you anyway,' she said in a stronger voice, drawing herself up to her full height. 'You left.'

'I don't like strange men around Paige.'

'You'd better be joking if you're trying to play the concerned father,' Bonnie growled, anger rising in her. 'It's a bit late for you to be worried about who may or may not be around Paige.'

'I never stopped being her father.'

'Actually, you did. You never even sent her a birthday card!'

Henri shot from the bed and started towards Bonnie. 'Can't you understand, I was depressed?'

'Depressed? How do you think I felt when you deserted us? I was pretty bloody depressed!'

'Now I am home again I can see why I was depressed,' Henri shot back.

'This is not your home,' Bonnie said in a low voice. 'This will never be your home.'

'Not ours soon,' Paige cut in, leaping between them. 'We're getting Jeanie's house!'

Bonnie groaned as Henri's eyes widened.

'You're moving into your mother's house?' he asked.

'Yes!' Paige said. 'She's moving to Spain and we're having her house. There'll be plenty of room for you there, Dad.'

Henri smoothed his expression to one of amiable charm. When he spoke this time, his voice was soft and his accent seductive. Bonnie knew the voice well; it was the one he used when he wanted something. That was, after all, how he had persuaded her to move him into the flat all those years ago, a mistake that had been costing her dearly ever since. By now, she was immune to his wily charms, but that didn't stop him from trying.

'Well,' he said, 'perhaps we should go into the kitchen and discuss what we are going to do to bring our family back together.'

'We can go into the kitchen,' Bonnie warned, 'and we can talk all you like, but don't think that you're staying here tonight.'

'Of course not,' Henri replied. 'As we agreed, I will get a hotel room.' He looked hopefully at Bonnie. 'Do you know somewhere locally that is not expensive?'

Bonnie sighed… same old Henri, probably didn't have a euro to his name. 'If you need to borrow some cash…'

'I'm sorry,' Henri said sheepishly, 'I have spent all my money on trains. And I had thought I might be able to come home and get a job.'

Bonnie almost laughed out loud but a glance at Paige's eager expression stopped her. *A job*. That was something she would have to see to believe. 'It doesn't matter,' Bonnie said instead. 'I have a little that you can borrow.' There was no way, even if she had to spend the entire month's electricity money, that she was letting Henri waltz back into their lives as if nothing had happened.

*

Bonnie massaged her temples as she gazed miserably at Linda.

'I'll say one thing for him, his timing is amazing,' Linda said dryly.

'What am I going to do?'

'About what?'

'Max.'

'Nothing. You're with Max now and Henri can go swing.'

'It's not that simple, though, is it?'

'Why not?' Linda asked, picking through a tray of grapes armed with scissors to cut the rotten ones from the stalks.

'Henri is Paige's dad. We were a family.'

'Until he ruined all that.'

'That's not the point. You'd understand if you'd seen how happy she was to see him. I owe it to Paige to try and sort things.'

'I think you're wrong,' Linda said darkly. 'I think it will be the worst move you've ever made to let that man back into your life... and especially back into Paige's life, just like that. If he goes off again, imagine how much damage that will do to her. It'll be even worse than last time.'

Bonnie sighed. 'That's not how Paige sees it right now.'

'Paige will come round to Max, and she'll see that he's twenty times the bloke Henri is. Just give her time.'

'That's one thing I don't have now that Henri is back.'

'He went to a hotel last night then?'

Bonnie nodded.

'Where the hell had he been anyway? I assume he offered some sort of explanation.'

'He said he needed some time to sort his head out, he went travelling around the South of France, like he'd planned to do before we met.'

'Oh, how lovely for him,' Linda replied, her tone dripping with sarcasm. 'What mental age is this man that you decided to have a child with? He has a bit of a bad day and decides that he needs to go *travelling…*' Linda made little speech marks in the air as she said the word, 'instead of looking after his kid like any decent bloke would have done?'

Bonnie was about to reply when the usual morning knock at the door announced Max's arrival.

Bonnie's expression turned to one of panic. It wasn't that she hadn't expected to see him this morning, but now that it was imminent, she didn't feel like she could face him. 'Oh, God, Linda, what am I going to tell Max?'

'Nothing,' Linda replied, walking calmly to the door. 'Because Henri turning up on your doorstep is nothing to do with you and Max.'

'But, Lind…' Bonnie's argument trailed to nothing as Linda slid back the bolts on the door.

Max stood on the step, wearing a huge grin. Bonnie felt her stomach lurch as she saw how happy he looked.

'Morning ladies!'

'Morning, Max,' Linda said brightly.

Max gave her a good-natured nod and then turned his attention to Bonnie. 'And how's my girlfriend this morning?'

His smile was so warm, so full of tenderness that Bonnie didn't know whether to run into his arms or burst into tears. She tried to force a smile back, but it felt stiff and unnatural. He noticed straight away.

'Are you okay?' he asked.

Bonnie nodded. 'I have a headache this morning.'

'Oh,' he said, 'then I suppose I'll have to sing your praises in a quieter voice today.'

'Oi,' Linda cut in, 'never mind *her* praises, what about the woman who made it all possible?'

Max grinned but Bonnie shot her friend a pained look which, luckily, went unnoticed by him.

'I think Fred was stressing about mouse poo again,' Bonnie excused. 'I'd better go and see if I can find where they're coming from.'

Linda frowned but didn't argue.

'If you don't emerge unscathed in half an hour, I'll call you later,' Max said cheerfully.

'Yeah, yeah, call me later,' Bonnie replied, and hurried into the shop.

'Right then, chief cupid,' Max turned to Linda, 'let's get the kettle on.'

Linda looked at him with a smile that was suddenly melancholy, as if she knew that very bad things were about to happen.

*

After managing successfully to stay busy until Max had finished bringing his delivery in and had left, Bonnie went about the rest of her morning in a daze. She worked on autopilot, serving customers, speaking and smiling in the right places, even from time to time getting orders right. But her mind raced as she worked through the tangled strands of her life. No matter how much she puzzled over it all, she was no nearer finding a solution that wouldn't hurt somebody. The fact that she had been inundated with texts when she checked her phone at lunchtime did nothing to lighten her mood – Paige, Max and Jeanie had all messaged her with different requests, and there was also one of Holden's now ubiquitous proclamations of undying love. Paige's and Jeanie's were easy enough to sort, and Holden's could be ignored, as always, but Max's was the one that gave her particular heartache.

How about a drink tonight? I know I'm not supposed to be this keen but I can't help being nuts about you!

Henri was supposed to come for tea that night so that they could talk everything through, so while she knew that she would have to talk to Max before things got out of hand, it looked as though it would have to wait. On top of that, Bonnie still needed to break the news of Henri's reappearance to her mum, and if she managed to do that without Jeanie heading off in the direction of her flat with a flaming torch and a pitchfork, that would be a minor miracle in itself. But it seemed cruel to put Max through another day of ignorance, and there was no way she could tell him what she needed to tell him in the shop.

She decided to message him to come and meet her at the Cheshire Cat – not the poshest pub in the world, but one of the few in town that had stayed free of noisy quiz machines and pumping music. At least in there it would be quiet enough to talk without eavesdropping daughters interfering. Telling Max about Henri was going to be hard enough as it was.

Bonnie took a deep breath, and then messaged Max with the details of the pub, telling him to meet her around nine, so that she would have plenty of time to get rid of Henri first.

*

When Bonnie arrived back at the flat, Paige was hoovering. Her face was bright red and the whole place smelled of a strange, clashing concoction of cleaning products.

'What's all this?' Bonnie asked as Paige noticed her come in and switched the hoover off.

Paige wiped a hand across her brow. 'I'm cleaning up.'

'I can see that. What I want to know is what you've done with my daughter. Or have I stepped into a parallel universe where a Paige Cartwright lives who likes housework?'

'Ha ha. Dad's coming over tonight, isn't he?'

'Yes,' Bonnie replied, 'but he lived with us before and he's sat in an un-hoovered room before.'

'I wanted to make it nice for him. Things are different now – I'm older, I can do stuff.'

'Paige...' Bonnie began gently, 'no amount of cleaning will make him stay. A dirty carpet isn't what made him leave last time.'

'Don't be stupid, Mum...' Paige frowned, but then she sighed and bit her lip. 'I just want to make things perfect. Whatever it was we did before that made him go, I don't want to do it again.'

'You really want him to stay, don't you? Even after all we went through you want him to stay.'

Paige nodded uncertainly. 'He's my dad, isn't he? Why wouldn't I want him to stay?'

'He may be your dad, but that doesn't make him a nice or reliable man.'

'He'll stay this time, I know he will. And we'll be happy, a proper family just like we were meant to be.'

Bonnie didn't reply. Instead, she glanced at the clock. It was six-thirty. She had an hour to make the decision that would affect Paige for the rest of her life.

*

How in the hell it had happened, Bonnie couldn't say, but before she had realised what she was agreeing to, Henri had somehow wormed his way back into the flat and arrangements had been made for him to bring his cases over from the hotel the following day. She had been determined to watch for his glib lines, the empty promises whispered in a dreamy accent, and she was determined that she would not fall prey to them this time. But here she was, driving now to meet Max after seeing Henri off with a huge grin on his face, with dread in her own heart and a terrible fear that she was about to make the biggest mistake of her life.

Pulling up in the car park of the pub, she was relieved to see that, being a week night, the place seemed relatively quiet. Max had insisted that they get some supper there and Bonnie hadn't known how to refuse without raising suspicions that would lead to the whole sorry business being blurted out on the phone, so she had reluctantly agreed. Now, however, her stomach churned and the last thing she wanted to do was eat.

Max's car was parked a short distance away. Bonnie had insisted that he let her meet him at the pub, making some excuse about not being caught out by Paige again, and he seemed happy enough to go along with it. It was like meeting Holden at the country pub all over again – some furtive, dirty secret that she had to keep hidden from everyone.

As she got out of the car, the wind whipping around her face, she looked up to see Max walking towards her with a huge grin. He almost ran the final few steps and pulled her into his arms.

'Hey gorgeous,' he said warmly, nuzzling into her neck.

Bonnie squeezed her eyes shut, tears burning them. It was almost more than she could bear – the smell of him, the feel of him this close, the affection that seemed to radiate from the very soul of him. She threw her arms around his waist and clung on, resting her head on his chest and breathing him in like she could never get enough.

He kissed the top of her head tenderly. 'It's freezing out here. How about we go and get warm?'

Bonnie clicked the lock on her car door and then let Max take her hand and lead her inside.

The pub was warm and cosy with homely, muted décor, split into a bar area and a separate dining room. Bonnie had always liked it here and another time she might have been pleased to see its old familiar interior. She swallowed the ache in her throat as Max led her to a secluded booth by a window.

'I've been saving myself since lunchtime, so I'm starving,' Max said, rubbing the cold from his hands. 'I hope they've got something left in that kitchen.' Bonnie forced a smile. 'How about you?' Max asked, picking up the menu, 'what do you fancy?'

'I'm not all that hungry, to be honest,' Bonnie replied.

'Aha.' Max grinned. 'Just hungry for me, eh?'

'I wanted to see you, yes…'

'And I wanted to see you, Bon. I haven't been able to stop thinking about you. I have such a good feeling about us, like I've never had before.' He paused for a moment, his expression earnest. 'I know we've only been together for days, but I feel like I know you so well, like I've been with you forever. Do you think that's weird?'

'No,' Bonnie said, struggling to keep her voice even. 'I don't think it's weird at all.' She fought to keep her emotions in check. She had known all along that letting Max get close to her was a stupid idea, that it would only end badly, and here was the proof. Never again would she let her heart rule her head. She paused, ready to continue, but Max interrupted.

'I'll get us a drink from the bar,' he said, giving her hand a squeeze across the table. 'What do you want?'

'Just a coke, thank you.'

'Shall I order food while I'm up there?'

Bonnie shrugged. 'I'll just have a plate of chips or something.'

'That's all you want?'

'Yeah, I'm really not that hungry.'

'You won't think I'm a fat pig if I have half a chicken with my chips?'

'Of course not.'

Max leaned across the table and kissed her lightly before he slid from his seat and strode to the bar. Bonnie watched him go – his tall, solid, ever-dependable figure scoring a knife through her emotions. This was torture; why couldn't she just tell him? The longer she dragged this evening out, the worse it would be for both of them.

Minutes later he was back with a coke and a pint glass. 'It's a shandy,' he said in response to Bonnie's questioning look. 'I'm a good boy, you see.' He placed Bonnie's drink in front of her and sat down with his own. 'Where were we?' he asked, grabbing Bonnie's hand and gazing at her with a broad smile.

Bonnie couldn't stand it anymore. She steeled herself.

'I don't know how to say this…' she began. She paused, watching as the smile slid from Max's face.

'Say what?'

There was another pause that seemed to drag on for hours. The only sounds were the murmur of other pub customers deep in conversation and the low rumble of a heater somewhere nearby. Bonnie took another deep breath and slid her hand from Max's grip. 'We can't see each other any more.'

'Why? What have I done?'

'You haven't done anything,' Bonnie cut in quickly. 'It's Henri. He's come back.'

'You have got to be kidding. When?'

'Yesterday.'

'And did he say where he'd been?'

'Not exactly. But it doesn't matter.'

Max stared at Bonnie. 'How can it not matter?'

'I'm so sorry,' she repeated miserably. 'I wish it could be different.'

'You're dumping me for a man who's been missing for two years and then just walks back in as though nothing has happened?' Max's voice went up an octave with incredulity.

'What else can I do?'

'Tell him to sling his hook, that's what,' Max growled.

'He's Paige's dad.'

'It's a shame he didn't think of that when he went running back to France and left you two in the lurch.'

'He didn't know what he was doing, his head wasn't right.'

'I'll bet half my business that he had a pretty good idea what he was doing.'

'Don't… Max, please,' Bonnie almost whimpered. 'Don't make this harder than it already is…'

'Oh, right…' Max replied, his voice now ice, 'how remiss of me to forget that in all this mess there's a seriously mixed up woman and a terribly jammy French git. Never mind the poor boyfriend who's wasted two years of his life waiting for this woman and when he finally gets her, his reward is a boot in the bollocks and his marching orders. Because we wouldn't want to make it any harder for little Bonnie than it already is…'

'Max –'

He held up a hand to silence her. 'Forget it, Bonnie. I understand perfectly where I fit in all of this; clearly a long, long way behind the French twat who deserted you and his daughter. But thanks for filling me in.'

'Max! I didn't mean it to be like this –'

'Really? I fail to see any other way you could have meant it to be.'

'I really liked you –'

'*Liked* me? Past tense? Gerard Depardieu turns up again and suddenly it's not *like*, but *liked…*' Max's voice grew in volume with his indignation and obvious humiliation. Bonnie stared miserably at him. If only it could have been anyone but sweet, kind, funny Max that she had to do this to.

'I'm sorry,' she said again. There was nothing else that could possibly make it any better.

Max's gaze softened. There was so much compassion in his eyes, it was almost harder for Bonnie to bear than the fury he had shown moments before. He shook his head. 'Forget it, Bon. I honestly hope you're happy with him.'

'You understand?'

'No,' he said ruefully, 'I don't, not one bit. But it's your life and your choice and I would never wish anything but happiness for you.' He smiled tightly. 'As they say in France, *bon chance*.' He pushed himself up and placed a twenty pound note on the table. 'This should cover the bill.'

'Max, I don't want –'

'I know what you're going to say. I said I'd treat you and I will. Indulge me, eh?'

Bonnie nodded, fighting the tears that were now stinging her eyes. She wanted to say thank you for being the most amazing, kind, understanding man she had ever met, she wanted to say that she was wrong and that she didn't want him to go, she wanted to say that Henri wasn't the right man for her and really, deep down, she knew that. But nothing would come out. Max walked away without another word and Bonnie simply watched him go.

Chapter Twelve

'Bloody hell, you look like death warmed over twice. Are you okay?' Linda asked as Bonnie shuffled into work the following morning.

'I haven't slept much,' Bonnie said.

'It looks as though you didn't sleep at all.'

Bonnie gave her a rueful half-smile. 'You guessed right.'

'Henri?'

'Sort of.'

Linda watched, a shrewd expression crossing her face as Bonnie shrugged off her coat and hung up her bag. 'Bon... please tell me you didn't dump Max.'

Bonnie turned to face her. She didn't need to reply.

'Bloody hell,' Linda said. 'Do you have any idea what an idiot you've been?'

'Don't... please.'

'I could smack you one!'

'Linda, you didn't see how Paige was with Henri. It means so much to her that we make this family work again.'

'Paige is fifteen! She doesn't understand yet what arseholes men can be, even her own dad. She doesn't understand how hard it is to come by decent men like Max... and you're letting her ruin your chance of happiness with one.'

'It isn't just about me!'

'No it isn't. And Paige is too young to realise that she'd be better off with Max in your family than Henri.'

'I did what I thought was right.'

'Then you're a moron.' Linda paused as she looked at Bonnie, as though she was trying to see right into her heart. 'Do you love him?'

'Which one?' Bonnie replied, aware of the irony of this question.

'Henri.'

'I honestly don't know. While he was missing, I thought I did. Now he's back… I don't know how I feel.'

There was a knock at the back door.

'Oh, God, Linda, I can't be here.'

Linda folded her arms. 'You can't be missing every morning. Sooner or later you're going to have to face him.'

'Please… just get the door today.'

Linda stepped aside. 'You do it.'

Bonnie shot her a pleading look, but Linda didn't flinch. A moment's stand-off ended with a second, more insistent knock. Linda marched into the kitchen and Bonnie had no choice but to go to the door.

Her heart was beating so fast that she felt dizzy as she undid the bolts. What would she say to him? How would he react when he saw her? Slowly, she pulled the door back.

Whether it was relief or more like sticking pins in her already wounded heart, she wasn't sure, but Bonnie felt her breathing calm again when she saw that Max was not outside the door.

'Are you going to let me in?' he said.

It was the surly youth that worked for Max in his warehouse. Bonnie stepped aside without a word. It seemed that Max was so angry and upset with her that he had sent his warehouse boy instead of coming himself. Was this how it would be from now on? What had she done?

*

Henri pushed his empty plate away with a smile. 'One thing I did miss was your cooking, Bonnie.'

'I'm glad to hear I could do at least one thing right,' Bonnie replied with a hint of sarcasm in her voice. Paige looked at her sharply but the moment seemed to pass Henri by. 'So, I take it you'll be looking for work tomorrow?' Bonnie added.

Henri shrugged. 'You know how difficult it was last time,' he said. 'I thought about placing an ad for language lessons.'

'But you'll try to get something in the meantime? The last time you did teaching you had hardly any students. Stavros wants help at the Bounty, he said so... how about that?'

'I will try to find something more suited to a man of my capabilities first.'

'You need to take what you can find,' Bonnie said scathingly. 'Jobs are hard to come by and you have no reasonable employment history to show anyone as it is.'

'Give him a chance,' Paige said defensively. Bonnie shot her a pained look. Why did Paige side with her dad all the time?

'I will find something,' Henri replied. 'I just need some time.'

'Well...' Bonnie said, getting up to clear the dishes away, 'don't take too long because I can't afford to keep us all like I did before. Things have changed – the economy is bad, everything costs a fortune and money doesn't go as far as it did two years ago.'

'But you won't have any rent to pay soon,' Paige put in helpfully.

'I will be paying your nan rent,' Bonnie said from the sink as she filled the bowl with hot water.

'But Jeanie said –'

'I don't care what your nan says. I'm paying her some rent whether she likes it or not. I'll put it in an account for when she needs it… and she will need it at some point, I'm sure. I'm not sponging off her, it's not right.'

Henri got up and moved to stand behind Bonnie at the sink. He kissed her lightly on the neck. 'You have always been too kind.'

'It's not being kind,' Bonnie said, trying to sidestep awkwardly away from the arms that were attempting to encircle her waist. She grabbed a teacloth and turned to face him. 'It's being a decent human being.'

Henri took the cloth from her and covered her hands with his. Paige watched them carefully from the table. Bonnie shot her a warning glance.

'I guess I'll go FaceTime Annabel,' Paige said, taking the hint that her mum and dad needed to be alone. She got up from the table and headed for her bedroom, a small, triumphant smile on her face.

Bonnie turned to Henri. 'You've been allowed back into the flat. But you need to work a lot harder to get back into my bed.'

He smiled, his dark eyes smouldering. 'I know that. And I intend to persuade you, whatever it takes.'

'I don't want persuading if it's the usual Henri Chasse method. I want you to show me that I can rely on you this time. Then, maybe we can talk about it.'

*

Max didn't show up at Applejack's all week. By the weekend, Bonnie was ready to slap Robert, his warehouse assistant, in his sullen face; the boy was no more pleasant than he had been the first time he had delivered to them, despite Linda's best efforts every morning to draw some sort of conversation from him. Linda had also tried to get some sort of information about Max from his uncommunicative employee, but he simply shrugged every time the subject was broached and said that Max had informed him that he was now the new delivery man until further notice. Bonnie tried desperately not to think about Max, but she could do little else. Once, Paige had caught her crying as she cooked bacon for Henri, but had accepted her reply that she was worried about Jeanie's imminent departure for Spain a little too readily.

Jeanie had reacted exactly as Bonnie had expected – with a long string of expletives and threats to remove certain valuable parts of Henri's anatomy – and it took Bonnie a long time to calm her enough to explain the reasons why she was letting him move back in. Jeanie sniffed and said that Bonnie was mad, that Paige clearly needed some kind of child psychologist, that she knew some very bad people indeed who could have Henri beaten up and left in an alleyway for twenty quid and a keg of Special Brew, and that she would rather set fire to her house before she left for Spain than see Henri move into it with them when she had gone. Bonnie nodded patiently to all this. She could see how hard it was for her mum to understand what Bonnie was doing. And if she was honest, sometimes, Bonnie couldn't quite see a clear way through her own muddled logic either. But her decision had been made, and she had to make the best of it.

Henri had well and truly settled in too. Bonnie had no idea whether he was job-hunting when she was at work, but every night when she got home, there was a suspiciously deep indent on the corner of the sofa that got the best view of the TV. It seemed that he had a total lack of insight into his previous wrongdoings and couldn't understand why Bonnie would not welcome him with open arms to settle right back into his old life, as Paige had done.

As for Paige's behaviour, Bonnie found it bewildering and frustrating in equal measure. While she was still as moody as ever with Bonnie, it seemed that Henri could do no wrong. Bonnie could only guess she had been so wounded when Henri left the first time that she was desperate not to be abandoned again and would do anything to make sure that didn't happen. But Paige steadfastly refused to talk about it during the rare moments Henri was missing long enough for them to do so in private, and without discussing how her daughter really felt, Bonnie couldn't be certain. The only positive thing the week brought was that Holden's texts seemed to have stopped and Bonnie silently wondered whether he had finally got the message. Any more of those would be a complication too far, and Bonnie's nerves were already close to breaking point.

*

Bonnie woke with a start as the bed moved. She turned groggily to see Henri's dark outline climbing in beside her.

'What are you doing?' she croaked.

'I was cold.'

'Get some more blankets then, you know where the cupboard is.'

'Please, let me sleep here tonight. I'm lonely.'

Bonnie hesitated. The pain in his voice sounded so genuine. Perhaps it was true. 'No touching,' she said finally, moving away as he lay down. 'Sleeping is exactly what we do.'

'Can I hold you?' Henri asked. 'I need to warm up. I won't do anything else.'

'No.'

There was a pause. 'Please…' He stroked a hand down her hair.

Bonnie suddenly ached with longing as his breath warmed the back of her neck. She desperately wanted someone to hold her at night, had wanted it for the two years she had spent sleeping alone. So what if Henri wasn't the right one? What was that old saying… *if you can't be with the one you love, love the one you're with*? Bonnie had never understood the meaning of that more than she did right now.

Henri took her silence as permission and slid an arm around her waist, pulling her in to spoon her, and laid his head next to her. No matter how much she fought it, no matter how much anger she still had towards him burning her insides, her resolve was beginning to crumble. It was so hard to be this lonely for this long and not melt under Henri's warm embrace, that voice in her ear, that seductive accent…

As she settled without pushing him off, Henri nuzzled closer. 'You still look so beautiful,' he whispered. 'This is why I could not stop myself from coming to your bed…' He kissed her neck; feather-light caresses sending thrills of desire down her spine.

'Stop it,' she hissed back.

'You don't mean that.'

Bonnie closed her eyes as he brushed her hair aside and trailed more delicate kisses across her back. This was so wrong, but it felt so good as the fire inside her began to burn, her body begging for much more.

'Please… Henri… don't do this.'

'We could be good together again. You know we could… *je t'adore, Bonnie*…' His hardness stirred against her as his hands moved lower, down to her thighs, softly caressing as he worked his kisses over the skin of her shoulder, faster now, more urgent.

Bonnie's insides ached, her thoughts jumbled into a blur of heat and longing… it would be easy to let him take her, and so, so good…

'Stop!' she gasped, pulling away and sitting up. 'Stop it, this isn't right.'

He sat up to face her and Bonnie reached for the lamp to flick it on.

'What is the matter with you?' he pouted.

'*This* is the matter!' Bonnie panted. 'You can't just come back into my life and do this to me.'

'It seemed that you liked it a moment ago.'

'You took advantage of me.'

'You're crazy! You wanted me.'

'I told you no.'

'Your body told me yes.'

Bonnie hugged herself and shivered slightly. 'Maybe my body doesn't know what's good for it,' she replied miserably. 'I've been on my own a long time.'

'Yes,' Henri said, 'you have. You are a beautiful woman who has needs. I understand that. I can fulfill your needs. We used to be great together…' He gave her a smouldering look. 'We used to have sex that woke the neighbours and broke the bed. Do you remember that? If sex is all you need, we don't have to make it about anything more than that – no strings.'

Bonnie's mouth fell open. 'You think that's okay?' she squeaked. 'You think I just need sex and you're prepared to go along with that, even though you're living under my roof as part of my family again?'

'I just thought –'

'Get out!' Bonnie said through gritted teeth.

'I don't understand.'

'No,' Bonnie cut in, 'you don't and you never will, and that's why you'll never get back in my bed. Get out!'

Henri pulled the sheets over his shoulder and turned to face away from her. 'I am staying here.'

'Fine,' Bonnie grimaced. 'Then I'll get out. Anything to be away from you.'

Grabbing her pillow, she headed for the sofa.

*

Bonnie woke to find Paige staring down at her holding a glass of water.

'What are you doing on there?' she asked.

'Your dad was cold, I let him have the bed,' Bonnie excused, pushing herself up to sit. It was lucky that it was Sunday, because at least it meant another terrible night's sleep wouldn't fall under Linda's scrutiny yet again. She rubbed her swollen eyes and yawned widely.

'You don't look like you've slept very well,' Paige observed as she sat down on the end of the sofa.

'It's not that comfy on here.'

'I know. But you let Dad sleep there for loads of nights.'

'Yeah, well your dad doesn't have to go to work the next day, does he?'

'I don't know why you can't just sleep in the same bed again. I won't be embarrassed, I know all about the birds and the bees now, you know.' Paige smiled. Bonnie tried to return the smile.

'I know,' she said. 'We're just not ready for that yet.'

'He hurt you, didn't he, loads more than you let on,' Paige said.

Bonnie stared at her for a moment. The way she had behaved since Henri's return, she hadn't felt that Paige understood it at all. Whatever her motives for welcoming Henri back, she obviously understood more about the situation than she admitted.

'He did. And I'm not sure how to forgive it.'

'But you're not still seeing Max, are you?' Paige asked.

Bonnie stiffened. 'It would have nothing to do with you or your dad if I was.'

'You are?'

'No, I'm not. But that's my choice and not up to anyone else.'

'Good, because Dad would go crazy if you were. He loves you and he wants us to be a family again.'

'He told you that?'

Paige shifted slightly. 'Not really. But I know it's true, or why would he come back?'

Bonnie could think of a few reasons, and none of them had anything to do with love. 'Are you happy, with him back in the flat?'

Paige nodded. 'It's weird, because I'm not used to a man being here, but I think so.'

'Okay.' Bonnie stretched and looked at the clock. 'Time for a coffee, I think. Do you want one?'

'I think I might go back to bed for a while,' Paige said, standing up.

'Not sneaking off to FaceTime Annabel with the latest gossip then?'

Paige grinned. 'I might be.'

'Don't be too long,' Bonnie said with a smile, 'or you'll miss bacon sandwiches.'

Paige bent to kiss her. 'I won't.'

*

Whether Henri had dismissed their nocturnal spat, or simply not attached as much significance to it as Bonnie had, he wasn't saying, but Sunday passed civilly enough with neither of them mentioning it. She wasn't certain why, but she found herself regularly checking her phone, whenever she had a quiet moment, only to find it empty of new messages. She knew that Max was not going to text her, of course, but the germ of hope was still there just the same. To know that he was thinking of her, that he didn't now completely hate her would have been enough. There wasn't even a text from Holden.

Later in the day, after lunch was over and Henri was curled up on the sofa watching a film with Paige, Bonnie, under the pretence of tidying some ironing away, found herself sitting in Paige's room staring up at the poster of Holden. He looked back down at her, with that cheeky, frozen grin. So that was it, after all she'd been through, Bonnie had found herself back where she'd began, with Henri and Paige and a steady job and nothing out of the ordinary. What had the past few months been about if fate had simply decided to throw her back after putting her through the emotional wringer? It didn't make any sense. Bonnie wanted to believe that Holden had moved on, but instead found his silence disconcerting; it seemed too neat to her that things would resolve themselves so easily. What was he up to now?

She looked up as Paige wandered in. 'That was an awesome night, wasn't it, Mum?' she said, sitting down next to Bonnie on the bed.

Bonnie turned to her. 'It was certainly memorable.' She smiled ruefully.

'I'm sad that Annabel didn't come… but I'm so glad I got to share it with you,' Paige replied.

Tears stung at Bonnie's eyes, but she swallowed them back. Her love for Paige had always been the most powerful emotion she had ever felt, right from the first second she had held her, fifteen years before, a tiny, fierce-looking bundle with huge lungs. Bonnie knew right now, looking at her daughter, just as she had always known, that she would do absolutely anything to make her happy. 'I'm so glad you let me,' Bonnie said, reaching to pull Paige into a hug.

Paige hugged her back and giggled. 'Blimey, Mum, I'll have to let you come out with me more often.'

Bonnie only held her tighter.

*

'Sofa or bed?' Bonnie asked Henri as bedtime arrived once again.

He raised his eyebrows in a questioning look. 'So I have to choose?' Bonnie nodded.

'What would you do if I chose the bed?' he asked.

'Then I'd sleep on the sofa.'

He paused, watching her with barely disguised amusement, as though he was confident it was only a matter of time before Bonnie caved in. Perhaps it was. 'Then I suppose I will take the sofa,' he said dryly.

Without a word, Bonnie took herself to bed.

*

Bonnie woke on another dreary Monday morning relieved that she had not been disturbed by an amorous Henri. She wondered whether he had finally got the message, but knowing Henri, she doubted it.

Paige joined her at the kitchen table for a quick and bleary-eyed breakfast. They hardly spoke, except for vague details of what time Paige would be in from school and what there was in the fridge for her to eat. Bonnie liked to make sure that the things Paige was happy to eat, which were limited, were all available and easy to find.

'What about Dad?' Paige asked. 'Shall I get him something when I get home?'

Bonnie shrugged. 'If he wants something I suppose.'

'I think I'll cook,' Paige said. 'He'd like that.'

He should be cooking for you, Bonnie thought. 'Just be careful,' she warned. 'I don't want any kitchen disasters.'

'Don't worry,' Paige said brightly, 'we'll be just fine.'

Somehow, Bonnie didn't like the idea of the two of them being alone while she was at work. She couldn't be sure what Henri might extract from Paige about their lives in his absence, that he could twist and store away to bring out when he needed emotional ammunition. But there was little she could do about it, and she left for work with a weary resignation that this was how life would be from now on.

*

The morning knock at the back door of Applejack's brought more disappointment as Bonnie opened it to Robert. She should have been getting used to Max not being there, but each morning that he stayed away only made her more miserable. It was clear that she would never get used to not seeing him, no matter how long he stayed away. She couldn't help but wonder whether he had gone back to Sarah. He deserved to be happy, and perhaps Sarah was the woman to make it happen. She tried to think of this and be pleased about it, but it was hard, no matter what she told herself.

Bonnie showed the boy in and made him a cup of tea before he started to bring the stock in (he might have been a sullen sod, but Bonnie and Linda had decided that it was no reason to make him die of thirst). Just as he was drinking it, a second knock came at the door. Bonnie and Linda exchanged worried glances. If it was Max, what would Bonnie say? What could he want?

'You want me to get it?' Linda asked, seeing the colour drain from Bonnie's face.

Bonnie nodded faintly and Linda went to the door.

'Henri!' Linda gasped.

Henri pushed past her into the stockroom. 'Paige tells me that Bonnie's boyfriend is the delivery driver.' Immediately, his gaze fell upon the spotty youth who was sitting on a bench and drinking tea while he glared at Henri. He wasn't glaring at Henri for any reason – he just glared at everyone that way. 'Is *this* it?' Henri asked with a scathing laugh as he pointed at the boy. 'I thought I would have more competition than that.'

'Who the hell are you?' Robert scowled.

Henri made a move towards him, his fists clenched and his jaw tight with anger.

Bonnie grabbed his arm. 'This is not him.'

Henri turned to her. 'Where is he then?'

Linda stepped forwards. 'Look here, you tit, don't you think you've done enough damage without coming in here threatening people?'

'Ah…' Henri replied, his voice dripping with sarcasm, 'how lovely to see you again, Linda…' He gave her a mocking little flourish.

'Get out,' Linda growled back. 'And take your sad ego with you.'

'Linda…' Bonnie stepped between them. 'Please, just leave it.'

'You think I'm going to stand here and watch while he screws up your life?' Linda shouted at Bonnie.

'Calm down,' Bonnie shouted back. 'This is not your battle.'

'Battle?' Henri cut in. 'Where is the battle in this? I am Paige's father; I was here before this *delivery driver*. It is my right to defend my woman!'

'I am not your woman!' Bonnie hissed.

'So you love this delivery man?' Henri asked savagely.

'I mean that I am nobody's woman! I'm not some trinket that you can take a fancy to and own! I'm sick of everyone thinking that they can own me!'

'You heard her,' Linda said, 'sling your hook.'

'Keep out of this, Lind,' Bonnie said.

'What do you mean, keep out?' Linda shot back. 'I'm saving you from yourself. And what about poor Max? He's heartbroken!'

Bonnie paused for a moment and stared at her. 'How do you know that?'

'I just do,' Linda replied, flustered. 'What I do know or what I don't, it doesn't change the fact that you were happy with Max and then *this...*' she threw a hand in the direction of a glowering Henri, 'turns up and you drop him with not even a decent explanation why.'

'How dare you!' Henri snarled, making a move towards Linda.

'Go on, tough guy,' Linda goaded, 'I'd love you to take a pop at me. Take a swing and I'll have you in prison faster than you can say *horsemeat.*'

'Linda! Stop it!' Bonnie shouted.

The delivery boy simply sat and watched the fireworks, a slow smile – the first he had ever displayed in Applejack's – spreading across his face. But then a voice cut through the tension and all four turned to see a furious Fred in the doorway.

'You!' he said, pointing a shaking finger at Henri. 'If you don't leave my shop now, I'll have you arrested... And you won't even have time to think about saying *horsemeat.*'

Henri glared at him, then took a breath and held his hands up in a gesture of surrender. 'I'm going.' He turned to Bonnie. 'Later, we talk.'

Bonnie watched him go in silence.

'Next time he comes in here kicking off,' Fred huffed at Bonnie once Henri had slammed the door behind him, 'you get thrown out with him.' He stormed back into the main shop.

Linda turned to Bonnie. 'He doesn't mean it.'

'I know he doesn't. He knows he wouldn't get anyone else to skivvy for him like I do.'

'He's fond of you really, you know that don't you?'

Bonnie sighed. 'It doesn't feel like anyone is fond of me right now.' Her attention was drawn by the delivery boy, who was making his way quietly to the door to fetch the stock from his van. 'Sorry about that,' Bonnie told him.

He looked round and shrugged. 'Don't worry, sug, I could have taken him.'

Bonnie gave him a wry half-smile. 'I'm sure you could.'

*

Linda pulled on her coat and glanced at Bonnie, who sat with her head in her hands at the table in the tiny kitchen of Applejack's. 'Come on, why don't you come down to the Bounty with me? The fresh air will make you feel better.'

Bonnie looked up at her with a weary resignation. 'I'm not hungry and I don't really feel like making small talk with Stav today.'

'Stay outside then while I go in and order.'

Bonnie shook her head. 'You go. I need to phone my mum anyway.'

Linda raised a questioning eyebrow. 'Is she okay?'

'Mum? Yeah, she's fine. I'm just worried about Paige going home to sit with Henri by herself after school.'

Linda's mouth dropped open as she stared at Bonnie with a horrified expression. 'You don't think he'd do anything to her?'

'Oh no,' Bonnie said. 'He wouldn't do anything physical, anyway. I'm more worried about the lies he might tell her, or what she'll tell him that he'll twist to suit his own ends. We've already seen the trouble that can cause.'

'This morning's little incident…'

'Yeah. I don't want anything like that happening again. And I know that Max is no pushover, but I don't want Henri anywhere near him… God only knows what he would do to him given half a chance.'

'Bonnie,' Linda said in a hard voice, 'do you honestly believe this is the sort of man who should be bringing Paige up?'

Bonnie shrugged. 'I don't have a choice, at least not right now. For today, I'm more concerned about this obsession he seems to have with Max.'

'What are you going to do then?'

'I'm going to ask my mum to meet Paige from school and take her back to her house. Paige won't like it, but I can't see any other way of keeping her away from Henri until I get home.'

'You can't do that forever.'

'I know. But at least it will give me a bit of time to talk to Paige first, make her understand that she has to be careful what she says to her dad.'

'That'll go down well.'

Bonnie grimaced. 'I know. They both have it in for Max right now so they might turn into a right poisonous double act.'

Linda laughed. 'That's one way of putting it.' She turned to head out the door.

'Linda…' Bonnie called.

Her friend halted and turned back. 'Yeah?'

'When you said before that Max was heartbroken… you've seen him, haven't you?'

Linda paused for a moment, clearly torn. 'Yes,' she finally admitted. 'I called in at the warehouse on the way home one night. I didn't think it would be open, but he was catching up on some paperwork.'

'Was he okay, though?'

'If you mean okay as in not slitting his wrists open, then, yeah, he's okay. If you mean is he happy and getting on with his life, then, no… he's really not okay.'

Bonnie hated herself for her next question, but it forced its way out. 'He's not back with Sarah, then?'

Linda shook her head. 'No. He's far too screwed up now for that.'

*

Three o'clock came and Bonnie's phone bleeped in her pocket just as she had finished bagging up a customer's order. Fred glared at her as she shrugged apologetically and hurried into the stockroom to check it.

Have picked up Paige, nothing to worry about. See you later. X

Bonnie heaved a sigh of relief. Paige hadn't kicked up too much of a stink then – that was one less thing to worry about. She tapped a reply:

Thanks. Will see you later and explain. X

She was just about to slide the phone back into her pocket when it bleeped again.

Robert told me about this morning with Henri. Are you ok?

The lump rose quickly in Bonnie's throat. She dragged a deep breath and swallowed her tears back. After all that she had done to him, Max still wanted to know if she was alright. She paused, re-reading the message. Eleven words. Eleven small, uncomplicated words that said so much more than they ever could by themselves. Replies formed in her head, but none of them seemed right, none of them were significant enough to convey how grateful she was that he still cared.

Finally, after staring at the phone blankly, she replied.

I'm fine. Thank you for asking. I'm sorry that Robert got dragged into it. I hope he was alright. x

It was nowhere near enough, but it would have to do. Bonnie shoved the phone back into her pocket and hurried out to the shop. Linda shot her a questioning glance, but Bonnie shook her head and tried to force a smile. Linda simply frowned in return. Bonnie knew she hadn't fooled her, not for a minute.

*

Paige sat glowering at Bonnie and Jeanie in turn as they shared a pizza, although, so far, Paige had refused to eat the slices on her plate.

'I still don't know why I couldn't go straight home,' she said. 'Dad will be all alone and starving by now and we're here munching crappy frozen pizza without him.'

'You know how he feels about your nan,' Bonnie reasoned.

'And the feeling is mutual,' Jeanie cut in.

Bonnie shot her a warning look. 'I thought we'd agreed not to bring all that up again.'

'Just saying. I still think you're both mad letting him back in the flat. And I'll tell you this now… he'd better not get any ideas about living in my house, because if I find out that he is…'

Bonnie sighed. She didn't see how she was going to get around that particular issue, but as her tired brain was already wrestling with more problems than it could handle, she had decided to cross that very rickety bridge when she came to it. She turned to Paige. 'The reason I asked your nan to pick you up is because I wanted to have a talk to you without your dad being there.'

'Why?' Paige folded her arms and frowned obstinately. 'What is there to say that Dad can't hear?'

'I need to talk to you *about* your dad. About what we do and do not say to him…'

'You mean you want me to lie to him about stuff?'

'Not exactly lie… just not exactly tell him everything…'

'But why?'

'Because…' Bonnie said carefully, battling with her waning patience. 'Your dad doesn't always react to things appropriately.'

Paige stared at her but didn't reply.

'What your mum is trying to say,' Jeanie cut in with a blunt tone, 'is that if your dad hears something he doesn't like, he doesn't wait to find out if it's true or not, he just goes out to smash someone's face in.'

Bonnie groaned. 'Yes, thanks, Mum. That wasn't quite how I would have put it.'

'I can't see the point in beating around the bush,' Jeanie said briskly as Paige's mouth dropped open. Jeanie ignored her granddaughter's reaction and looked at them both in turn. 'Now that's sorted, who wants a cuppa?'

Chapter Thirteen

Tuesday at work had been quieter and at least there had been no repeat of the previous morning's drama. Max's text had raised some hope in Bonnie that he might show for delivery that morning, but as was usual now, Robert had come instead. Bonnie was almost disappointed that Henri had stayed away too – it meant that there was no reason for Max to text again.

Bonnie mused on all this as she stood at the kitchen counter later at home, chopping peppers for a chilli. Interrupting her thoughts, Paige sidled in and sat at the table.

Bonnie stopped for a moment and glanced over her shoulder. 'Alright Paige?'

Paige nodded. 'Annabel wants to me to go over.'

'You know you can go to Annabel's whenever you want as long as I know about it.' Bonnie turned to her now with a puzzled look. 'Why are you looking so unsure about asking?'

Paige shrugged. 'Well… Dad will be here.'

'Yeah?'

'And he might think it's rude if I go out again.'

'Of course he won't.' Bonnie smiled. 'You're fifteen; he knows that you have a life of your own now.'

Paige scuffed her feet under the table as she bit her lip thoughtfully.

'Stop worrying,' Bonnie said, wiping her hands on a cloth and joining Paige at the table. 'You can't walk on eggshells your whole life in case you upset your dad.'

'Eggshells?'

'It means that you have to get on with your life as normal. Which means going out with your friends, throwing dirty pants under your bed and stealing my lipsticks.'

'I don't steal your lipsticks!'

Bonnie raised her eyebrows and Paige grinned.

'Okay, maybe I borrow your lipsticks.'

'Yes, very long-term borrow.' Bonnie leaned to kiss her on the forehead. 'Go and see Annabel. Your dad will still be here when you get back.'

'I wish I could be sure about that,' Paige said darkly.

'We're none of us sure that our loved ones will always be here for us,' Bonnie replied, 'but that doesn't mean we should live our lives in fear.'

'You know what, Mum…' Paige said with a cheeky look, 'sometimes you're really thick…'

Bonnie laughed.

'But sometimes,' Paige continued, 'you're really smart.'

'What am I today?'

'Pretty smart.'

'Coming from you, that's a huge compliment. So, what time are you going to Annabel's?'

Paige glanced towards the half-prepared ingredients on the worktop. 'Her mum says I can go for tea… if that's okay.'

'Oh that lot will keep,' Bonnie said, waving a dismissive hand at the food. 'You go for tea and I'll save you some for tomorrow.'

Paige smiled and got up. 'Thanks Mum.'

Her expression was so much lighter than it had been ten minutes previously, but Bonnie's darkened as her daughter left the room. It was only right that Paige should get on with her life, but now Bonnie faced the test of eating dinner alone with Henri. They were playing this happy family game well enough for everyone outside, but the atmosphere between them was as taut as piano wire. Henri had made it quite clear what he wanted from Bonnie, and she had made it equally clear that she wasn't about to give it to him. With Paige out of the way, Bonnie had a horrible feeling that tonight was going to end badly.

*

With dinner eaten in a reasonably civil atmosphere, Bonnie cleared away the plates while Henri uncorked a bottle of wine. He poured a glass and then looked at Bonnie questioningly.

'Not for me,' Bonnie said. 'I'll never get up for work tomorrow.'

'Go on.' Henri smiled. 'Just one tiny glass won't hurt.'

'Really, I'm fine.' Bonnie squeezed some washing up liquid into the bowl and ran the hot tap.

Henri came up behind her moments later and placed a glass of wine next to her on the worktop. 'For when you've finished washing up.'

'I don't want one,' Bonnie said, her eyes fixed firmly on her task.

'Please…' Henri pulled her by the shoulder gently to face him. 'Drink with me. It's been so long since we drank together. I promise I will be a good boy.'

Bonnie paused, ready to argue. But then she simply sighed. 'One drink. Don't think you can get me tipsy and have your way with me.'

Henri pouted. 'There was a time I could have my way without getting you tipsy.'

'Don't…' Bonnie warned.

Henri stepped away with his hands in the air. Against her better judgement, Bonnie turned off the tap and dropped the dirty dishes into the water to soak before grabbing her wine and following him into the living room.

Henri was sitting on the sofa, his wine on a small side table. He patted the seat beside him. 'Come and sit with me. It's time we talked properly.'

'That reality show about DIY is on in a minute,' Bonnie said, grabbing the TV remote and sitting on the other end of the sofa. 'It's supposed to be hilarious.'

Henri reached over and took the remote from her. Then he took her wine and placed it next to his before reaching for her hands. 'Never mind the television. We need to talk.'

'Okay,' Bonnie said, sliding her hands from his and folding them in her lap. 'What do you want to talk about?'

'Us.'

'I thought we'd sorted all that.'

'We sorted the practical things.'

'What else is there?'

Henri lowered his voice into a seductive drawl. 'I miss you, Bonnie. I need you.'

'Not this again…'

Henri put his finger over her lips. 'Stop. Let me talk.'

Bonnie frowned but was silent. She waited. But Henri simply reached for a lock of her hair, tucking it gently behind her ear. The action fired tiny pulses through her and she couldn't help but close her eyes. His touch was still so good, and he knew it. Then his lips were close to her ear, his hot breath on her neck. 'I want you back. Not only to live with… I was wrong to leave. I want you back as my lover. I will do anything...' He kissed her earlobe lightly and she shivered, fighting the ripples of desire that fired up and down her spine. 'Anything... to have you...' His lips moved down her neck, and onto her mouth, kissing her forcefully. She could taste the wine on his lips.

Bonnie shook herself and pulled away. 'This is not going to happen.'

'You can't fight it, Bonnie. You want me; I feel it when I touch you.'

'You're wrong.' Bonnie stood up. 'Stop trying now, because it will only end with you losing your temper.'

Henri followed her back out to the kitchen. 'Why are you doing this?'

'Doing what?' Bonnie asked as she plunged her hands into the washing up water.

'Denying me.'

'Because you left.'

'That's the only reason?'

'It's enough, isn't it?'

Henri exhaled loudly. 'You know why I left.'

'Yeah, your head was messed up. What do you think it did to me and Paige when you went?'

'Paige is not complaining.'

'Paige doesn't understand. She's so desperate to keep you here she'll say anything. She'd swear black was white if you told her to.'

'This is not about Paige. This is about you and me. I love you, Bonnie and I know you still love me.'

Bonnie swung around. 'You don't love me. Stop saying that! And I don't love you, so get that into your thick head.'

Henri narrowed his eyes. 'This is because of the delivery man.'

'Stop going on about Max! It's over between us, you saw to that, so leave him out of it!' Bonnie turned back to the sink and threw a handful of cutlery into the bowl, bubbles exploding over the worktop.

'I don't believe you,' Henri said quietly. 'Why else would you refuse me?'

Bonnie spun around again and fixed him with a blazing stare. 'You're so arrogant that you think the only reason I could possibly refuse sex with you is that I'm seeing another man? God, Henri, I thought I knew you, but this is a whole new level of why I hate you.'

'You don't hate me, Bonnie.'

Bonnie glared at him, but deep down, she was afraid he was right. The truth was she didn't know what she felt about him. But she did know for sure that getting back together with him was a very bad idea. She could keep up the pretence of being a family for as long as she needed to, for as long as it took Paige to get her head sorted, but to let herself fall for Henri again? It would almost be too easy to let him back in, especially when giving up Max had left such a huge hole, bigger than she'd ever imagined it would.

'This is imbecilic,' Henri growled as she stared him down. He reached past her for the half-full wine bottle and stalked into the living room, leaving Bonnie to finish the dishes, her mind swimming with confusion and wishing dearly that Paige would come back from Annabel's so that she wouldn't have to be alone with him for a moment longer.

*

In the living room, Henri refilled his wine glass and took the lot in a huge glug. Just as he was about to start on Bonnie's abandoned glass, a sound caught his attention. He looked up to see that Bonnie's phone was on the mantelshelf, and it had just bleeped the arrival of a message. Throwing a quick glance towards the kitchen door to make sure the coast was clear, he picked up the phone and unlocked it.

Are you ok? I'm worried about you and I'm here if you need anything. It doesn't matter if Henri is back, please don't shut me out. X

Henri's jaw clenched as he read the text. He tapped out a reply.

I love Henri. Don't message me again.

Then he deleted the incoming message and placed the phone carefully back on the shelf.

Still glowering at the phone, Henri knocked back Bonnie's wine in one gulp and poured himself some more.

*

'Mum…' Paige sidled up behind Bonnie as she dropped some toast on a plate the next morning.

Bonnie turned and handed her the plate. 'Uh-oh. I know that voice. What do you want?'

'Nothing…'

Bonnie raised a disbelieving eyebrow.

'Oh, okay. Every Which Way are finishing their tour in Birmingham. Annabel is trying to get tickets from Ebay because she missed out last time and they're sold out everywhere else. Can I go with her?'

Bonnie frowned. 'They'll cost a fortune from ticket touts on Ebay.'

'What if they don't? Could I go if they don't cost too much?'

Bonnie looked at Paige's pleading expression. She could see that Paige desperately wanted to go. For a crazy moment, she considered texting Holden to get some tickets. But, of course, that was a ridiculous idea and asking for trouble, not to mention totally immoral, considering she had told him to get lost and never speak to her again.

'When is it?' she asked instead.

'Saturday night.'

'What! This Saturday?'

Paige nodded.

'No way. Sorry, but I can't get the money together that quick. If you'd given me a bit of warning…'

'I didn't know before…' Paige began to whine.

'Sorry, Paige. I'd love to say yes but I can't. Maybe you can go to a date on the next tour.' Bonnie silently hoped that the next tour would be soon. Holden had been quiet for the remainder of this one, and the danger of him having nothing to occupy his time and picking up where he had left off with Bonnie was a worrying one.

Paige pouted. 'Where's Dad?'

'In bed, of course. I'd have more money to spare if he hurried up and got a job.'

'It's not his fault,' Paige said defensively. 'He says he has trouble getting work because of visas and stuff.'

'Hmmm,' Bonnie replied noncommittally.

*

Paige mentioned the concert at every available opportunity throughout the remainder of the week, dropping hints big enough to cause tsunamis in the Indian Ocean. Bonnie skilfully ignored every one and Henri seemed oblivious to any of it.

By the time a blustery Sunday arrived, alternate snatches of bright sunlight and steel grey colouring the sky, the flat had turned into an emotional battlefield. Paige was fuming that Annabel had managed to get the Every Which Way tickets and taken Nicola Clayton (who'd just had timely birthday money) in Paige's stead; Henri glowered every time he looked at Bonnie and Bonnie was ready to run away to France herself with the excuse that her head wasn't right. Lunch was a largely silent affair, shortly after which Paige retired to her room and Henri settled in front of the TV, leaving Bonnie to clear up.

As she put away the last of the dishes, Bonnie heard her phone bleep from the shelf in the living room. Going through to see what the message was, she was furious to find Henri had picked it up. He shot her a guilty look.

'What the hell are you doing?'

'Your phone went off… I was bringing it to you.' Henri made no move to give the phone back, but Bonnie flew over and snatched it from him.

'This text has been opened!' Bonnie said, reading it quickly. Her heart felt as though it had stopped as the colour drained from her face. 'Oh, God!'

'What is this new secret you're keeping?' Henri said, regaining his cold composure. 'No name on this text, only a phone number.'

Bonnie had never stored Holden's number in the phone memory, but she recognised it just the same. She read the text again. Surely he couldn't be serious?

'If you think you can hide your boyfriend's messages from me, you are sadly mistaken.'

'It's not Max…'

Bonnie's hasty explanation was cut short by a knock at the front door. She froze, staring at Henri in some kind of weird *High Noon* stand-off as they both waited to see who would answer the knock first. Before either of them had a chance, Paige called through, 'I'll get it,' in one of her misguided attempts to appease her dad by appearing to be helpful.

There was a deafening squeal from the doorway.

'OH MY GOD!'

Bonnie ran but wasn't quick enough – Henri shoved her aside and got there first.

Holden Finn was standing in the doorway holding an enormous bunch of red roses. His cap was pulled low over his eyes and he wore sunglasses, but there was no mistaking him.

'WHAT IS THIS?' Henri shouted.

'What the hell are you doing here?' Bonnie gasped.

Paige stared as he removed his sunglasses and looked pleadingly at Bonnie. 'You never replied to my messages, what else was I supposed to do?'

'You've been messaging Holden Finn?' Paige stared at Bonnie in total disbelief.

'No,' Bonnie began, but then stopped as she saw Henri move menacingly towards Holden.

'Henri… No!'

'This… boy… is the reason that you won't take me back?'

'No, it's not what you think…'

But Henri wasn't listening to Bonnie anymore. Holden took a step back.

'I don't want trouble. I'll just leave these and go…?' He put the roses on the step. Henri snatched them up and threw them out into the apartment corridor. Paige grabbed Henri's arm.

'Dad, what are you doing?'

Henri shook her off and shoved Holden in the chest. 'Stay away from my family.'

Then Holden said the worst thing he could possibly have said…

'Listen, *prick*, do you have any idea who I am?'

It was all over before either Bonnie or Paige could do anything to prevent it. Henri's eyes flashed with anger, and he swung at Holden, hitting him with a clean, hard punch that sent him flying out into the corridor, his sunglasses skittering across the marble floor. His head thudded into the wall and he was still.

'OH MY GOD, MUM! DAD KILLED HOLDEN FINN!' Paige screamed.

Bonnie ran to Holden, her heart frozen in panic. Paige followed and Henri stood in the doorway with his hands still clenched into fists, breathing heavily, his nostrils flared. Bonnie gently lifted Holden's head and took off his hat.

'Holden,' she said softly, tapping his face lightly. 'Holden… can you hear me?'

Holden groaned a little but didn't wake.

'Phone for the ambulance, Paige,' Bonnie snapped.

Paige stared at her in shock.

'Paige!' Bonnie commanded, 'Call the ambulance. Now!'

With that, Paige seemed to snap out of her trance and ran for her phone. Bonnie turned her attention to Henri. 'Help me get him into the flat.'

'Why should I?'

'Because, you idiot…' Bonnie snarled, 'you've just knocked out Holden Finn.'

'Who is this *Holden Finn*?'

'The man who has the power to make sure you end up in prison for assaulting him. And believe me,' she continued as she turned back to Holden, tapping his face gently, her voice lower now, 'he probably will, and I'd be sorely tempted to help him out. So if you know what's good for you, you'll at least pretend to be sorry when he comes round.'

Henri stared at Bonnie, incomprehension on his face. But doors opening along the hallway and curious neighbours emerging from their flats spurred him into action. He helped Bonnie pull a still unconscious Holden from the floor and together they dragged him into the flat to wait for the ambulance.

After they had made Holden as comfortable as they could on the sofa, Bonnie ran to the bedroom to fetch some blankets. While she arranged them over Holden, Henri stared at her as though she had turned into an alien.

'What are you doing?'

'He could be in shock,' Bonnie said, 'so I'm keeping him warm.'

Paige came from her bedroom, white faced, and stared down at Holden. 'Oh my God, Mum,' she whispered. 'What the hell is going on?'

'Did you phone the ambulance?' Bonnie asked.

Paige nodded, still staring at the unconscious figure stretched across the sofa.

'Who is this man?' Henri asked in an exasperated tone. 'If this is not the delivery man either, how many men do you have, Bonnie?'

'It's Holden Finn,' Paige said in a dazed voice.

'You keep saying this name! But who is Holden Finn?' Henri demanded, the volume of his voice creeping up.

Paige turned to Bonnie. 'He was here for you, he said so.'

Bonnie sighed. 'It's complicated.'

'So you have two boyfriends?' Henri cut in.

'No… for God's sake, Henri, will you just forget the boyfriend thing for one minute and grow up! You've knocked the poor boy out!' Bonnie snapped.

'He should not have come to our flat with roses for you,' Henri said.

Bonnie stamped her foot. 'That doesn't give you the right to punch his lights out!'

Their argument was cut short by a low groan from the sofa as Holden began to stir. Bonnie knelt beside him. 'Holden,' she said gently, 'Are you okay?'

His eyes slowly opened. He looked at Bonnie but didn't seem as though he was focusing properly. 'Where am I?' he croaked.

'You're in my flat. The ambulance is coming.'

'What for?'

'For you.'

'Have I hurt myself?' Holden asked in a small, dazed voice.

'Um… sort of,' Bonnie said. 'Lie still and don't try to talk.'

Holden's eyes closed again and he seemed to drift back into unconsciousness.

Bonnie turned to Paige. 'How long did the ambulance say they'd be? And Paige, you didn't tell them it's Holden, did you?'

Paige seemed to squirm as Henri watched the exchange in confusion.

'I didn't tell the ambulance people, but I might have just messaged Annabel…'

'Bloody hell!' Bonnie shouted, leaping to her feet. 'You told her Holden was here?'

Paige nodded uncertainly.

'You go and message her again right now and tell her it was a joke!' Bonnie ran a hand through her hair, almost crying with frustration. Why was she the only person here who could see how bad their situation was?

'I can't do that, she'll think I'm an idiot,' Paige pouted.

'You are,' Bonnie yelled. 'Don't you understand that your dad is in enough trouble already? If this gets around, there'll be hell to pay!'

Paige looked as though she would argue for a moment, but finally sloped off to her bedroom again.

Bonnie looked at Henri, who had now sat himself down and was staring at Holden on the sofa. 'I can't believe you'd do this to us.'

Henri shrugged. 'I still don't know who he is.'

'He's incredibly rich and incredibly famous. You're quite possibly the only person on the planet who doesn't know who he is.'

'If that is true, what is he doing here?'

Bonnie put her hands on her hips. She was sick of pussyfooting around Henri, with his demands and uncontrollable jealousy. 'What do you think?'

Paige sidled into the room quietly. Bonnie turned to her.

'Well?'

Paige paused for a moment. 'It kind of might be on Snapchat…'

Bonnie threw her hands in the air. 'Delete it!'

'I can't,' Paige said. 'It kind of might be on loads of different people's stories now.'

Bonnie slumped into an unoccupied armchair. 'That's it then,' she said miserably. 'We're doomed.'

Holden's eyes opened again and this time he lifted his head from the cushion and looked around in bewilderment. 'Bonnie?'

Bonnie jumped up from the chair and knelt on the floor beside him. 'How are you feeling?'

'Weird,' he replied, looking utterly spaced out. He put a hand to his jaw. 'Ow! And in pain too.' His gaze settled on Henri, now standing up and watching them carefully with a dark scowl. Holden seemed to suddenly remember what had happened and his eyes widened. 'Keep that mentalist away from me!'

Bonnie laid a hand on his chest. 'He'll be on his best behaviour from now on.' She threw Henri a warning glance as she spoke.

Paige touched Henri's arm. 'Come on, Dad, let's get a cup of tea.'

'Get Holden a glass of water while you're there, Paige,' Bonnie said.

Holden managed a small smile at Paige, who returned it as she led a reluctant Henri to the kitchen.

Moments later Paige returned with a glass, which she handed to Bonnie.

'How did last night go?' Paige asked Holden in a small, shy voice.

'Last night?' Holden frowned. 'Oh, you mean the tour?'

Paige nodded.

'Great. You didn't get there?'

'We couldn't get tickets.'

Holden gave her a half-smile. 'I bet you could have if your mum had phoned me.'

Bonnie shot Paige a worried glance. She was still uncertain how Paige was going to react to this new and unexpected situation once all the drama of having an injured Holden Finn in their flat was over. Paige simply shrugged.

'I guess she didn't want to use you like that.'

'I guess not,' Holden said quietly, looking at Bonnie, who then put the glass to his lips and helped him to drink some water.

'Go and see if your dad is okay,' Bonnie said to Paige.

Paige hesitated for a moment, looking at them both in turn as if working out some puzzle, and then went to the kitchen.

'She's a good girl,' Bonnie said.

Holden gave her a quizzical look.

'Are you going to press charges?' Bonnie asked in a blunt tone.

'I don't know,' Holden replied with equal frankness.

'Only…' Bonnie began, 'it'd kill Paige to see her dad go through that.'

Holden gazed at her thoughtfully. 'Why didn't you tell me about him?'

'There was nothing to tell. He was missing for two years and then he just turned up one day. We're not back together as such, but we're a family again as far as Paige is concerned.'

'And you're happy?'

'I'm…' Bonnie paused, searching for the right reply. 'I'm content that it's the right thing to do.'

'That means you're not.'

'Leave it, Holden, please.'

'You'd do this for Paige?' he asked shrewdly.

Bonnie nodded. 'She's my daughter. I'd do anything for her.'

Holden gazed at her. 'You know you're amazing.'

'That's silly. You don't know anything about me.'

'I know enough.'

'Holden… you have to forget about me.'

'I can't.'

'You must. Because I'm with Henri now and that is not going to change.'

'You want to be with him?'

'Yes.'

Holden sighed and pushed himself up. 'If that's really what you want, then I'll leave you alone.'

Bonnie's eyes filled with tears. She felt as though she was hurting him so much, but she knew that this infatuation with her was nothing more than just that – it wasn't love that he felt, she was certain of it – and in no time he'd have some supermodel hanging from his arm. 'Yes, it's what I want.'

He traced the shape of her jaw line with a gentle finger and smiled. 'It was fun while it lasted, eh?'

'Yeah, it was in a strange sort of way,' Bonnie laughed through her tears.

'Don't cry, Bonnie Cartwright,' he said, wiping her cheek with his thumb. 'I won't press charges against your caveman in there.'

Bonnie laughed properly now. 'Thank you,' she said, leaning to kiss him lightly.

'Ow!' he said again, holding his jaw, but he was grinning slightly. 'And next time you want tickets for a gig, you make sure you call me, okay?'

They were interrupted by a knock at the front door. Paige raced through from the kitchen to answer it. They could hear voices and then two paramedics came in.

Holden's eyes widened. 'You called an ambulance?' he asked Bonnie in a slightly panicked voice.

'I told you so before,' she replied. 'You were unconscious; I didn't know how badly you were injured.'

'You don't need us?' one of the paramedics asked in an irked tone.

'No…' Holden began.

'Yes,' Bonnie cut in. She turned to Holden. 'Let them check you over.'

'I'm fine.'

'Please, for me…'

Holden looked up at the paramedics, clearly torn.

'Don't worry,' the female paramedic said with a conspiratorial smile, 'we're bound by patient confidentiality rules.'

'I don't care. I don't need checking over.'

'We'll decide that,' the male paramedic replied. 'Let us take a look.'

'NO!' Holden almost shouted.

'Okay,' Bonnie cut in. 'Calm down. You've got to let them do their job.'

Holden hesitated for a moment. 'Okay. But not here.'

'You can come with us and we can sneak you into A&E by a secret entrance,' the female paramedic said. 'We'll get you treated if you need it and make a few phone calls to get you taken home.'

'There are forms we have to fill in, though,' the man added gruffly. 'If you refuse treatment at the incident scene we don't want to be held accountable.'

Holden waved a hand vaguely. 'Whatever…'

'But we can sort it,' the woman said, giving her partner a barely concealed glare.

Holden looked at her gratefully; she clearly knew who he was and what sort of pandemonium his appearance at the hospital would cause, not to mention the embarrassment of being discovered somewhere he obviously wasn't meant to be.

'Perhaps that would be a good idea,' he admitted. 'Bonnie,' he asked, 'I don't suppose you could phone my PA; ask her to arrange for my car to be collected?'

'You left your car on this estate?' Paige squeaked. She exchanged a look with Bonnie. Once word had got across the internet that Holden had been at their flat, the appearance of a car with a personalised number plate nearby would corroborate that fact.

Both Bonnie and Paige seemed to realise this at the same time.

'You'd better give me your keys,' Bonnie said to Holden. 'I'll drive it wherever you need me to.'

One of the paramedics pulled out a treatment case.

'I said not here,' Holden insisted, glancing at the kitchen doorway. 'I'd rather just go straight to the ambulance.'

The ambulance crew hesitated, looking at each other uncertainly for a moment, before the male gave a sigh of defeat.

'At least let me get a wheelchair or something for you.'

'No way, that would draw even more attention.'

The man opened his mouth to argue, but then seemed to realise the futility of it. 'I'll go and get the paperwork from the ambulance. If we're going ahead with this, we'd better document it properly.'

While he was gone, Paige retrieved Holden's hat and glasses from the hallway outside.

'You're probably going to need these.' She handed them over with a small smile.

'And you're going to need these...' Holden said, turning to Bonnie and handing her his car keys. 'And thanks... you know, for everything.'

Bonnie resisted the impulse to raise her eyebrows in surprise as she took the keys from him. Her overly possessive partner had punched him in the face and he was thanking her? Could this day get any weirder?

*

Holden managed to get out of the building with surprisingly little fuss, Bonnie slipping out shortly afterwards to drive his car back to the point arranged with his PA, leaving Paige alone to explain, as best she could, to a thoroughly confused Henri what was going on. Within the hour, Holden had texted Bonnie to say he'd been treated, told there was no serious damage, and a driver was coming to collect him. She could only hope that this would be the end of the whole sorry business, and that Holden would keep his promise not to involve the police.

When she arrived home, Bonnie was horrified to find a group of about twenty teenage girls outside their flat talking to Paige.

'What's going on here?' Bonnie asked. The day had gone from crazy to crazier and all Bonnie wanted was for the dust to settle while she had a quiet cup of tea. And she needed to have a serious heart to heart with Henri too – he had always been volatile, but this tendency to lash out at every man who spoke to her had got a lot worse… and it had to stop.

'Is it true?' one girl asked.

'Is what true?' Bonnie said carefully.

'That he was here?'

'Who?' Bonnie glanced at Paige, who was blushing furiously. 'What's my daughter been telling you?'

'That Holden Finn has been here. That…' The girl stopped as Paige shot her a warning glance.

'Whatever Paige has told you is complete rubbish,' Bonnie said sternly. 'So you can all go home.'

There was a collective groan as they all looked towards Paige, who simply shrugged and looked slightly mortified. Bonnie pushed past them and into the flat.

Henri was sitting at the kitchen table waiting for her. 'I think you need to explain why that man was at our house with flowers.'

'Didn't Paige tell you who he is?' Bonnie said, dropping into another chair and taking her coat off.

'What Paige told me doesn't explain why he was here looking for you.'

'I'm too tired for this now,' Bonnie sighed as she pushed herself away from the table to put the kettle on.

Henri grabbed her wrist. 'Sit down.'

Bonnie pulled her arm free. 'What the hell is wrong with you?'

'You're driving me insane, that is what is wrong with me. You make me think that you want me and then you turn cold when I come near you. Strange men appear from all over the place and claim to be in love with you...' He stared at her, suddenly making her feel chilled to the bone. 'You are meant to be with me.'

Bonnie snatched her coat up from the chair. 'That all ended when you abandoned me. Now if you'll excuse me, I need to go and talk to our daughter.'

*

Bonnie found Paige in her room, lying on her bed and typing on her iPad.

'Have you come to tell me off for dropping you in it?' Paige asked, looking up as she heard Bonnie come in.

'No,' Bonnie said, sitting down next to her on the bed. 'I've come to say sorry.'

Paige sat up. 'What for?'

'I'm sorry that you had to be here when all that madness just happened.'

'It's okay, Mum. I know you couldn't help it.' Paige put the iPad to one side. 'So...' she continued, 'what was going on?'

'Me and Holden...' Bonnie paused. How ridiculous was it going to sound when she told Paige the truth? But there was nothing else she could tell her that wouldn't sound just as ridiculous. 'We sort of had a *thing*.'

'Like a dating thing?'

'Kind of.'

'So he liked you?'

Bonnie nodded and Paige's eyes widened.

'And you liked him?'

'I thought I did at first,' Bonnie replied. She looked thoughtfully at Paige. Her daughter was growing up fast. Perhaps it was finally time to start treating her as an equal, to start confiding in her. She took a deep breath. 'You see, when your dad left us, it hurt me, more than anything ever did before. And I felt like I would never love again. But then there was Holden – this perfect man that I would never have. And if I loved a perfect man I could never have, then he could never hurt me…' She watched as Paige listened intently. 'Does that make sense?'

Paige nodded. 'I suppose so. But then we went to the concert…'

'Yes. And God only knows why, but Holden seemed to take a shine to me that night.' Bonnie carefully edited the story as the memories came back to her. It was one thing treating her daughter as an equal, but some things were not to be shared with anyone else.

'Did you have dates with him?' Paige asked, her dark eyes wide.

'One, sort of date.'

'Just one? Why didn't you carry on seeing him?'

Bonnie shrugged. 'It didn't feel right.'

'It wasn't because Dad came back?'

'No.'

'Was it because of Max?'

'It wasn't because of anyone. I realised that even the most perfect seeming person isn't perfect.'

'Was he horrible?'

'Not horrible… just not right for me. And I wasn't right for him either, he just couldn't see it.'

'Dad was really angry when you'd gone to take Holden's car back.'

Bonnie gave her a half-smile. 'I bet he was.' Her smile faded. 'Are *you* angry with me?'

'For going out with Holden Finn?'

'For not telling you about it.'

Paige grinned. Of all the reactions Bonnie had expected, this was the least likely.

'You think I'm angry about it?' Paige laughed. 'It's amazing! How many girls can say Holden Finn has a crush on their mum?'

*

Exhausted from all the excitement, partly to escape from the continued black looks from Henri, and partly in readiness for work, Bonnie had fallen into bed at around nine and had, against all odds, slept as soon as her head hit the pillow. When the alarm had gone off at six the following morning, it felt as though she had barely climbed into her bed five minutes before.

Yawning and shouting a last warning to Paige that she needed to get her backside out of bed if she was going to make school on time, Bonnie opened the door of the flat to leave for work.

That's when the flashes started. She leapt back in shock as she was confronted by a crowd of people, pointing microphones and Dictaphones at her, taking photos and filming, all shouting at once.

'Bonnie... is it true that you're seeing Holden Finn?'

'Bonnie, what sort of kisser is he?'

'*Daily Mail* here... is it true that your husband and Holden had a fight over you?'

'How long have you been seeing each other?'

'Are you going to get married?'

Bonnie slammed the door shut again and leaned against it, her mind in a whirl. How the hell was she going to get to work? Outside, she could still hear frantic chatter and people calling her name.

She took a deep breath and opened the door again. The noise doubled immediately, flashes popping and people waving in her face for attention. Bonnie held up her hands for quiet but nobody seemed to take any notice. She began to explain, struggling to make herself heard over the din. Finally, she shouted at the top of her voice.

'QUIET!'

A shocked silence fell over the gathering.

'I don't know who has given you this information,' Bonnie began, trying not to show her nerves, 'but it's wrong. I'm not and never have been seeing Holden Finn.'

She paused, waiting for them to disperse, but the din simply began again, the questions louder and more insistent this time.

'Have you slept with him?'

'Did you go on tour with him?'

'What does the future hold for you both?'

'What does your daughter think?'

Bonnie hurried back inside and shut the door again. Sod the common sense approach, this situation called for some creative thinking.

Bonnie paced the hallway, turning the problem over in her mind. But then a slow smile spread across her face as she pulled her phone from her handbag. With a bit of luck her neighbour, Tina, who was always game for an unusual situation, might just be up and dressed and willing to help.

'Hello? Hi Tina… I'm sorry to phone you so early and this is rather a strange request but… you remember yesterday when Henri sort of got into a fight outside in the corridor? Yeah, I know… there's a huge bunch of journalists outside our door and I need a distraction so that I can get to work. I'm sorry I can't explain right now, but I promise to call round with a bottle of wine and fill you in later. Do you think you can spin them some sort of yarn to get them to come to your flat so I can nip out?'

Bonnie ended the call and put an ear against the door. She could just make out the sound of Tina's front door opening, then her call out something about cups of tea and that she knew everything there was to know about Bonnie and the man who called yesterday and before you could say *gullible* there was a rumble of footsteps and it sounded as though they had all gone.

Bonnie cautiously opened the door. She looked out to see two journalists still looking uncertainly at Tina's now closed front door. As soon as they saw Bonnie they made for her, shouting questions again.

Two of them, Bonnie thought. *Now that's odds I can cope with.* And she slammed the front door behind her and sprinted for the car, the two journalists in hot pursuit shouting questions and requests as they ran.

*

The next few days were possibly the most annoying and inconvenient of Bonnie's life. Journalists hounded her at every turn, including while she was at Applejack's (until Fred threatened them with a sweeping brush), at Jeanie's house (until Jeanie threatened them with a sweeping brush) and at home (making Henri wish he knew where their sweeping brush was kept and forcing him to charge at them with a butter knife instead). The only place that Bonnie seemed able to get five minutes' peace was on the toilet, and her visits had been getting longer and longer, something which made Linda howl with laughter, just as she had when Bonnie had unfolded the whole sorry tale.

'It's not funny,' Bonnie had snapped.

'It is from where I'm standing,' Linda replied. 'It's Bonnie Cartwright all over – never one to do things by halves.'

Bonnie had considered a reply, but eventually had to concede that there wasn't one that would make things sound less ridiculous than they already were.

Not only that, but Applejack's had suddenly become the trendy place for teenage girls to be seen – hordes of them crowding in, buying single apples or bananas while they stared at Bonnie, and then hanging around outside to stare some more through the windows. Strangely, Fred wasn't quite so averse to this particular nuisance, probably something to do with the healthy increase in his daily profits. The omnipresent journalists had even, at one point, congregated outside Linda's car, and followed her to the Bounty as she went on a solo sandwich run to spare Bonnie the awkwardness of trying to get out. The tongue lashing they got from Linda made sure that it didn't happen again – an impressive array of swearwords and derogatory names that made even the hardiest of them blush.

It wasn't until Holden himself released a statement denying any kind of relationship with Bonnie and explaining that he had got the impressive bruises on his face from a particularly clumsy round of golf that things began to settle down and the interest gradually waned. Bonnie was happy to see that Holden had kept his promise not to press charges, and seemed to have given up any ideas of their having a relationship. But he had sent a text to thank her for her discretion, to say that he would never forget her, and hoped they could remain friends. This made her smile. At least someone other than Henri cared about her, because Max's lack of texts over that week, considering that she was a high-profile woman named in the middle of a strange and messy love triangle, suggested that he had moved on. Either that or he was so disgusted by her behaviour that he couldn't bring himself to contact her. Whatever his reasons, it looked like the end of the road for them.

On the other hand, Jeanie and Paige had both been so impressed by the idea of Bonnie dating a famous musician (no matter how many times Bonnie wearily reminded them that she hadn't actually dated him at all) that they both secretly enjoyed the inconvenient press intrusion, and were almost disappointed when it stopped.

Chapter Fourteen

Bonnie had never been so relieved to see a weekend looming than she was when the *closed* sign was finally displayed in the door of Applejack's that Saturday evening.

With the coast clear of reporters or silent, staring teenage stalkers, and pretty certain that whatever damage leaving Paige with Henri might cause it couldn't come close to what had already happened that week, Bonnie decided to grab half an hour with her mum before she headed home from work.

Jeanie stood with her hands on her hips, looking critically at a teetering pile of crockery on the kitchen table when Bonnie walked in.

'What's all this?' Bonnie asked. 'More clearing out?'

Jeanie nodded. 'I wondered what you might need, so I thought you could go through it. What you want I'll keep in the cupboards, the rest can go to that Salvation Army charity shop in town.'

Bonnie sighed. 'You want me to do it now? I'm knackered.'

Jeanie raised her eyebrows. 'I'm not surprised after the last few months of creeping around like some double agent. Here was I thinking you were lonely – turns out you'd got men stashed all over the place.'

'Very funny, Mum.' Bonnie took her coat off and hung it on the back of a chair. 'I told you what happened with Holden.'

'And you used to shout at me for *going groupie*, as you used to call it. I think you've trumped anything I got up to backstage.'

'I didn't do it deliberately. Who could ever have seen that situation coming?'

'That's true,' Jeanie mused. 'And I bet your photo is on a few teenage dartboards right now too.'

Bonnie smiled. It wasn't the first time they'd had this conversation; in fact, it seemed to be Jeanie's favourite topic at the moment. But even Bonnie had to see the funny side of it all. And as Holden had replied to her text asking if he felt better without once mentioning the fact that he couldn't remember dance moves or words to songs, she took it as a good sign that he was moving on to pastures new.

Bonnie grabbed the kettle and took it to the sink. She was filling it when the house phone rang out in the hallway.

'I'd better get that, I'm expecting Juan to call,' Jeanie said, running a hand over her hair and flicking her dreadlocks into place as if he could somehow see her.

Bonnie shook her head with a wry smile. Humming to herself as she ran the tap, she wondered silently when her turn would come. Perhaps the best thing for all of them would be a nice quiet end to the year and a well-earned breather.

Jeanie returned a few moments later and her expression was grim. 'That was Paige,' Jeanie said tensely. 'She's been ringing your mobile but you didn't answer. You need to get home, right now.'

Bonnie felt the blood leave her face. She remembered guiltily that she had put her phone on silent for a bit of peace. 'What is it?'

Jeanie was already heading for the hallway. 'I'll come with you,' she called behind her, 'I can tell you on the way.'

*

Paige was sitting on a chair twisting her fingers together, staring at a woman who sat on the sofa opposite. The woman looked to be in her early-to-mid-twenties, blonde, petite, and very pretty. She was cuddling a tiny baby who was sound asleep and wrapped in a thick, powder-blue fleece.

'Mum!' Paige wailed as she leapt up and threw her arms around Bonnie's neck.

Bonnie gave her a fierce hug. She only had the barest of information supplied by Jeanie on the way over, but her daughter's reaction told her that even she knew there was some truth in this new revelation.

'Where's your dad?' Bonnie asked, gently prising Paige's arms from her neck so she could look at her. Paige's cheeks were tracked with tears and her eyes were puffy.

'I don't know,' Paige said. She threw a glance at the woman, who had said nothing at all but simply stared at them, her look a mixture of fear and determination. Paige nodded her head at the stranger. 'There was a knock at the door. I went to get it and *she* asked for Dad. As soon as he saw her, he started shouting that I shouldn't have let her in. Then she told me that the baby...' Paige's breath hitched as she started to cry again, but she swallowed hard and continued, 'is my dad's. She kept asking Dad when he was going home. I told her that Dad *was* home, but she wouldn't listen and just kept going on about it. Then Dad lost his temper and went into the bedroom. He was in there a few minutes, and then he went out. He didn't say a word about where he was going.'

Jeanie shot a look at Bonnie. 'You think he's done a runner?'

'Would you go and check in the wardrobe?'

Jeanie nodded and left them. Bonnie looked again at the silent stranger. She didn't have to ask; she already knew that the woman was telling the truth. Bonnie sat down next to her and peered at the baby.

'How long has this been going on?' she asked quietly.

'He's been living with me for a year,' the woman replied in an even tone, Bonnie's calm seeming to rub off on her. The accent wasn't local, but it was British. Bonnie tried to place it, theories quickly forming in her head as she did so. 'Where was this?' Bonnie asked.

'York.'

'And he was with you until a few weeks ago?'

The woman nodded. So Henri had come straight from York back to Bonnie, not from France at all. It seemed like a reasonable guess.

'Did he say anything about his life before he met you?' Bonnie asked gently with no malice in her voice. 'He's much older than you, I'm guessing. Didn't you wonder where he'd been all those years before? Did it occur to you that he might have children or a partner elsewhere?'

The woman shrugged. 'He said he'd travelled a lot for his job. He said that he'd never settled long enough to start a family. But then he'd come to York to teach French and he moved into my flat because he had just started up and he was waiting for the clients to start coming.'

'That's when you got pregnant?'

As the two women spoke, Paige watched them miserably. Bonnie looked up and caught her eye. She tried to give her an encouraging smile. It had been a weird enough week for her daughter already, without this on top of everything. She had the feeling that Paige's entire world was about to crash in on her. Paige would deal with it either by sinking without trace, or rising above it all stronger and better equipped to fight her way through the emotional minefield that adult life could be. Bonnie desperately hoped it would be the latter option.

Jeanie hurried back into the living room. 'All his stuff has gone,' she said grimly.

The young woman's eyes filled with tears. Bonnie laid a hand on her arm. 'He's not worth it.' The woman looked up and nodded, sniffing hard. 'You want a cup of tea?' Bonnie asked. The woman nodded uncertainly again. 'Sorry,' Bonnie said as Jeanie disappeared to put the kettle on, 'I don't know your name.'

'Lauren,' the woman replied as she cuddled the baby a little closer. 'And this is Zach.'

'Zach, that's a great name,' Bonnie said.

'He's eight weeks old now.' Lauren gave Bonnie a proud if watery smile.

Bonnie paused for a moment, looking at the baby thoughtfully. 'So that means he was only just born when Henri left you.'

Lauren's eyes began to fill again. 'He said he was going to visit his parents in France. He said I couldn't go with him because his mum was ill and it wasn't a good time to introduce me, but that he'd be back soon. When he didn't come I was worried sick because I thought that something had happened to him, but I had no idea where his parents lived and the French authorities couldn't tell me anything.'

It all sounded so familiar. And yet, Bonnie couldn't help but be thankful that Henri had at least stuck around until Paige had been much older than Zach. She thought back to all the times over the years he had said he was going back to France on family visits. Just what *had* he been doing?

'How did you find him?' Bonnie asked, her curiosity piqued.

Lauren gave a wry smile. 'You were all on telly. I saw Henri chasing off some reporters and they mentioned the town of Millrise on the report. Pretty much the first person I spoke to locally told me where you lived.'

'I had no idea I was so famous,' Bonnie said with a smile.

'Well…' Lauren began, suddenly a little shy, as if she was in awe of Bonnie, 'it *was* Holden Finn.'

'I suppose it was,' Bonnie agreed.

From the corner of her eye, Bonnie noticed Paige slip away into the kitchen to join Jeanie. Bonnie guessed that the conversation was one she wasn't quite sure how to deal with. She turned back to Lauren, satisfied that Jeanie would be able to say the right thing to make Paige feel better. 'Have you travelled all the way from York today?' she asked.

Lauren nodded. 'I came by train. I probably should get back soon or I'll miss the last one.'

'Sorry… I don't mean to criticise, but what did you think Henri would do when you got here?'

Lauren's shoulders seemed to sag and she looked down at Zach, still sleeping soundly. 'I don't really know. I just wanted him to tell me what I did wrong.'

'You did nothing wrong. It's just Henri. He left me too, you know, and I didn't know where he was for two years.' She gazed down at the baby. 'I suppose that's one bit of the mystery solved anyway.'

Jeanie came back in, followed by Paige. They'd laid out tea things on a tray which Jeanie now carried.

'We thought it would save disturbing the baby if we brought the tea in here,' Jeanie explained.

Bonnie nodded and smiled.

'You're being so kind,' Lauren said, her eyes filling with tears again. 'I thought you'd go mental when you found me here.'

'Nonsense,' Jeanie said, 'it's not your fault. We should be making voodoo dolls of that bastard and sticking pins in it together, all four of us.'

'If you thought that, why didn't you run off when Henri left?' Bonnie asked Lauren curiously. 'Why not get out before I arrived home?'

Lauren glanced at Paige. 'Your daughter was so upset… And… well, she's Zach's sister really, isn't she? I suppose I thought that maybe, if we could work things out, they could get to know each other one day… I don't have much in the way of family myself…'

Bonnie and Jeanie both turned to Paige, who was still standing at the living room door. The ghost of a smile played about her lips. 'I never thought about it like that,' she said quietly. 'I suppose I have a brother.'

'What do you think?' Bonnie asked.

Paige's smile spread a little. 'I'm not sure. I think it's okay though.'

*

Bonnie and Paige spent Sunday together, crying, discussing, hugging, crying more and generally trying to understand what Henri had done to them. It seemed that Paige had finally learned the hardest lesson of her life so far, and one that Bonnie only wished hadn't been taught in such a heartless and brutal way. Now, Paige understood that people aren't always what they seem, and that even those you trust can let you down.

They heard nothing from Henri, but this time, both Paige and Bonnie agreed that there was no need to chase him down. Lauren was keen that Paige and Zach shouldn't lose touch, and Paige had even seemed hopeful and excited about the prospect of visiting them in York when Lauren had suggested it.

For the first time in two years, on Monday morning Bonnie rang work to tell Fred she was sick, and then phoned Paige's school to tell them that she was sick too. They were glue for each other's souls, and even after the entire Sunday together, Bonnie felt that they needed more time to mend what had broken. So she went out to the shops and bought as much terrible food as she could, and then got back into her pyjamas, pulled a mattress and duvet into the sitting room, where she and Paige lounged for the entire day, watching TV, eating sweets and talking until they were both hoarse. In a strange way, Bonnie felt a kind of deep contentment by the end of it all, and she sensed that Paige felt it too, as though their shared pain had brought them closer together.

Perhaps there would be a silver lining to this stinking great black storm cloud after all.

*

On Tuesday Bonnie was back at work. A worried Linda had called the flat on the previous evening, and Bonnie had filled her in on the details. By the time she had spent an hour on the phone, she was sick of hearing herself talk about Henri and what he had done.

When Bonnie arrived at Applejack's, Linda had a big bunch of flowers and an even bigger hug waiting for her. Bonnie could not find the words to tell Linda how grateful she was that she still had some people who would never let her down. She thought about Lauren and Zach and only hoped they would be as lucky.

After Fred had read the riot act about Bonnie's absence, which she took remarkably well in the circumstances, she went through to the stockroom to help Linda pull out the cold stock. In a strange way, it was good to see things settle down to normality, and Bonnie was almost looking forward to a dull week at work. Just as they were about to start, the knock came at the back door.

'I'll get it,' Linda said, practically bouncing over to the door and yanking it open wide. 'Hello stranger!' Linda stepped back to reveal Max, grinning awkwardly.

'I thought it was about time Rob stopped having all the fun and I got out a bit myself.'

Bonnie watched as Max came in and shook the rain from his hair. She didn't speak – her heart was thumping too fast and too loudly.

'This calls for a celebration cuppa,' Linda said with a broad smile. 'I might even crack open the biscuits.'

'I have missed your tea, Lind.' Max was speaking to Linda, but he never took his eyes off Bonnie.

'Right…' Linda said in a significant tone, 'I'll get the kettle on.'

As soon as she had gone into the kitchenette, Max spoke. 'I heard about what happened,' he said in a low voice.

'Which bit?' Bonnie asked, trying to ignore the fact that her heart was ready to burst at the sight of him. Despite how terribly she had missed him, the violence of her emotions now was a complete shock.

'Henri's little surprise package.'

'Oh. I suppose Linda told you.'

'She might have mentioned it on the phone last night.'

Bonnie threw a glance at the doorway where Linda was busying herself with teabags and mugs and trying to look as though she wasn't listening.

'I just wanted to see for myself that you were okay.'

'I'm fine.'

'Only… your last text…'

'What text?' Bonnie frowned.

'You said you loved him. I suppose you're pretty cut up now.'

Bonnie shook her head slowly, realisation suddenly dawning on her. 'I'm beginning to realise what an idiot I am. I never sent any such message, but I have a feeling Henri might have done it for me…'

'Oh…' Max replied. 'Well… I thought…'

They were silent for a moment, the only sounds those of Fred grumbling loudly about something in the front of the shop and the kettle bubbling in the kitchen.

'So… Henri has gone for good?' Max asked finally.

'Looks like it.'

'You and Paige are okay with it?'

'It's hurt Paige. That was one lesson she could have been spared from. But I think that she understands now just what sort of a man he is.'

'You wouldn't have him back?'

'No.'

Max smiled slightly. 'What about Holden Finn?'

Bonnie couldn't help a little laugh. 'So you heard about that too.'

'*Everyone* heard about that.' He gave her a lopsided grin. For a moment, he looked like the old Max, the one who hadn't had his heart pulled inside out by Bonnie and her mixed up life. She wished they could rewind time somehow and get back to when they were just like that – able to laugh and joke together with no awkwardness. She didn't suppose things could ever go back to that now. Henri had gone, but perhaps the damage his reappearance had done to her and Max was beyond repair.

Linda came out and handed them both a mug. 'Are you friends now?' she asked with a devious grin.

'Oh no… 'Max said, stepping back from her and making the sign of a cross with his fingers, 'don't you dare think about locking us in the fridge again.'

Linda laughed. 'I wouldn't use the same trick twice, I'm not that stupid.'

'So you are planning something?' Bonnie asked, trying to look stern but hardly able to keep the smile from her lips.

'Maybe…' Linda grinned.

Bonnie glanced at Max. She wondered how happy he would be if Linda *did* lock them in the fridge together. But he said no more on the subject, and simply put his cup on the bench before making for the back door.

'I'd better move it; those carrots won't bring themselves in.'

*

Bonnie wondered whether Max's appearance at the shop was simply a one-off, and expected to see his surly assistant, Rob, back the following morning, but Max turned up again. Although he appeared to be his usual wise-cracking self, Bonnie could sense the tension that hummed in the air between them. Linda seemed to be watching them carefully too, but if Bonnie and Max expected her to step in and engineer some trick to get them back together, they were both to be disappointed. Whether she had decided that her interference last time had been ill-advised, or whether she just couldn't be bothered again, she did nothing.

Weeks passed, and Christmas came and went. Max was a regular again and Bonnie felt a curious mix of embarrassment, awkwardness, affection and relief. Their relationship slowly began to transform and, although they didn't share the easy banter that they had once done, it was getting close. As they closed the shop on Christmas Eve, Max rushed in with three bottles of wine, as he did every year, handing Fred and Linda theirs with a jovial greeting and Bonnie's with an awkward, hopeful smile.

'Happy Christmas, Bon,' he said.

'I didn't get you anything,' Bonnie replied, blushing a little.

Max shrugged. 'Maybe next year, eh?' he replied before hurrying out onto the windswept street.

Jeanie decided that she was going to move at the end of January so Bonnie and Paige spent a quiet Christmas with her, knowing that next year, everything would be different for the three of them, wherever they decided to spend it.

Lauren sent a Christmas gift box for Paige from Zach – a silver framed photo of him, a bottle of perfume and a nail varnish set – which Paige scowled at, though Bonnie could tell that she was secretly pleased. One morning shortly before Christmas, another parcel containing an anonymous gift arrived for both Bonnie and Paige – an incredibly expensive watch each. They both had a fairly good idea who had sent them, but neither of them said a word about it. So long as the gift didn't come attached to a popstar boyfriend, Bonnie was happy with that. Not that it was likely – the last she had read in the papers, Holden was now dating a singer from an up-and-coming teen band called Love Note. Nothing arrived from Henri – not a card, not one solitary gift, not even a phone call to Paige. It was as though he had never been back at all. And Bonnie was pretty happy with that too.

Chapter Fifteen

It was a bright, frosty Tuesday morning in mid-January when Max knocked as he always did, but instead of his usual carefree demeanour, he wore a deep frown and seemed to be steadying himself against the doorframe. Bonnie clapped a hand over her mouth when she saw that he looked so ill he was almost grey.

'What on earth are you doing working?' she squeaked. 'You look terrible.'

'Someone's got to do it,' he said gruffly. 'I'll be okay, it's just a stomach ache. Probably ate something dodgy last night.'

Bonnie stepped aside to let him in. 'What did you eat last night?'

'Toast.'

'And?'

'Just toast. I wasn't hungry.'

'That doesn't sound very dodgy,' Bonnie chided. 'For God's sake, come and sit down; me and Linda can get the stock off your van.'

'No way,' Max said, gently moving her arm from his. 'I'm not having Fred on my case about his staff doing my work. I'm honestly fine.'

But the violent shudder that suddenly doubled him over told Bonnie that Max was far from fine.

'Lind…' Bonnie shouted. 'Come and give me a hand…'

Linda emerged from the fridge, wiping her hands down her tabard. 'God, Max,' she gasped as her gaze settled on him, 'what the hell were you drinking last night?'

Max gave her a weak smile. 'I wish it was down to drink. I've had this stomach ache all morning. Went to bed okay and woke up at about four o'clock in agony.'

'Have you been to the loo?' Linda asked practically.

'Yeah, thanks, nurse,' Max replied, clutching at his abdomen as a film of sweat began to form on his brow. 'I'll be fine, I just need to get the deliveries done this morning and then I can go to bed and sleep it off.' He gritted his teeth and stumbled against the wall. 'Bloody hell!' he cried, doubling over again.

'Max!' Bonnie led him to the bench to sit. 'You need to go home, right now.'

'He needs to go to hospital,' Linda said bluntly, 'never mind home.'

Bonnie made him sit, real fear beginning to grip her as she faced Linda. 'What do you think?'

Linda glanced at him. He now had his head almost on his knees, holding onto his stomach and groaning. 'Appendix,' Linda said. 'I'd bet my life on it.'

Bonnie's eyes widened. 'Are you sure?'

'John's brother had it and he was exactly the same. You stay with him and I'll phone the ambulance.'

Bonnie rubbed an awkward hand on Max's damp back. It seemed such a pointless thing to do and was clearly giving him no comfort at all, but she had to do something. She was so rigid with fear that she could hardly think straight. Max was almost oblivious to her now as he groaned and clutched at his stomach, mumbling words to himself that made no sense at all.

'Max,' Bonnie whispered into his ear. 'Max…'

There was no reply. She rubbed his back again, then stroked a hand over his burning forehead before kissing him gently on his damp cheek. 'I can't lose you now… not like this. You just tell that bloody appendix of yours to hold on for a bit longer because…' Bonnie felt tears blurring her vision, but she wouldn't let them fall. It was Max who should be crying now, not her. She swallowed hard. 'I don't want to lose you. If anything happens I'll never forgive myself for not telling you what I should have told you a long time ago…' Bonnie paused. 'Max, you great daft dolt, I –'

'Ambulance is on its way,' Linda said, rushing in.

Bonnie sniffed back her tears and gave a strained smile. 'That's good. You told them to be quick?'

'I told them to stop off at Tesco first to pick me a loaf up… Of course I told them to be quick!' Linda snapped. She glanced at Max, who seemed to have become even worse in the last couple of minutes, and then back at Bonnie. 'I think we're going to need a miracle, though.'

*

Three long hours later, Max stirred and opened his eyes. The doctor who'd performed his surgery had told Bonnie that, under the circumstances, it had gone well, but the appendix had already burst by the time Max had arrived at A&E. Another half an hour and he would have died. This meant the possibility of many post-surgery complications in the weeks to come. For now, Bonnie was content that he was alive, and her heart leapt as his gaze flitted around the hospital room, as if trying to work out some complicated puzzle, before coming to rest on her.

'Hello.' She smiled.

He didn't reply for a long time, but simply watched as she smoothed his hair from his forehead and stroked his hand. When there was still no sound from him, she busied herself pouring a glass of water, which she left in readiness on the cabinet beside his bed and then straightened out his sheets. It wasn't that any of these things needed doing, but keeping occupied was the only way to stop herself from crying.

'I'm in hospital?' Max asked finally.

Bonnie nodded. 'You were unconscious when we got here. In fact, you were out of it by the time the ambulance arrived at the shop.'

'Ambulance?'

'Lights, sirens and everything.'

'Kind of embarrassing…' he croaked.

Typical Max, thought Bonnie, no matter how serious the situation was, he'd always try to make light of it. 'We'll forgive you this once.' She squeezed his hand gently. 'I didn't know how to contact your parents or anything, so I'm afraid it's just me here for now.'

Max gave her a tired smile. 'I don't mind. Thank you.'

'It's okay.'

Max's eyes began to close again. 'Don't leave me, Bon,' he murmured.

'I won't,' Bonnie said, her eyes filling with the tears that kept threatening to fall. 'Not ever.'

And as Max went back to sleep, she finally wept.

Chapter Sixteen

Bonnie stamped her feet as she waited at the glossy black door. It had taken her a while to find the right street, tucked away as it was at the far end where the Waterlands housing estate met nearby farmland. Max had warned her it was tricky to locate, but even with his directions, it had taken her a frustrating half hour longer than she had anticipated. She tried to breathe slowly. Getting herself in a flap was not going to make her useful to anyone and Max needed all the help he could get.

Max's house was almost brand new – period-styled, exclusive and detached on a corner plot overlooking a broad expanse of empty fields. The cul-de-sac was quiet and peaceful. His garden was green, but bare and functional – the odd easy-care shrub breaking up the sweeping lawn but little in the way of colour. Bonnie had half expected him to have a vegetable plot and a goat tied up… Perhaps they were round the back, she mused.

Just as she was wondering whether he had heard her knock, the door opened. He looked tired and drawn, his skin, if possible, paler than it had been during his time in hospital, but his face lit up as he gave her a weak smile.

'I didn't think you were going to make it.'

Bonnie's tension evaporated and she returned his smile with one of her own. 'Nurse Cartwright reporting for duty.'

Max shuffled painfully into the hallway, allowing Bonnie to follow him. She wondered whether to help him back to his living room, but in the time she took hesitating, he had veered into a doorway off the hall and already dropped into a chair with a heavy sigh.

'Sorry,' he said ruefully. 'I'd have baked a cake but… y'know…'

Bonnie took off her coat and laid it on the arm of the sofa. 'Don't be daft. I just wanted to see how you were. It's me that should be looking after you.' She ran an appraising eye over him. 'When was the last time you had a drink?'

'G&T for breakfast,' he said, the ghost of a cheeky grin appearing.

'But you've got people who can come in and help you?' Bonnie asked, ignoring the quip.

Max sighed. 'People have got their own lives, their own worries. Everyone I know works or has family commitments. It's bad enough that I'm expecting the warehouse staff to keep everything ticking over at work without getting people involved at home. I'll be absolutely fine.'

Bonnie looked at him sternly. 'Yeah, sure you will. Now what do you want for your dinner?'

*

'Max will be far too ill to come,' Bonnie told Linda for the third time. 'He's still recovering from a burst appendix, remember.'

'He'll be okay,' Linda replied sagely, ignoring Bonnie's warning, as she had done every time it was issued.

They were sitting in Linda's brand new conservatory. The smell of fresh paint still clung to the walls, and the windows, with their stark white frames, overlooked a new decked patio area. Linda had insisted that they take their mugs of coffee in there as they planned Jeanie's leaving party. She checked over the list again. Without looking up from it, Linda asked carelessly, 'Have you told Max any of this stuff you told me?'

'Like he's going to give me a second chance,' Bonnie replied. Her friendship with Max had grown stronger than ever since his illness, but Bonnie was convinced now that she had blown her chances of anything more. She didn't blame Max; she blamed herself, and had to be content with what they now had.

'I think you'd be pleasantly surprised,' Linda replied airily. 'He's never stopped being nuts about you, as far as I can see.'

'I'm just glad he's okay,' Bonnie said. 'And that he's talking to me again.'

'He was talking to you before.'

'Not properly, like he is now.'

'He hasn't got much choice when you visit every day, has he?' Linda looked up with a wry smile. 'If I didn't know he was still recovering from his operation, I'd think you two were having it away or something.'

'Well,' Bonnie excused, colouring. 'There's nobody else to check on him, is there? Not since his mum and dad went back to France. Anything could happen to him while he's all alone in that house.'

'He's not that ill now,' Linda remarked. 'Personally, I think he's milking it so that you'll carry on going round.'

Bonnie frowned but Linda cut off any argument she was about to make.

'Speaking of France,' she asked, 'still no word from *Le Grand Dick*?'

Bonnie laughed. 'No, thank God.'

'How about Hot Holden?'

'He's all loved up now with a girl from another band. She's as empty headed as they come by all accounts but she seems sweet enough.'

'That was one crazy year,' Linda remarked as she sipped her coffee.

'It was,' Bonnie said with a distant smile, 'but this year is going to be nice and quiet.'

'That's what you think.'

'Now, don't be getting any ideas at this party.' Bonnie wagged a finger at Linda. 'No locking me in fridges or getting me so drunk I'm trying to snog your garden gnomes.'

'Moi?' Linda put on a shocked tone.

'Come on, then,' Bonnie said, tapping the list with her finger, 'let's get this sorted some time this weekend.'

'So…' Linda went back to the page where hastily scribbled notes vied for her attention. 'Your mum has let all her friends know it's at my house?'

Bonnie nodded. 'Friends – check.'

'Paige is doing music…'

'She's putting together a playlist on her iPod of all Mum's favourite stuff.' Bonnie grinned. 'As you can imagine, she's loving every minute of that.'

'Serves her right for making me listen to terrible music every time I come round to your flat.' Linda scribbled on the paper. 'Music and friends… I'll sort the food out.'

'I can help with that.'

'I've watched you make butties, Porthole Jim,' Linda said. 'I'll take care of the food. You can go on a booze run and do balloons and stuff.' Bonnie was silent and Linda looked up at her. 'What?'

'I can't thank you enough for doing this for my mum. You're so good to me. I really don't know what I'd do without you.' Bonnie's voice began to tremble slightly. 'I don't know what I'm going to do without my mum either…'

Linda dropped the list and pen onto the rattan table and put an arm around Bonnie. 'You're going to be just fine,' she said gently. 'Your mum is going to Spain, not Saturn. And you know that I'll always be here for you. We're mates, and that's what mates do.'

Bonnie looked up and tried to smile. 'I know you're right. It's just that whenever Mum talked about it, I felt like it would never really happen. And now it's almost time for her to go.'

'Yep. It's hard but you're going to have to get used to the fact that things will be different now. But Paige is not a baby anymore and hopefully, Henri is finally out of your life, so maybe things will be easier in a lot of ways too.' Linda squeezed her shoulder. 'And there's all those lovely free holidays to look forward to as well.'

'You're right, as always,' Bonnie sighed.

*

Bonnie and Paige arrived at Linda's house early to set up the music and unload the booze from her car. They had been a little surprised that Jeanie had made an excuse to come later by herself when Bonnie had offered to pick her up on the way, but Jeanie had seemed adamant that they go on without her. Linda was already dressed in a sequined black top and palazzo pants, her hair piled elegantly on her head. Bonnie smiled to herself – if Linda's other parties were anything to go by, at the end of the evening that elegant hair would be hanging around Linda's face in sweaty ropes and she'd be wearing a pair of plastic boobs over her own as she staggered drunkenly around the house singing *My Old Man's a Dustman*.

'You look lovely,' Bonnie said as she kissed Linda lightly on the cheek.

'Ta, ducky, so do you.' Linda smiled. 'And Paige... wow!'

Paige had opted for understated elegance too, as opposed to her usual jeans and t-shirt or tiniest hotpants available. She wore a short, ditsy flowered dress, fitted at the bodice and flaring out from the waist. It showed off perfectly her newly budding curves. The addition of opaque tights had made the dress look classy, rather than tarty, and Bonnie's heart had almost burst with pride when she saw how beautiful her daughter looked. Bonnie herself had gone for a tried-and-trusted number – her forest green vintage dress. She had wanted to buy something new but in the end decided that she couldn't justify the expense, and it wasn't like anyone was going to be there that she needed to impress.

Paige gave Linda an embarrassed but pleased grin. 'Thanks, Linda.'

'Everything is done,' Linda said with obvious pride.

'Blimey, you don't mess about, do you?' Bonnie said as they followed her into the kitchen where plate upon plate of bright and tempting finger foods lined the surfaces.

'Mum went to Iceland,' Linda grinned.

Bonnie laughed and went to inspect a plate of chicken kebabs. 'I think mum cooked these from scratch! They look amazing, Lind. I wish I had your catering skills.'

'Well, when you live to party like me, you have time to practise. Unlike some of us who are too busy chasing pop stars around town…'

Bonnie grinned. That particular standing joke between her and Linda was one that was likely to take a long time to be forgotten. It was funny, but Bonnie didn't mind it so much now, in fact, she had begun to look back on her encounters with Holden almost fondly. They had done a lot to change her life in some ways, and for the first time in many long months, Bonnie actually felt happy and content with her lot. She had begun to realise that happiness could be found in many places, and you didn't always need a man to make it happen.

'Mum is coming later by taxi.'

'How come?' Linda asked as she popped a cherry tomato into her mouth.

Bonnie shrugged. 'She just said she wasn't ready and for me to go on without her. She wouldn't hear of me waiting.'

'Who's coming tonight?' Paige asked.

'Your nan's crowd from Leathers all said they'd be here. Some people she used to work with at the tyre factory… Fred even said he might call for an hour. And Stavros is coming…' Linda winked.

'Stav? But he hardly knows my mum.'

'I know,' Linda said, 'but I thought it would keep John on his toes to see that another bloke fancies me.' Paige's mouth fell open and Linda laughed. 'You've got a lot to learn about men, young Paige.'

'I'm beginning to see that,' Paige said.

There was no mention of Max and Bonnie didn't push it. She had seen him earlier in the week, but with the last-minute preparations for her mum's departure, there hadn't been much time to get round as often as she had been. And at that last visit, although he was brighter and had made coffee for her for the first time, instead of the other way around, it was obvious that he was still too ill to be going out anywhere. Bonnie couldn't shake a small, needling feeling of disappointment all the same.

*

An hour later the first guests started to arrive. For a short while, Bonnie began to feel as though she was in an episode of *This is Your Life* as people that she hadn't seen for many years began to pile into Linda's spacious living room. Linda had removed as much furniture as was practical, and pushed the sofas back against the walls, to make as much floor space as possible. Now the room was easily as big as the function room of the local pub where they had first considered having the party. But Linda's house was far more welcoming and Jeanie had been so touched by Linda's offer that she agreed enthusiastically as soon as Bonnie had relayed it to her. There had been much oohing and aahing at Paige, and embarrassing tales of things she had done as a younger child, things that Paige couldn't remember and suspected many of her grandmother's old friends were making up. Still, she did her best to listen politely and smiled where she thought she ought to. Bonnie was certain that she would be grumbling later at home, but was just glad Paige was behaving herself for now.

The last expected guests arrived with no sign of the guest of honour, and Bonnie was about to phone her mum when there was another knock at the door. It went unheard by Linda, who was involved in relaying an anecdote about the time John broke his toe in a hilarious swimming pool incident in Turkey to a group of ageing rockers, and so Bonnie went to answer it.

Jeanie stood in the porch, smiling awkwardly, on the arm of a man.

'This is Juan,' she said, with uncharacteristic shyness. 'Juan, this is my daughter, Bonnie.'

Bonnie stood at the door, staring stupidly at the pair of them. The moment had caught her completely by surprise. 'When... what... how did you get here?'

'They do have this invention called the airplane,' Jeanie laughed.

Bonnie shook herself and stepped aside to let them in.

'I am pleased to meet you,' Juan said. 'I have heard much about you.'

His accent was strong, but his English perfect, and he had a pleasing baritone to his voice that was almost soothing. Bonnie instantly felt at ease in his presence. She offered a hand to shake but he pulled her toward him and kissed her lightly on both cheeks. As he stepped back, she took a moment to appraise him. He was a little on the chubby side, but in a way that looked cuddly and comforting rather than fat, his shoulder length hair was thick and wavy but steel grey and his dark eyes were full of kindness. Bonnie could see straight away why her mum had trusted him so much at that first meeting, and she instantly relaxed. If first impressions were anything to go by, Jeanie was going to be very happy indeed. This was the best gift her mum could have given her before she left, and it seemed that both Jeanie and Juan had understood the need for Bonnie to meet him before they started their new lives together in Spain; for Bonnie's peace of mind it meant so much.

'It's so wonderful that you could come,' Bonnie said warmly. 'Come and meet everyone else.'

A great cheer erupted from the gathering as Jeanie and Juan walked in, and Jeanie was bombarded with greetings and hugs. Juan looked slightly overwhelmed at first as Jeanie's curious friends fired questions at him, but he soon seemed to relax and was chatting easily amongst them in no time.

Paige took this as her cue to fire up the music and as Bon Jovi kicked in to *Livin' on a Prayer* another cheer went up. Paige rolled her eyes, but then shot a glance at Bonnie, who gave her a thumbs up which turned her frown into a grin.

Paige had cautiously greeted Juan as soon as the music was set up, and then told Bonnie in confidence that he looked like an absolute loser and that, in her opinion, Jeanie would be back home in no time and the whole party would have been pointless. Bonnie listened patiently, but then caught a small smile from her daughter as, a few minutes later, Juan accepted a drink from her and called her beautiful. Paige was just being Paige, and she would come around soon enough. It had been a long time since Bonnie had seen her mum look this happy and radiant, and she quite clearly adored Juan. From the way he looked at her, it seemed the feeling was mutual.

Nine o'clock came. Bonnie and Paige were about the only sober people in the room by now. Paige's iPod was doing most of the DJ duty for her, and so she sat on a sofa with her head leaning on Bonnie's shoulder, watching the other guests get drunker and more rowdy.

'Jeanie's friends are mental,' Paige observed in a bewildered tone.

Bonnie stroked her daughter's hair. 'They are. But in a good way.'

'What do you think of Juan?'

'I think he seems nice,' Bonnie said carefully. 'Do you still think he's a loser?'

Paige shrugged slightly as they watched Juan twirl a laughing Jeanie on the makeshift dance floor that Linda's living room had become. 'Maybe he's not so bad.' She suddenly lifted her head from Bonnie's shoulder and cocked it to one side. 'Was that a knock at the door?'

Bonnie listened but couldn't hear anything over the music and chatter. 'I don't think so.'

Paige's head went back to Bonnie's shoulder again. 'I just thought I heard something.'

'Nobody else is meant to be coming tonight,' Bonnie replied thoughtfully. She glanced around the room. 'Unless it's Stavros, of course, but I wouldn't have thought he'd be coming this late… or Fred, but I don't think he's sociable enough.'

Juan came over with Jeanie trailing behind. 'Paige…' he called, rolling Paige's name out with his glorious accent, 'come and dance with us, *senorita*…'

'Not bloody likely,' Paige grumbled, clinging onto Bonnie's arm.

'Bonnie, you dance,' Juan said, turning his attention to her instead.

'I'm only coming if Paige does,' Bonnie laughed.

Jeanie grabbed Bonnie's hand and pulled her up, and in turn, Bonnie grabbed Paige's and pulled her up too. As they reached the middle of the throng, Paige protesting loudly that she didn't dance, and especially not to *this crap*, the song changed and everybody started to roar with laughter as Bonnie Tyler began to sing *I Need a Hero*.

'Ha ha,' Jeanie shouted at Paige, 'you remembered!'

'I wish she bloody hadn't,' Bonnie said, hiding her face as everyone started to grin in her direction. 'Bane of my life, that woman.'

'She's brilliant,' Jeanie shouted, grabbing Bonnie to hug her, 'and so are you!'

As Jeanie let go and Bonnie started to dance awkwardly, far too sober not to feel self-conscious, there was a loud rap at the living room window.

'I told you someone was knocking,' Paige called to Bonnie.

'Go and tell Linda,' Bonnie said.

Paige was only too happy to have an excuse to stop dancing and went to find the party host while Bonnie was twirled around by an inebriated Juan.

Moments later, Linda came back into the room with a wicked grin. Bonnie stopped mid-twirl. She could feel the blood rush to her face and her pulse suddenly race as Max's gaze settled on her. She should have been laughing, as others were, at the fact that he had turned up in full white American naval uniform, but she wasn't. She could only stare.

He had lost weight through his illness, but his now trim figure buttoned up in the suit looked incredibly sexy. She had been used to seeing him slope around in pyjamas and track suit trousers since he'd been in hospital, but now he was clean and groomed and looked healthy. It was like a scene from a film, and if he had come and swept her into his arms at that moment, Bonnie would gladly have let him. She would have kissed him until the end of time.

But instead of striding across the dance floor and sweeping Bonnie up, Max threw a murderous glare at Linda, who simply laughed and went off to join John on the dance floor. Bonnie Tyler was still singing about her hero as Max made his way towards his Bonnie.

'I didn't think you'd come,' she said, still amazed by the sight of him.

He pulled off his cap and mussed his hair. 'I wasn't going to, but then Linda persuaded me at the last minute.'

From the corner of her eye, Bonnie caught Paige staring at Max too, grinning broadly.

'Did she now?' Bonnie asked, shaking herself from her stupor and looking Max up and down meaningfully.

'She told me it was bloody fancy dress, didn't she? I wasn't going to bother but then she offered to go and get me something to wear from the hire shop.'

Bonnie giggled. 'It could have been worse; she could have got you Scooby Doo or something.'

'It's not funny. Wait till I get hold of her.' He shrugged as he looked down at himself. 'I have a feeling that this was a very deliberate choice, though,' Max added, unable to prevent himself smiling a little now.

'I never told her about my man in uniform fetish, honest,' Bonnie said.

'Oh… so you *do* have a man in uniform fetish?' Max replied impishly.

'I didn't think so until tonight…' Bonnie gazed at him. This, standing right in front of her, was the old Max, *her Max*, the one she had missed so desperately. 'Come on,' she said, taking his hand, 'I suppose you're allowed a drink now you're out?'

'I'll need one to forget the fact that I'm wearing this ridiculous outfit.'

'I don't know why you still swallow everything Linda tells you,' Bonnie said as they made their way to the quieter, cooler kitchen. 'You know how she loves to wind you up.'

'Well,' he said ruefully, 'she did warn us that she hadn't given up on matchmaking just yet.'

Bonnie grabbed a can of lager from the fridge and handed it to him. The kitchen was empty, the plates of food almost reduced to crumbs and the leftovers of the less popular dishes.

'Don't worry.' Bonnie grinned. 'There'll be plenty of opportunity for revenge.' Her grin faded as she found her gaze drawn to the gold buttons fastened over his lean torso.

'Are you alright?' Max asked, taking her sudden lapse into silence as distress.

She looked up into his clear blue eyes and nodded. 'Never been better, actually.'

'The party looks like it's been good,' he commented as he cracked open his beer.

'It has,' Bonnie said absently. Her mind was not on the party at all. She was about to take the biggest gamble of her life, and right now, she was wondering whether it was the most inspired or the stupidest thing she'd ever do. All she knew, as she found herself lost in Max's eyes, was that she had never been more certain of what she really wanted. She loved Max. She had loved him for a long time. It was simply amazing that it had taken her so long to realise it, and she could only hope that all the idiotic things she had done over the previous months hadn't ruined things between them forever.

She laid a tentative hand on his chest, and even through the starched uniform, she could feel the solid beat of his heart. It seemed to quicken just a little as he gave her a quizzical look. He opened his mouth to speak but she laid a finger over his lips.

'Don't say anything. Not one word until I've done this, and then you can tell me what you think.' Bonnie's own pulse was racing. She wasn't drunk, but she felt suddenly lightheaded as she reached to kiss him.

As she pulled away, Max's eyes were still closed. When he opened them, a mix of surprise and lust reflected back at her. 'I thought…'

'I know,' Bonnie said quietly. 'So did I. But over the last few weeks I've had time to figure out what's important.' She stepped away from him, her gaze never leaving his. 'So, what do you think?'

He put his beer down carefully and leaned against the worktop. 'You're sure you're not drunk?'

'I'm driving.'

'Hmmm, so I'm safe to do this and you won't forget in the morning…' He pulled her close and grazed his lips over hers.

'Quite safe,' she whispered.

'Okay,' he said, 'what about this?'

He kissed her again, harder, deeper this time, his hand finding the nape of her neck and then moving up into her hair. She sighed, her body melting against his, the warm scent of him intoxicating, the explosion in her gut sending her senses wild with desire. Everything else was forgotten – there was only this perfect moment, and this perfect feeling, here and now, a moment that seemed like it would never end.

They only stopped kissing when Bonnie suddenly became aware that they were not alone. Grudgingly, she parted from him and they both looked around.

Standing at the doorway of the kitchen was a small crowd, including Jeanie and Juan, Linda and John, and Paige. Linda started clapping her hands and chanting.

'*Duh, duh, duh, another one bites the dust…*'

Howling with laughter, the rest of them joined in, stamping their feet and clapping, singing, very badly, the words to the Queen song. Only Paige folded her arms, scowling.

'Oh my God, Mum,' she said as the ribbing finally died down, 'that's so gross!'

Bonnie wrapped her arms around Max's torso and nuzzled into him. 'Gross or not, I'm afraid you're going to have to get used to it.'

Linda let out a squeal and clapped her hands excitedly. 'I knew the uniform would do it!'

'About that…' Max pretended to frown sternly at her, but Linda only laughed.

'I'll take payment in cheques or visa, or good old pounds sterling,' she quipped.

Bonnie looked up at Max and he kissed her lightly on the nose.

'Bloody hell,' Linda said, rolling her eyes, 'you can do better than that. Kiss her like you really mean it!'

Bonnie blushed furiously as Max laughed. 'I'm saving that for later.'

And then Linda started the chanting again: '*Kiss her, kiss her, kiss her…*'

Max looked at Bonnie and shrugged. 'I'd be an idiot to refuse an order like that.'

He kissed her again, and this time Bonnie didn't care who was watching.

A Letter from Tilly

I want to say a huge thank you for choosing to read *The Time of My Life*. If you did enjoy it, and want to keep up to date with all my latest releases, just sign up at the following link. Your email address will never be shared, and you can unsubscribe at any time.

www.bookouture.com/tilly-tennant

I'm so excited to share this reworked edition of *Hopelessly Devoted to Holden Finn*, now titled *The Time of My Life*, with you, and I don't mind saying that editing it again after all these years brought a little tear to my eye! This book means so much to me – it was the very first Tilly Tennant book to be published and a story I loved telling.

I hope you loved *The Time of My Life*, and if you did I would be very grateful if you could write a review. I'd love to hear what you think, and it makes such a difference helping new readers to discover one of my books for the first time.

I love hearing from my readers – you can get in touch on my Facebook page, through Twitter, Goodreads or my website.

Thank you!
Tilly

tillytennant

@TillyTenWriter

www.tillytennant.com

Acknowledgements

The Time of My Life started out as an experiment, which doesn't sound like a very good way to start a novel, but as I'd never written anything with the intentions of trying to be funny before or, for that matter, anything that was about ordinary folk, the truth has to be told. I'd written about fantastical adventures and far-off worlds, I'd written about the past and the future, I'd written about ghosts and aliens and I'd even written about love, but I'd never simply looked at the world around me and thought, there are stories to be told here. That is, until Holden popped into my head.

As most writers will tell you, there are some stories that refuse to stay in your head, no matter how you try to ignore them, and *The Time of My Life* was one of those. I didn't know if anyone would like it and I didn't even know if I'd end up liking it, but this became the book that would change my life. This was the book that got me my first agent, and this was the book that launched a new career in a genre I now absolutely love writing. I have a lot to thank Holden, Bonnie and Max for.

There are people I must thank for their support on this journey, and I want to apologise in advance if I forget you – that doesn't make you less important, it just means I have a brain like a sieve! My heartfelt gratitude goes out to each and every one of you whose involvement, whether small or large, has been invaluable and appreciated more than I can express.

My family, of course, are always first on any list of special mentions for the patience and tolerance they show when I'm working. I know I'm not easy to live with when I'm deep in story territory but they support me and love me nonetheless.

I also want to mention the many good friends I have made and since kept at Staffordshire University. It's been over ten years since I graduated with a degree in English and Creative Writing but hardly a day goes by when I don't think fondly of my time there. I'd also like to shout out to Storm Constantine of Immanion Press, who gave me the opportunity to see my very first book in print, and Philippa Milnes-Smith and the team at the Soho Agency, who did such a wonderful job of supporting me in the early days of my career and continue to do so where they can.

I have to thank the remarkable team at Bookouture for their continued support, patience and amazing publishing flair, particularly my editors Cara Chimirri – who has been responsible for *The Time of My Life*'s wonderful new lease of life – Lydia Vassar-Smith and Jessie Botterill. I'd also like to shout out to Kim Nash, Noelle Holten and Sarah Hardy and the rest of our amazing publicity folks. Last but not least I want to mention Alexandra Holmes who keeps my schedules and my wandering attention on track, and the most wonderful Peta Nightingale – if not for a chance meeting with her I'm certain I would not be where I am today. It was Peta who first read *The Time of My Life* all those years ago and worked so hard to help me make it the best book it could be. I know I'll have forgotten someone at Bookouture who I ought to be thanking, but I hope they'll forgive me. I'll be giving them all a big hug at the next summer bash whether they want it or not! Their belief, able assistance and encouragement mean the world to me. I truly believe I have the best team an author could ask for and I'm so grateful every day for them.

My friend Kath Hickton always gets an honourable mention for putting up with me since primary school, and Louise Coquio deserves a medal for getting me through university and suffering me ever since, likewise her lovely family. I also have to thank Mel Sherratt, who is as generous with her time and advice as she is talented, someone who is always there to cheer on her fellow authors. She did so much to help me in the early days of my career that I don't think I'll ever be able to thank her as much as she deserves.

I'd also like to shout out to Holly Martin, Tracy Bloom, Emma Davies, Jack Croxall, Carol Wyer, Clare Davidson, Angie Marsons, Sue Watson and Jaimie Admans: not only brilliant authors in their own rights but hugely supportive of others. My Bookouture colleagues are all incredible, of course, unfailing and generous in their support of fellow authors – life would be a lot duller without the gang!

I have to thank all the brilliant and dedicated book bloggers (there are so many of you but you know who you are!) and readers, and anyone else who has championed my work, reviewed it, shared it or simply told me that they liked it. Every one of those actions is priceless. Some of you I am even proud to call friends now – and I'm looking at you in particular, Kerry Ann Parsons and Steph Lawrence!

Finally I'd like to give a special mention to my agent, Madeleine Milburn, and the team at the Madeleine Milburn Literary, TV & Film Agency, who work so hard on my behalf.

Made in the USA
Coppell, TX
06 December 2021

67321189R00166